ALSO BY EMILY SNOW

Tidal

All Over You (A Devoured Novella)

DEVOURED

a novel

EMILY SNOW

A Touchstone Book
Published by Simon & Schuster
New York London Toronto Sydney New Delhi

Touchstone
A Division of Simon & Schuster, Inc.
1230 Avenue of the Americas
New York, NY 10020

First Touchstone trade paperback edition May 2013

TOUCHSTONE and colophon are registered trademarks of Simon & Schuster, Inc.

For information about special discounts for bulk purchases, please contact Simon & Schuster Special Sales at 1-866-506-1949 or business@simonandschuster.com.

The Simon & Schuster Speakers Bureau can bring authors to your live event. For more information or to book an event, contact the Simon & Schuster Speakers Bureau at 1-866-248-3049 or visit our website at www.simonspeakers.com.

Designed by Claudia Martinez

Library of Congress Cataloging-in-Publication Data is available.

ISBN 978-1-4767-4408-7
ISBN 978-1-4767-4409-4 (ebook)

For my family,
who have never stopped believing in me.
I love you guys.

DEVOURED

1

"Your baby brother called. Three times."

My gaze snaps up from the mail I'm holding to meet Tori's dark eyes. She's ten feet away me, sitting behind the Formica countertop in the kitchen that we share. My cool, confident roommate—whom I met four years ago when she rescued me from a wasted and touch-happy frat boy—fidgets anxiously with the rim of a supersized shot glass that boasts a raunchy quote: LIQUOR GOGGLES: MAKING FUGLY GUYS HOT SINCE THE 19TH CENTURY. Tori knows my brother well enough to realize something is going on. It must be important because Seth wouldn't stop avoiding me for anything else. He's owed me two grand since July, seven months ago, and the last time I actually spoke to him was Labor Day.

Even when Seth had backed out of visiting me for Christmas break, he'd done so via e-mail.

God . . . this can't be good.

"Did he say what he wants?" I croak. I press my body up against the steel door behind me, the long row of deadbolts poking hard into my back. Crisp envelopes crumple between my fingertips, but I'm powerless to stop myself from obliterating the stack of shared bills and postcards for Tori, from her parents who are vacationing in Mexico. I'm much too worried about why Seth has called me.

Three times.

Tori shrugs her bare, shimmery shoulders, squints down at the splash of clear liquid in her glass, and then downs the shot in one swift flick of her wrist. There's no bottle in sight, but I know she's drinking peppermint schnapps. Her telltale bottle of chaser (Hershey's sugar-free chocolate syrup) sits next to her phone. Plus, schnapps is her usual Friday night pregamer. Sometimes—when my boss has an off week that inevitably rubs off on me—I let Tori talk me into drinking a little. I'm in no mood to even consider touching the stuff right now, though.

There's already a migraine building in that frustrating spot between my eyes.

"He just said call him . . ." she says. But as her voice trails off, I know she's thinking the same thing I am.

What the hell has my mom done this time?

Because last time I received a frantic call from Seth, a year and a half ago, he'd told me that Mom had made a suicide attempt. I'd taken the first available flight out of Los Angeles, only to discover that she had lied to my brother and grandma for attention. Even now, I can vividly recall how Mom had laughed

2

at me for being naïve and stupid enough to come running, and I ball my hands into tight fists.

"Always so quick to please," she'd said in her thick Southern accent. Then she took a long drag of a cigarette for which she'd probably had to do unmentionable things to earn, and blew the smoke over my head.

Forcing thoughts of my mother out of my mind for the time being, I offer Tori a strained smile that I know isn't fooling anybody. "You going out tonight?" I ask.

The answer is obvious. It *is* Friday night, and even though only her upper body is visible, I can tell Tori is dressed to kill. Immaculate long black hair and makeup that would make Megan Fox weep, check. Strapless red dress that's probably no longer than my top, double-check. I can almost guarantee she's wearing a pair of her mile-high, "screw-me" shoes, too.

"Vanguard with Ben, Stacy, and Micah." Her jet-black, perfectly arched eyebrows knit together as she parts her lips to say something else. I shake my head stubbornly and she snaps her mouth shut. We both know it is pointless for her to invite me. Tonight, no amount of sweet-talking will convince me to leave the apartment. There's a good chance that whatever Seth is about to tell me will ruin my night and the rest of my year, too.

I swallow, over and over again, in my best attempt to get rid of the sudden dryness in the back of my mouth.

It doesn't help.

"That's it," Tori snaps. She reaches across the counter to grab her phone. "I'm calling to cance—" But I lunge forward and pluck her massive Samsung Galaxy out of her hand. I drop the balled-up pile of mail beside her empty glass. Thanks to my sweaty palms, it's practically fused together.

"Please, just . . . *don't*. You look way too hot to spend your night with me. I-I swear I'll be fine." She doesn't seem too convinced because she presses her full lips into a thin, scarlet line. I slide her phone into her hands, curling her fingers around it. I coax my face into an even brighter smile and tell her in the most chipper voice I can muster, "Go, and have a good time."

She's talking, protesting, but I can barely hear her exact words. I'm already walking down the narrow hallway to my bedroom, my own phone clutched in a death grip as I dial my brother's number.

Seth picks up on the second ring. On those rare occasions that we speak, he always lets my call go to voicemail and then responds to me five or six hours later.

This is *definitely* not good.

"Is everything okay, Tori said that—" I begin, ducking into my bedroom and shutting the door behind me.

"Thank God," he hisses before I can get another syllable out. "Where've you been, Si? And why the hell didn't I have this number?"

Less than ten seconds into our conversation and my brother is already arguing with me. I slam my oversized bag onto my bed. My wallet along with a bunch of tampons and makeup spill out onto my lavender cotton sheets and some fall on the carpeted floor. I'll clean it up later, even though clutter annoys me.

"I work. And I've tried to call you from this number several times. You just didn't answer," I point out.

I don't sound angry, which is how I feel, but like I'm explaining myself to my brother. Like I'm the one who should be sorry for *him* ignoring me.

I really hate myself for sounding like that.

"Sienna, it's Gram," Seth says.

And this—*this* is when I literally freeze in place, standing between my bed and desk. I must look like one of those tragic, serious statues in the cemeteries back home in Tennessee. My heart feels as if it's stopped. The first thing I'd assumed when Tori told me Seth was trying to reach me was that my mom had somehow gotten herself in trouble again. I hadn't even thought of my grandmother because she's so strong and resilient and wonderful.

She's also seventy-nine years old.

I try to say something, anything, but there's a lump the size of a lint-flavored golf ball clogging up the back of my throat. Is Gram sick? Is she—?

I can't even bring myself to think *that* word.

I'm still choking and wheezing when Seth finally releases an exasperated sigh and snaps, "She's fine, Si. Well, physically fine."

I don't get a chance to exhale in relief or yell at my brother for scaring the hell out of me before he launches into the story of what's going on. Seth says words like *foreclosure* and *eviction notice. New owner*—some douchebag musician from California. *Court on Monday*. And then he tells me that I need to be there for her, for him.

"I have to work," I whisper. Tomas, my boss, is like the Michael Bay of wardrobe, and he's been telling me ever since he hired me how many people would literally kill to work with him. I can't imagine what he'll say if I ask for time off for anything besides a funeral or the certain impending demise of an immediate family member. I might get fired. Or worse, my boss could possibly give me a horrible reference and I'll never get another wardrobe job for the rest of my life.

"No, you've *got* to be here," Seth says stubbornly.

"I can't just . . ." But I'm already sitting in front of my laptop with my bank statement pulled up on one tab and a discount airline Web site on another. I'm already entering in my debit card information for an early Monday morning flight, biting down so hard on my lower lip that I taste blood. I'm broke. Half of what's in my account—half of my *total* savings—will have to go to Tori for my share of the bills.

And before I hang up with my little brother, I'm already shoving my belongings inside the beaten Coach suitcase my grandparents had given me five years ago as an eighteenth birthday present.

It's mind-numbingly cold in Nashville—thirty-three degrees, to be precise—and snowing lightly when I scoot into Seth's messy Dodge Ram 1500 on Monday afternoon. From the way I'm sweating, though, you would think it was the middle of August and that I'd arrived in Nashville dressed from head to toe in wool. The flutter-sleeve top I'd so carefully selected because I thought it would make me look professional, clings uncomfortably to my skin and the tops of my thigh-high tights sag to just above my knees.

The sudden spike in perspiration is my own fault. I spent the majority of the four-hour flight from Los Angeles to Nashville fretting over how I'd convince Gram to come back to California with me. And the more I thought about it, the more doubtful I became. My granddad had given her that cabin and land as a gift after my mother was born, back in the early seventies. There's no way in hell Gram's giving it up without a fight, even though from what Seth has said, the house is already gone.

"What'd your boss say?" my brother asks as he turns onto the interstate. He slams on the brakes to avoid hitting another car. The Dodge skids on the slippery road, jostling us around, but Seth manages to get the pickup truck under control halfway into my frantic gasp.

My brother doesn't so much as flinch. He squints straight ahead, the same way our dad always does when he drives in crappy weather, and rubs the tips of his thumbs on either side of the steering wheel—yet another Dad trait. With his dark blond hair, brown eyes, and year-round tan that puts my easily burned skin to shame, Seth even looks like Dad now.

I've got red hair and what Tori calls "Amazon height" and don't resemble either my mom or my dad. Not that I mind.

"Damn, Si, you going to answer me or just sit there with your mouth wide open?" Seth demands.

Digging my hands into the hem of the dark tweed pencil skirt I'm wearing, I shrug my shoulders. "I worked through Christmas and New Year's, so he didn't have much of a problem. Besides, I'm just an assistant." I don't add that I had to beg Tomas for the time off and that he'd pointedly said I better take care of my family drama and have my ass back in L.A. before the end of the month—two and a half weeks later.

"Echo Falls is ranked first in females aged eighteen to thirty-four. There are people willing to trade their own offspring for a chance to work on this series. Replacing you with a new wardrobe assistant who covets this career won't be too hard a feat," Tomas had said, *punching something into the iPad he carried around everywhere. He never even spared me a glance, so when he shoved a newly inventoried wardrobe rack against a brick slab wall, he didn't see me startle. "Don't force me to find that person, Jensen."*

"I'll wrap it up in two weeks, Tomas," I'd promised.

"You'd better."

Telling Seth any of that is simply a waste of oxygen. He would either not get why I can't neglect my job whenever I please or simply not care. Knowing my brother, it would be both.

"Got anything I can wipe my face with?" I ask.

Seth twitches his head to the right side, toward the center console. "In there."

I find a package of wet wipes in between a half-empty thirty-count box of condoms and a completely empty bottle of Jose Cuervo. Before I can stop myself, I whirl on my brother and blurt, "I hope you're not stupid enough to drink and drive. You're only nineteen and you—"

"Don't start, Si, okay? Today is not the day for your bitching."

I could remind Seth that I am older than he is. That out of

just about everyone in his life—aside from our grandmother—I care about him the most. I could keep talking in an attempt to get my point across.

I don't.

Instead, sinking my teeth down on the inside of my cheek until the nauseating taste of copper floods my mouth, I turn my attention to the bumper stickers plastered on the little Ford Escort in front of us. HONK IF YOU HATE PEOPLE, TOO one of them says. How fitting.

There's only eight miles between the airport and the courthouse, but the drive takes forty-five minutes due to the traffic and snow. Seth and I spend just about every minute of the ride in silence, like we usually do when we're around each other. The only time he says something to me is after I switch the radio on. Seth lets The Black Keys serenade us for a minute and a half and then abruptly cuts the volume.

"I can't listen to this and drive," he grumbles.

"Fine."

As I dab at my face with wipes and smooth my long red hair back into a low ponytail, I mentally kick myself for being such a dumbass and lending him money. Not only has he been nothing but terse toward me since I got in his car, he hasn't mentioned the cash I gave him.

I doubt he will.

Seth's smart enough to realize that I'll never bring up the money he owes me because I'd rather gouge myself in the eye than get into a confrontation with him.

There's a reason, actually a few reasons, why I rarely come to town and baby brother is just the smallest part of them.

By the time Seth and I arrive at the courthouse and find the correct courtroom, the hearing is coming to an end. My brother and I sit on opposite ends of one of the wooden benches at the back of the room. He's got his arms crossed tightly over his chest, staring ahead with a stony look in his dark eyes. I hate that he's irritated at me, but there's nothing I can do about it. Giving him a sad smile, I lean forward until my chin brushes the top of the next pew up and listen attentively to what's being said.

From what I manage to piece together, this is the second hearing. The new owner, whom I've decided to refer to as Asshat, and his lawyers are both here, and they're seeking a formal eviction. My grandmother and her attorney Mr. Nielson (the same one she's had since before I can remember) are across from them on the left side of the room. Even though I know I shouldn't be angry with him, I find myself glaring death rays at Asshat.

Then again, I shouldn't be checking him out, either.

Since his back is turned to me, there's a depressing limit to what I'm able to ogle, but I know that he's *built*. And with a backside like his, the rest of him is bound to be equally as gorgeous. Dressed in an impeccable black business suit that molds a little too perfectly to every inch of his body, he's got dark, tousled hair that brushes his neck and long fingers. He taps them rapidly in some type of rhythm on the mahogany table in front of him. I'm tall, but this guy must tower over me by a good six inches—he's easily six foot three or six foot four.

And his ass . . .

Ugh, I'd bet the last thousand dollars in my account (and would even overdraw it a few hundred bucks) that the attorney who's standing beside him would be staring at it, too, if she could get away with doing so. Or if she could stop beaming up at him with her chest thrust out for longer than five seconds.

Hot-faced and utterly reluctant, I drag my gaze back to Gram's side of the courtroom. If Seth catches me staring at Asshat, he'll never let me live it down. Knowing him, he'll probably accuse me of conspiring with the enemy.

I frown, because I know that's *exactly* what Seth would say to me.

"Mr. Nielson, your client has ten days before the court issues a possession order," the judge is telling my grandmother's lawyer in a deep Southern accent that rivals the one I used to have. "After that, the sheriff will carry out the eviction within a week."

When she hears those words, my grandmother's shoulders sag. She grips Nielson's shoulder for support so hard that even from the back row, I can see her knuckles turn white. It takes every ounce of my willpower not to bolt out of my seat. I hate this. I hate my mother for this, because at the heart of things, it really is all her fault.

I was right when I assumed she'd done something stupid. Mom's the reason my grandmother is losing her home. She is the reason everything in this family turns to shit.

And then the hearing is over. Gram's bright blue eyes widen

in stunned surprise as she makes her way toward me and Seth, and her drawn expression softens. She gives me a melancholy smile that's full of defeat. I've only seen her look at me like this once before. There's a sour taste in my mouth when I realize it was in this exact courthouse. Before Gram has a chance to utter a single word, I pull her to me and bury my face into her puff of gray hair, inhaling her familiar scent of vanilla and Chanel No. 5.

"Did you drive?" I ask. I won't say anything about what just happened—not in here, at least—because I don't exactly trust my emotions or Gram's. She nods into my shoulder, so I say, "I'll take you back home then." Loosening my grip, I glare over her shoulder at Asshat. Now his back is no longer turned to me. Instead, I have a side view that's just as nauseatingly sexy as the back.

He's speaking to his female attorney, and they're both laughing. She's got her hand on his arm and her boobs are still jutted out. If we were *anywhere* else I'd snort aloud at how ridiculous she looks. He's probably thanking her. And she's more than likely suggesting they celebrate the easy win against an old woman and her equally ancient lawyer over drinks and then a quick screw at her place. I'm about to draw away from Gram and lead her out of the courtroom when the man turns his face, lifts his eyes. Our gazes connect. His hazel eyes challenge my blue.

Predator and prey.

He draws himself up to his full height.

My chest seizes up. I was right, the full package is devastatingly handsome. And when I decided to nickname him Asshat I was being much too lenient.

I pray my grandmother doesn't feel the change in my heartbeat, the sudden hitch in the way that I'm breathing. This exchange isn't one of those love-at-first sight moments. No, it's nothing at all like that. This is one of those moments where fate has roundhouse kicked me in the face yet again. Why is *he* here in Nashville? In the same courtroom as *me*?

God, please, please *don't let this man remember me.*

For a moment, I'm sure he has no clue who I am, that he'll go back to chatting it up with Boobs McBeal. *By now there would've been tens,* hundreds, *of other girls. I'm nothing to him. I'm the only one who remembers,* I tell myself.

But then, a slow, animalistic smile of realization stretches across Lucas Wolfe's face.

It makes me feel like he'll devour me whole at any second.

That grin—it's the exact same one he gave me two years ago, right after I refused to let him cuff me to his bed, and just before he literally told me to get the fuck out of his house.

2

I'm numb as my family and I leave the courtroom; my body feels on autopilot, going through the motions. I give my grandmother's attorney a robotic greeting when he catches up to us and asks me how my work in New York is going—I don't correct him and say that I work in Los Angeles, not Manhattan. As Seth and I wait for Gram when she goes to the restroom, I'm especially quiet—almost to the point of being creepy.

"Are you sick?" my brother questions me as he props his arms against the wall on the other side of the hallway. Supporting his weight against it, he narrows his brown eyes and motions his head to the bathroom door. "Si . . . you're fucked up on something, aren't you?"

Now it's my turn to glare at Seth for asking such a stupid question. I shake my head to each side and look at a fingerprint smudge on the water fountain two feet away so I no longer have to face my brother's intense gaze. "I'm just tired," I say in a weak voice. And to be honest, I am exhausted. Seeing Lucas after two years—even for such a brief moment—has somehow managed to drain the energy out of my body, replacing it with confusion and frustration.

And a feeling of humiliation that I thought I'd gotten over months ago.

"Well, you look like you're high on *something*," Seth points out.

"I'm not, so drop it." There's a nasty bite to my voice, but it does the trick. My brother doesn't ask any more questions and Gram comes out to join us a second later.

As soon as we get outside of the courthouse and reach the bottom steps, Seth announces that he's bailing on us. I'm not surprised. "I've got an afternoon class," he explains. I'm positive that's total bull. He's probably just going to drink away his worries. I don't confirm my suspicions as our grandmother speaks to him, thanking him for being there for her.

A razor-sharp sensation scrapes the wall of my chest, as I once again try to come to terms with the fact Seth knew more about what was going on with Gram than I did. Standing by myself, a few feet away from them, with snowflakes melting the second they kiss my pale skin, I feel left out—literally like the redheaded stepchild. As quick as the thought entered my head, I squash it down.

What am I, a jealous ten-year-old?

"Make sure you get some rest," Seth yells out to me, waving good-bye before he takes off in a graceful sprint in the direction of the parking garage where he left his truck.

"Sure will," I grumble under my breath. I'll be fine as soon as I have the opportunity to collect my thoughts about everything that's happened in court today. As soon as tomorrow comes and Lucas Wolfe is once again an unpleasant memory.

"Keep making that face and it'll get stuck like that," Gram says. She used to say the same thing when Seth and I were kids, and the corner of my mouth twists upward.

"Are you ready to go?"

Smiling up at me with a grace and fortitude I've always been envious of, my grandmother jangles the keys to her ancient black Land Rover into my palm and closes my fist around them.

She pulls an umbrella out of her bag and opens it. Turning right, in the direction of her lawyer's office, she says, "Nielson wants me to stop by for a strategy meeting. I'm sure you don't want to waste your time in a boring meeting with an attorney." Gram forces a throaty chuckle, adding, "I don't even want to waste my time going to this meeting."

I may not return home nearly as often as I should, but I know my grandmother better than just about anyone else. This is her way of telling me she doesn't want me around for whatever she and Richard Nielson have to say to each other.

She doesn't want me involved.

My muscles tighten. I swallow hard, pursing my lips into what I hope passes for a good-natured expression. "Sure. I'll just"—I squint through the snowflakes at our surroundings until my eyes land on a two-story café directly across the street from Nielson's office and the courthouse—"go grab something to eat over at Alice's. I'll keep an eye out for you."

in a few minutes," Gram says. "And Sienna?"

. . . y you've come home."

Tears burn the corners of my eyes. I squeeze them shut, whispering, "Me, too." There's so much else I want to say and do, but there are people all around us heading into the court-house and to various attorneys' offices. If I speak, there's a 90 percent chance the waterworks will start.

So I give Gram a cheerful wave as she walks away from me.

It's only after she disappears into Nielson's building that I let my shoulders slump and drag ass across the street to the café. I haven't been inside this restaurant since my mom's legal woes a few years ago, so I'm stoked to find it's now decorated in an *Alice in Wonderland* theme. My roommate and I are complete opposites, but one of the places where we find common ground is fantastical movies and books and . . . you know, Johnny Depp.

The woman behind the counter, wearing an elaborate velvet Mad Hatter hat, smiles up at me and yells, "Go ahead and seat yourself, hon. Someone'll be right over." I nod my head appre-ciatively and then find a booth in the far left of the café that gives me the best view of Nielson's office and easy access to the heater. After I order a double slice of the special—Cheshire pie—and a cup of coffee, I send a series of texts to Tori that sound more than a little neurotic.

> Lucas Wolfe is the person who's bought the house. That shitface bought my grandma's house.
>
> The universe has to be plotting against me.

WTF is he doing here?

Tori???

There's slush melting inside my pumps and I realize I was so distracted by merely seeing Lucas that I forgot to get my bags out of the back of my brother's truck. And yet . . . still the only thing I can think about is Lucas. Not only about how he's trying to throw Gram out of her house, but how he threw *me* out of his one January night two years ago.

I'm deep in thought and waiting for Tori to text back when I hear footsteps shuffling next to me. I slide my cell phone from the edge of the table over toward the salt and pepper shakers in order to give the waitress enough room to set down my order.

A large and incredibly unfeminine hand covers mine, fingers callused from playing the guitar gliding across my knuckles. It's a familiar touch that sends an unwanted—and very delicious— jolt through my body. I snatch my fingers away from Lucas's, angry at my body's obvious betrayal, and knock over a porcelain bowl of sugar packets. The sugar scatters across the linoleum and he chuckles. It's a musical and deep and sensual noise that tugs at the pit of my stomach.

I feel the sudden urge to vomit.

Gesturing to the empty seat across from me, he asks, "Room for one more?"

"Not much for spending my free time with strangers," I say through clenched teeth as I shake my head. "So, sorry, there's not."

He slides into the booth anyway, stretching out his long legs so that his calves straddle mine. I open my mouth to protest, but he holds up his hand. "Before you try to bullshit me, you should probably know I never forget a face." Then he lifts his eyebrows wickedly and says, "Or a body."

Who does he think he is? Feeling a sudden need to come right out and ask him, I demand, "I guess you're not used to hearing no, huh?" My voice packs a hell of a punch, shocking me. If this were anybody else I would have already separated myself from the situation. Lucas has an unnerving way of tearing away the layers of my nervousness—my need to shy away—until I'm raw and wanting to lash out at him.

He grins, cocking his head to one side as if he's carefully studying me. "Do you really have to ask me that?"

My lips part as my senses and every inch of my skin flood with heat. Swiping a sugar packet from the tabletop, I squish my thumb and forefinger into the grittiness and glance away from Lucas's hazel eyes out the window toward Nielson's office.

"You're sexy when you're nervous."

"I'm not," I say.

"Sexy?"

My head jerks back, away from the window, and I give him a wide-eyed stare. "No . . . nervous." But I'm sure he can hear the tremor in my voice, feel how my legs are shaking between his underneath the table as we speak.

The corners of his lips pull into a sardonic smile that's infuriating and ridiculously sensual. Once again, I feel electricity flow through my body. I hate myself for having any response toward this man other than blatant hatred. "Tell me why you're here, Sienna," he demands softly.

"Why do you care?"

Placing his forearms on the table, he leans forward. His sleeves ride up just enough for me to see the tattoos on his right wrist—black five-sided stars surrounded by elaborate tribal patterns. I squeeze my eyes shut, vividly picturing the rest of the tattoo sleeve on his right arm and the heart that's full of daggers inked in the center of his muscular chest. Anyone who follows his band, Your Toxic Sequel, would know about each of Lucas's tattoos. I mean, just a few months ago he and the drop-dead gorgeous female lead singer of Wicked Lambs were on the front cover of some rock magazine—he was shirtless and so was she, with him standing behind her, cupping her breasts.

But at another time, I'd seen Lucas's ink up close. I'd gotten to trace my lips along the intricate patterns that ran along his hard body as he wound his fingertips into my hair and whispered for me to kiss, to taste. I shiver.

I wish I could say it's because of the thirty-three-degree weather.

Lucas finally answers me, untangling me from the memories. I hate myself for being disappointed at losing the images of my hands, and my tongue, on his body. "You want to know why I give a shit about you being here, Sienna? Because being around you is—"

He stops speaking so that the waitress can put my lunch on the table. He grants her his trademark buy-my-album-and-vibe-off-to-it grin. She fumbles, blushing as she asks him if there's anything she can get for him. I frown. If he orders, that means he'll stick around and really, I just want to hurry this along so Lucas and I can go back to being . . . well, nothing to one another.

Luckily for me, he declines, sending the waitress on her way.

"Being around me is what?" I demand the moment we're alone again.

Twirling a spoon around in my coffee, he flicks the tip of his tongue over his top teeth. I can't tell whether he's smiling or grimacing. And I have no idea why I should care either way.

My cell phone plays the ring tone I've assigned it for calls and messages from Tori—a Taylor Swift song that she swears she loathes but sings in the shower every morning after she does Pilates. I reach for it, but Lucas captures my hand in his, threading his fingertips between mine.

"You could be bad for music," he whispers, bringing my fingers to his lips. "And that's what I'm here to do. Make music."

"I can't be bad for anything if we don't see each other after today."

"You really think that's possible, Sienna? You think it'll be easy for you to walk away from me?"

Instinctively, my teeth grind together. His hazel eyes go dark but he says nothing, even though I can tell he wants to. "Are you saying you'll follow me if I get up and leave right now?" I demand. "Because I've got to admit, that's not the Lucas-fucking-Wolfe I met a couple of years back."

Lucas doesn't jump to answer me. Instead, he kisses each of my fingers slowly, raveling my stomach into hundreds of knots with each touch. We're in public, and there are people all around us. But for what seems like a thousand years, he and I are the only people in the world.

"No, Sienna, I won't follow you. I'm just asking if you're really going to leave when you're looking at me like you want to wrap yourself around me right here, right now."

"Lucas—" I start, my voice threadbare. Staring down at the sugar packet disaster on the table, I take a deep breath and then rake my teeth over my top lip. I don't know what to say to him so I don't appear weak. When I glance up in time to see his beautiful face break into a smile that makes my chest clench, I realize it doesn't matter. He already knows he's my kryptonite.

He's known that for two years.

"The second I saw you, I promised myself I wouldn't do this with you again, Sienna," he growls.

Do what—lead me on? Boot me out of his life without so much as a proper good-bye? I'm about to demand an explanation, but then I see the door to Nielson's office swing open and Gram comes out. I immediately feel like the worst granddaughter in history because at some point during my exchange with Lucas, I managed to forget she's the reason I'm in this café to begin with.

Pulling my hand away from his, I toss my phone into my bag with a little too much force. "I'm here because some douchebag musician from California bought my grandmother's house."

I can't mistake his sharp intake of breath or the way his long legs go stiff beneath the table, applying more pressure to my own. "I see."

"So you'll understand why I'm saying this: Go fuck yourself, Lucas," I say.

Our eyes lock. His are mocking and angry and something else. Something that I'd seen two years ago, the night I went home with him. Something I'll pretend I don't see right now because I don't want to handle the feelings it evokes in me.

"I've only heard you that forceful once, so I've got to ask: Was that for your grandma or for what happened with us?"

I untangle my legs from his, stand, and put money under the untouched platter of Cheshire pie. "Both," I whisper.

I'm so flustered—emotionally, mentally, and dammit, physically—by my encounter with Lucas that I'm only half tuned in to my conversation with my grandmother as I drive her home. I hear her ask if my flight was comfortable, how long I'll be staying in Nashville, and I listen to myself respond mechanically. "It was great, Gram. . . . I'll be here as long as it takes. . . ." Then she starts asking me a new series of questions, and I give her even more mechanical answers. Our entire exchange sounds like a hazy dream to me, but Lucas's voice plays loud and static-free in my head. It's teasing me, warning me that I'm bad for music.

Whatever that's supposed to mean. Maybe I inspire him to write angsty stuff where the rocker *doesn't* get to screw the girl or something. When I think of it that way, I guess that is a career drainer.

The only thing I'm entirely sure of is that I wish the person snatching away the home my grandparents loved so much was anyone else in the world but Lucas.

Turning the Land Rover down the private drive that leads to the house where I spent most of my childhood, I draw my brain away from Lucas Wolfe and back to the important issues at hand.

"Why didn't you tell me about the foreclosure?" I ask Gram quietly. "You came to L.A. to see me for Christmas, you must've known then."

My grandma faces me with guilty eyes. "I thought I could fix things. What am I saying? I can *still* fix things. The last thing I wanted to do was burden you with something that would make you stress."

"Oh, Gram . . ."

"Don't you dare give me that pitying voice, Sienna Jensen. There's still time left. It's not over yet," she says, her voice hard as steel. But when I look at her out of the corner of my eye, I notice her cheeks are wet. She's gripping the armrest for support.

And she seems so much smaller than she was when I last saw her a couple of months ago.

"You're right."

"Of course I am," she replies.

But she sighs. We both know the land around us, the house we're drawing closer to, is all but gone. In less than two weeks, maybe a little more if we're fortunate, Gram will be homeless. I refuse to leave Nashville until she's settled somewhere else. I'll swallow my own inhibitions and go to battle for my grandmother's happiness.

Even if the person that I'm fighting is Lucas.

Shutting off the engine, I pull the keys out of the ignition and stare out at the cabin, which really isn't a cabin at all but what can only be described as a log mansion. For the last few years, I've told Gram that it's way too much house for her and she needs to downsize. Now . . . I feel like shit for even joking with her like that.

"You make yourself at home, sweetheart. I'm going to go on upstairs and lie down. I've not been feeling like myself lately," Gram says as we walk inside of the stifling hot house. She's hanging her coat on the rack in the foyer, so she doesn't see the way I pull at the high collar of my blouse.

"Room still the same?" I ask, and as soon as the words leave my mouth, I kick myself. What an awkward, horrible thing for me to say.

She makes an unnatural noise that's probably supposed to be a chuckle, but it makes me cringe. "For the next couple of weeks it is."

"Then I'll make myself at home," I say. Without my bags. Because I couldn't stop thinking about the sexy rock star who now owns this house long enough to remember anything else. I just hope like hell some of my old clothes from high school and college are still packed away upstairs.

"Are you sure you don't need—" Gram starts to say, but I shake my head, pointing my finger at the staircase in front of us.

"You get some rest. I'll be fine, okay?" If I'm so fine, though, why does it feel like someone's stomping up and down on my chest right now?

While I help myself to a frozen meal in the kitchen—my grandmother is obsessed with convenience—I call Seth. He doesn't answer, so I have to leave him a message. "Hey, Seth, it's me, Sienna. I left my bags in your truck. Can you bring them by ASAP?" And because I know he'll complain at having to drive across town, I add, "I'll give you twenty bucks for gas money." I rerecord the message two more times until I'm satisfied with how it sounds, and then I call Tori. The first ring is not even halfway through when she answers. Immediately, she starts talking rapidly.

"Oh my God, Sienna, where've you been? Don't you check your texts, woman? I've been trying to get in touch with you for the last hour! You don't just send a bunch of messages like that and completely disappear." She pauses for a moment and takes a deep breath. I can actually picture her right now, fiddling with one of the random whatnots she keeps on her desk because she's so worked up. If stress balls didn't exist, Tori would self-implode because it's absolutely necessary for her hands to stay busy. A nasally female voice says something to her, and Tori hisses back that she'll do it when Jenna, her supervisor, confirms the instructions.

"Please, please, please, tell me you're kidding me about Lucas Wolfe. Please tell me that this is a let's-screw-with-Tori moment," Tori finally says in a low, breathless whisper.

"Nope. Not joking. Definitely him. And sorry for not calling you back sooner, I was . . . occupied." I flush, thinking of the way Lucas had stopped me from answering my phone earlier—how the feeling of his lips and tongue against the tips of my fingers had managed to separate me from reality for far too long.

Tori groans, and I hear a door slam closed, followed by the loud clacking of her high heels. When she begins to speak again, there's an echo, and I realize she must be hiding out in the stairwell. "Sorry, had to get away from the donkey witch in the next cubicle. So . . . does he remember you? I mean, it was two years ago and you didn't actually fu—"

"He remembers," I snap.

She makes a noise that's a hybrid of a groan and a squeal, like she's both disgusted by the prospect and excited. "Well, what did he say? What did he *do*? Holy shit, why is he in Nashville of all places? No offense, babe, but it's not exactly L.A."

Since I'm still wondering the exact same thing, I give her the explanation Lucas gave me: "He's here to make music. Apparently, my grandma's house is the right place for him to hole up in while he does it."

She's silent for such a long time I have to pull the phone from my ear to make sure the call hasn't dropped. It hasn't. The moment of Tori inserting dramatic silence gives me time to load my chicken pot pie and a Coke onto a breakfast tray. I start upstairs, toward the bedroom I slept in as a kid. At last, Tori whispers, "And that's *it*?"

I pause at the top of the steps, supporting my weight against the banister. There's a major part of me that's just dying to confide in her about how Lucas had made me feel in that café, how the attraction between the two of us was just as fierce and thrilling as before.

But then, the other part warns me not to touch that subject at all. Hadn't Tori been the person I bawled to after the disastrous night with Lucas? Not to mention when I found out Your Toxic Sequel never wanted me on the set of any of their music videos again and I thought my career was ruined.

If I told my best friend that I still felt the slightest bit of magnetism toward Lucas Wolfe, she'd be on the first available flight to Nashville to slap some sense into me.

"Sienna?" Tori asks pleadingly. "What else?"

"Well, I did tell him to go fuck himself," I say. It's somewhat true, even if it had been uttered after Lucas had deliberately frustrated me.

I hear her clapping her hands together slowly. "Badass, Jensen. See, that wasn't so hard, was it?"

Ugh, she has no idea.

"Look, I'd better go, but I'm proud of you, Si, for not letting Lucas run all over you and telling him off. I'll text or call you tonight."

But I feel like crap when I hang up the phone and walk into my bedroom, closing the door carefully behind me so I won't wake Gram. With my appetite suddenly a thing of the past, I leave the tray sitting on the edge of my dresser.

It's comforting to see that Gram's left my room the same as it was in high school and college. The same furnishings, same pink and orange hibiscus bedspread and Have a Day posters and the same scent of apple cinnamon, thanks to the Bath & Body Works plug-ins that were placed throughout the house.

Too bad even comfort won't do anything for the dull ache in my chest.

I curl up in the fetal position on my old bed, burying my face in pillows that smell like fabric softener, and listen to the bitter sound of nothingness in a house that I'll miss as much as my grandmother will. Silent prayers for the next couple of weeks to be easy roll through my mind. For me to be strong for Gram as she loses this place, the warmest home I've ever known.

But more than anything, I pray that today is my very last encounter with Lucas Wolfe.

3

My hope of avoiding Lucas Wolfe is nothing more than wishful thinking.

Not only is he dominating the majority of my thoughts, but he's suddenly everywhere I turn—like my iPod, on a random playlist that includes him and his band by some freak accident; on Fuse, where they've dedicated a whole day to Your Toxic Sequel's best videos; on my favorite local radio station giving an interview, his voice low and intimate, like rough sex over the airwaves.

And the next day—a little less than twenty-four hours after our run-in at Alice's Café—Lucas is at Gram's house, too. I don't realize he's come by until I hear him talking with other people outside. There's a luxury silver SUV—a Cadillac—parked in the driveway, and a white work truck behind it with some type of logo on the side.

At first, I have no intention of letting Lucas know I'm here. My grandmother is out running errands, and he, along with whoever is with him, hasn't tried to gain access to the inside of the house. I follow the muffled sounds of their voices until I'm able to hear bits and pieces of what they're saying. And this is when I totally freak out.

"Demolish this section of . . ."

". . . completely do away with for the recording studio."

". . . better off just knocking down the whole damn house and starting over with what you want."

For the better part of a minute, I'm breathing heavily at the thought of my childhood home being ripped apart for the sake of a recording studio. Even though I'm dressed in a too-small set of pj's I found stuffed in a bottom drawer in my room—Seth still hasn't brought my luggage or called me back, for that matter—I shove my bare feet into a pair of my brother's oversized boots that I find in the foyer.

Cursing under my breath, I stalk outside into the cold, letting the voices guide me. Lucas is at the back of the house along with his entourage—no other rockers or a bodyguard like he would have in Hollywood, but two men in khaki pants and contractor shirts and a tall woman with dark eyes and black and blue hair. She's rapidly taking notes of everything being said on a tablet.

It's his assistant, Kylie.

I remember her well, and she must know who I am because when our eyes connect, she mouths a silent "Oh" just before breaking into a huge grin. I dart my gaze away from her before she succeeds in making me feel even more awkward. It won't take much for me to lose my nerve right now, and if that's going to happen, I'd prefer to dig my foot halfway into Lucas's ass first.

"Just what the hell do you think you're doing, Wolfe?" I demand before he can completely spin around to face me. For a moment, he looks as shocked as Kylie to see me. His momentary silence gives me a chance to appreciate how incredible he looks in light, blue-wash jeans and a dark burnout T-shirt, how his eyes seem more green than brown today, how his muscles are so completely obvious even under the loose shirt.

I stop ogling a couple of seconds after he regains his composure, granting me the smile that's likely dropped panties across the world. "You're still here," he says. His voice is a mixture of two things—surprise and relief. I'm not sure I like either one.

"Why would I leave?"

"Hmm, let's see. Maybe because the judge said this place is—"

"It's not yet," I snap. Clenching my hands by my side, I count to ten to steady myself before peering up into his eyes. "So, like I said, what do you think you're doing out here?"

Lucas opens his mouth, as if he wants to say something, but one of the contractors interrupts him.

"Mr. Wolfe, we have a limited amount of time because of other appointments this afternoon . . ." the man begins, but Lucas shoots him a dark look. Holy hell, even grown, two-hundred-fifty-pound men lose their confidence around this guy.

Lucas nods to Kylie. "Finish up with these guys. I have . . . shit to take care of."

Kylie pecks a few additional notes into her tablet and then ushers the two men off, talking up plans of renovations and additions and completely gutting Gram's house. She gives me an apologetic smile as she shuffles past, probably because she knows her boss and I are about to get into it, and the odds are out of my favor. How the hell can someone so pleasant work for someone so . . . *Lucas?*

What a stupid question to ask yourself, Jensen, I think. *He's gorgeous and talented, and you came all over his bed without even getting down to the* actual *deed.*

Those type of thoughts—yeah, they're the ones that get me flustered and in trouble. They're the reason why I'll always have a hard time letting this man go. "So I'm shit?" I ask, my voice a jumbled rush.

"Don't be ridiculous, Sienna. You know exactly what I meant."

"You know you have some jumbo balls coming out here today. God, don't you have a soul? I don't care if you're the legal owner now or not. If my grandmother had heard you talking about tearing down walls and demolishing, she would have been devastated."

When he crosses his muscular, tattooed arms over his chest, I repeat the gesture, trying to ignore the dizzying feeling that he's slowly undressing me with his hazel eyes.

It's the same way he looked when we first met a couple of years ago, on the set of one of his band's music videos. To this day, "All Over You" is my favorite Your Toxic Sequel song. Every time I listen to it, hearing Lucas rasping taboo promises, I think of how his eyes drank me in on that video shoot.

"You're cherry red. And your nipples are hard," he growls. My arms automatically hug myself tighter. He chuckles, then whispers, "Hearing about the stripper pole in the living room turned you on, huh?"

I gasp, because for some messed-up reason, I can't help picturing svelte women in G-strings grinding their asses against my grandmother's furniture. It's a ridiculous thought—even if Lucas did install a pole, it's not like Gram's belongings would still be inside of the house. I'm still furious.

"Are you fucking with me?"

Before I realize what's happening, he moves forward, pulling my arms from their protective position over my body and pressing me up against the wooden door that leads into the basement. His scent—a mixture of the Polo cologne he wore and sweat—fills my nostrils, makes all my senses blur. He's close. So close that I can feel the fabric of his jeans scratching my bare legs. When his lips brush my right temple, my breath comes out in ragged puffs, and to my surprise, so do his.

"Do you really think I'm that classless to put a pole in my living room?" Lucas demands, tilting my face up until we're eye to eye. I glare darkly at him, dropping my hands to his shoulders, and he grins. "On second thought, don't answer that."

"Why couldn't this have waited until after all this was over? Lucas, my grandmother is almost eighty. If something had happened to her, if you had gotten her upset . . ." I inhale deeply, until my lungs are about to explode, and then exhale.

Hesitantly, he lifts his hand up and traces it along my cheek. "Do you know how bad I want you, even when there's green shit all over your face?"

For a second, I'm utterly confused, but then he holds up two of his fingers for me to examine. Mortification sinks in as I realize I'd failed to wipe off the spot corrector I put on earlier. When

I move my hands from his broad shoulders to cover my face, he shakes his head abruptly.

"Don't," Lucas orders, and I dig my fingertips into his flesh the moment his hands return to my face. "Do you know how much I want to taste you right now?"

"No," I murmur, "I don't."

Touching his lips to my temple, he caresses my skin with rough fingers, his breath ruffling wisps of my hair all the while. A shudder that's agonizing and pleasant, hot and cold, all at once ripples through my body. I squeeze my eyes together. Start a slow mental count to ten.

My head is spinning so violently that I only make it to six.

"If something happens to my grandmother because of you, I will kill you," I say, trying to bring our conversation back to the reason why I'm out here and away from his need to touch me. I open my eyes when he pulls his mouth away from my skin. From the expression he's wearing, he's shocked by my threat.

"Funny, I would've taken you for the passive type, but then again"—he leans backward, letting me go, and crosses his arms over his chest—"there was that little incident you're still so pissed off about. Guess you're not very passive after all, huh?"

"You asked me to let you handcuff me to your bed. And sorry, Wolfe, but I'm not some fucking toy you can do with whatever you please."

Snorting, he wrinkles his nose. By the way he's skeptically looking at me, I know he's about to say something mocking. "Don't think that's exactly what I said. I told you I was *going* to handcuff you to my bed, and you refused. Actually, I'm pretty sure you would've started screaming if I hadn't asked you to leave."

"Get the fuck out."

His eyes narrow into thin slits. "This is my house, Sienna. And technically, I'm not in."

"No." I shake my head so hard that my high ponytail starts to shake loose. He lifts a strand of my red hair, sifting it through his fingers, his eyes never leaving mine. It's yet another intimate gesture, and I feel that frustrating need in the pit of my belly. Silently, I curse my body for wanting him so much in spite of everything. "You didn't ask me to leave, you told me to get the fuck out," I whisper.

He cringes. "Well, I'm sure I wasn't that—"

My voice is five times as strong as before when I say, "You were."

"You know, I misjudged you."

I'm getting sick of Lucas's riddles, and we've spent a total of five minutes in one another's company today. "What is that supposed to mean?"

"The entire time we were shooting 'All Over You,' you were very obedient and . . . Ah, shit, let's put it this way, Sienna—I didn't expect you to say no to the fucking handcuffs."

Why does he have to bring up that night? Why does he have to drag my mind, and my heart, back to the way I'd wanted him to take me under?

Glancing down at a spot of earth that's nothing but bright

red mud due to the snow, I say in a quiet voice, "Isn't it time for you to leave?"

I hold back a strangled sound when Lucas reaches out and strokes his thumb across my cheek once again. "Is that what you really want?" he implores.

No. I don't know what I want because you confuse the hell out of me.

"Yes," I whisper, lifting my head, "I want you to go."

Lowering his hand from my face, Lucas takes a few more steps backward, and motions his arms out in an overtly grand gesture toward the hill that will take us back to the front of the house. I grit my teeth together, and shake my head.

"I thought I'd be nice and let you go first, but whatever," he says. His voice doesn't sound too polite. It's rough and hard and dangerous. And just a few moments ago, his voice and words and touch succeeded in completely getting to me. Giving me one last sardonic smile, he turns abruptly and stalks up the hill, tracing his fingers alongside the log siding. I shake away the images of him running them along my bare skin instead.

Halfway to the front of the house, Lucas pauses. He doesn't turn around to face me when he calls out over his shoulder, "You might think I'm shit, but I'd have never brought anyone up here to upset your grandmother. She's gone every Tuesday, like clockwork."

Squeezing my eyes together to shut out the sight of Lucas's muscular backside, I pinch the bridge of my nose. The fact that he knows Gram's schedule well enough to figure out the best time to come here without disturbing her is unnerving. It only makes me wonder how many times he's slunk around this place, plotting what he'd destroy first.

I wait until I hear both vehicles leave before I go back up the hill and inside the house. As I track down cleaning supplies, hundreds of thoughts flicker through my head, burning my brain like poison. Every one of them centers on a single question: Where is Gram right now?

Though I wish I could say that wondering about her whereabouts is better than thinking of Lucas Wolfe, it's not.

Because if Gram is going somewhere I should be concerned about, it's not like she'll ever tell me. She's always protected me, even if it means shielding me from the truth.

When I was a child, and my mom and dad would argue or Mom would throw one of her tantrums, my grandparents were my salvation. They had spoiled Seth and me rotten. After my parents divorced when I was twelve, and my mother just flat-out disappeared, my brother and I were given the chance to move in with Dad and his new wife.

It was a shitty opportunity.

Not that there's anything wrong with my dad or Margaret, but they'd moved to Bar Harbor, Maine—over a thousand miles from home. Luckily, even at eight, Seth was bullheaded. My brother told Dad that not only did he hate him and his new wife, but he'd rather be ripped apart by wild dogs than live with them in Maine. That's when our grandparents, Mom's parents, stepped in. Dad wanted to be with his new wife. Our grandparents wanted us. And we wanted to stay because it was the only thing we *knew*. And because no matter how she treated us, we both were hopeful that Mom would come back someday.

It was one of those fairy-tale moments where everyone was happy, and there was no animosity.

But three years later, when Mom finally returned to Nashville with her new husband, I quickly learned how completely stupid I'd been for hoping she'd ever come back.

Now, I just want to know where the hell my grandmother is. And I want to know what else Lucas Wolfe knows about my family's history. Whether he knows anything about my mother, since he's learned so damn much about Gram.

I tighten my grip around the scrubber pad in my hand, until the steel prickles painfully into my palm, and attack a spot of invisible soap scum on the shower wall. Ever since Lucas left a couple of hours ago, I've kept myself busy, alternating between cleaning and watching reruns of some zombie TV show on Netflix. Neither have been very good distractions from thinking of Lucas or where Gram's weekly Tuesday errands are actually taking her.

"You rushed me over here with your bags for . . . ?" The sound of a voice behind me just about pulls me out of my skin. Splaying my wet palms over my chest because my heart is pounding so hard it burns, I scramble around on my hands and knees to face my brother.

"Don't you knock? Or ring doorbells?" I sputter. "I could've—"

"What? Attacked me with household cleaner? The papers would have a shit-fest with that one. 'Pissy redhead mauls popular Vandy student with the remains of a Brillo Pad. Charges are pending.'" Seth doesn't seem daunted by the fact that he'd scared the hell out of me. In fact, he's smiling like an idiot. Begrudgingly, I take his hand when he reaches it out to me, and he pulls me up to my feet. My brother isn't exactly a good-natured person, so when he's in a decent mood I might as well take advantage of it.

"You wouldn't press charges against me," I point out, leaning against the sink.

Scratching one of his hands through his short blond hair, Seth tilts his head to one side. "Why's that?"

"I'm a girl. And I'm betting you have some screwed-up idea that admitting a girl kicked your ass makes you a lesser man. Am I right?" I demand, grinning all the while.

"First time you've gotten something right about me in, what? Four years?"

Ignoring the jibe, I follow him down the stairs. I almost expect him to take a ride on the wooden banister, like he was so fond of doing when we were kids, but he jogs instead. The coatrack in the foyer topples over from the motion.

We squat down at the same time to pick it up. As I work on collecting the jackets that have fallen to the floor, I make up my mind to confront him about what Lucas pointed out earlier. There's a chance Seth knows something about Gram that I'm not aware of, though I'm almost hoping he doesn't for the sake of not getting jealous again about being so out of the loop.

"Where does she go every Tuesday?" I blurt out.

Seth cocks a light brown eyebrow, and he gives me a half smile. "Um, Si . . . you know I'm not psychic, right?"

Hugging a bright red fleece jacket to my chest, I take a deep breath before I continue, "I'm talking about Gram. I'm just curious about where she goes on Tuesdays."

My brother's light mood seems to change in a matter of seconds. His relaxed smile disappears, suddenly replaced by a tight frown, and his shoulders stiffen. He pops to his feet, but this time he doesn't help me to mine.

"How do you know she goes somewhere *every* Tuesday?"

"Sh-she mentioned something about keeping to her usual Tuesday schedule this morning at breakfast," I lie, hanging the jacket on the coatrack and avoiding Seth's eyes. Whenever my brother takes on the brooding expression he's wearing right now, I know he's only a matter of moments away from going over the edge. I don't want to pair whatever is bothering him with letting him know Lucas was out here this morning.

Lucas could beat the hell out of my brother with his eyes closed and both of his tattooed arms tied behind his back.

Releasing a growl, Seth drags his hands through his wheat-colored hair and then stalks past me into the dining room. He sits down at the antique table where we used to eat dinner every night and slides out the chair beside him, motioning for me to sit, too. I scoot it back in and opt for the seat at the other end of the table, directly across from him.

"I take it this isn't good," I say at last.

Seth shakes his head in agreement. "Do you think she's been going to see Mom?" he asks.

Of course I think that, but I was hoping Seth would reassure me otherwise. Instead, my brother is so upset about the prospect that he's flushed, shaking. Out of the two of us, his bitterness toward our mother is twice as bad. But then again, I wasn't the kid who Mom had almost convinced to take the fall for her sins.

Yet I'd still found myself smack-dab in the middle of it all.

And for the first couple of years after everything happened, I was the kid who let Mom bully her around even from inside of a prison cell.

I place my hands together, rubbing them on either side of my nose. I must look like I'm praying because Seth rolls his brown eyes dramatically and releases a deep groan. "So what do we do?" I demand, my voice sounding desperate.

"She's not a kid, Si. There's nothing we can do."

"You're a pretentious ass. You always know what to do."

"I'm not going to ask her if she's visiting Mom because I've got no proof. If you want to, you can, but I'm sure you won't."

I slam my hands down on the wood, glaring across the table at him. "Why's that?"

"Come on, Si. You're scared of your own shadow. Gram didn't want to tell you about the goddamn foreclosure because she thought it would just upset you. Do you remember how you were in court during Mom's trial? All nervous and nodding and staring down at your lap and—"

Shaking my head, I cut Seth off, speaking in a low, clipped voice: "Thanks, but I don't need a character evaluation. And I'm stronger than you think." Still, when I touch my hands to my cheeks, my face feels like there are flames burning beneath my skin. This is the second time today someone's blatantly pointed out negative traits about me.

My stomach tangles into taut knots.

Quirking up the corner of his mouth, Seth starts to say something, but then thinks better of it. He shrugs his broad shoulders nonchalantly and then rises to his feet. He can try and pretend like he's not upset all he wants, but I know different. His hands are clenched. As soon as he leaves here, he'll head straight to the gym to blow off some steam.

It's better than blowing up and punching someone's face, like he was notorious for after Mom was sentenced. It's a wonder he isn't locked up in a juvenile detention center somewhere.

"I left your bags in the living room," he tells me, sliding the dining chairs back where they belong. He doesn't look up at me when he adds, "Hey, do me a favor—when Grandma gets in, can you tell her to call me?"

Realizing that our heart-to-heart has come to a definite close, I nod my head. "I will. You drive safe, okay?"

He rolls his eyes and mutters something under his breath where I only make out the words *not, fucking,* and *mom,* then says, "I'm going to start looking around for places for . . ." His voice dies away, and once again, I bob my head up and down.

Like a broken little bobble-head doll.

Seth goes to the door, starts to leave, but then turns around, his expression softer. "You should rent a car or something, Si. Might do you some good not to be stuck here all day."

"I don't mind it," I lie, and he shrugs before walking away.

When I hear him start the engine to his truck a minute later, I trudge back upstairs. I finish cleaning up the mess in the bathroom, throwing the used scrubbing pads in the wastebasket, and run a cold shower to wash away the neon blue soap that's dried to the porcelain.

After I'm finished, I return to my bedroom and climb onto my bed, sliding under the pink and orange comforter. Resting against the mass of pillows leaned against the headboard, I open my laptop, determined to see what the damage will be if I go ahead and reserve a compact rental car for the next thirteen days. As much as I hate to admit it, Seth is right—getting out of the house would be good for me, especially with Gram being gone so often and her not wanting to take me along with her. I'll simply have to chalk up spending a couple hundred dollars for the sake of convenience.

"It's just money," I tell myself. "I'll make it back quickly and all will be well in the world again." Silently I add, *If Tomas doesn't do a one-eighty and fire my ass.*

I'm in the middle of typing in Enterprise Rent-A-Car's Web address when I notice the red notification in the left corner of the Facebook page I'd left up earlier after returning a message to Tori. It's a new friend request.

From Kylie Martin, Lucas's blue-and-black-haired assistant.

Is she screwing with me?

"Dear social media: piss off," I mutter, moving my finger over the mouse to decline the request. But then I see the message just below Kylie's request, and I freeze. I lean in closer to the screen to read.

Hey Sienna,

I know you really want to just tell me to go get hit by a bus (or you know, decline being my friend) but please accept. I have a way you might be able to save your grandmother's house. All I need is a few minutes of your time.

—Kylie

Without a second thought, I accept the request.

And just like that, I'm friends with the enemy's little worker bee.

4

Less than an hour after I accept Kylie's friend request, my curiosity gets the best of me. She hasn't sent me any replies, and I have to know what she meant when she wrote she has a way to save this house. Biting the inside of my cheek, I send her a response that simply reads: *Will you tell me how?*

A shrill ding indicates that I've received a brand-new message approximately seven minutes after I clicked send. Tossing the fitness magazine I'm attempting to read (and failing miserably because I'm so worked up by Kylie's cryptic message) on top of my nightstand, I watch the screen and shift my teeth together as Kylie sends me a series of instant replies.

> **Kylie Martin:** Hmm . . . to be honest, what I've got to tell you is probably something that should best be said in person and not online. Are you free this evening?

I decide to wait before I write anything back because the instant messenger says she's still typing.

> **Kylie Martin:** I can pick you up at, say, 7 p.m. and we can go into all the nitty-gritty details over dinner. My treat. Order the most expensive prime rib on the damn menu, if you want. It's on Lucas's dime.

This time, I don't immediately answer because there's something that chafes me raw about going out to dinner and using Lucas's money to do so. It makes me feel . . . well, sort of cheap, though I know that's ridiculous. I'm sure his assistant takes other people out on all sorts of dinner and lunch dates, swiping Lucas's credit card at as many restaurants as she can reasonably get away with. If I go, tonight won't be any different.

Except for the glaring fact that it's obviously very different.

> **Kylie Martin:** Just let me know something in the next hour, before 6 p.m., okay?

I ease my butt down on the edge of my bed. The mattress dips down a bit in that particular spot, and even though I know it's because the bed is old, I make a vow to go for a run first thing tomorrow morning. With my lack of funds there's no way I can afford going up another dress size. Clutching the sides of my laptop, I stare at Kylie's messages at the bottom of the computer screen, unable to look away, even when the words start to blur into one another and all I'm able to see is a dizzying swirl of blue and white and black.

Does Kylie genuinely know something about Lucas that might delay the foreclosure? Hell, even if she does, why would she betray her boss like that to help me? She's been working for Lucas for a long time—at least a couple of years—and I'm no one special to her. Other than this afternoon, I've only met her one other time in my entire life and we hadn't had much to talk about other than the usual pleasantries.

Then, another possible reason behind Kylie's invitation comes to me, knocking me upside the head like a brick. My thoughts shift to a completely different, sinister direction.

What if her inviting me out is some sort of setup just to get me out of the house for some reason? Like Lucas and those two contractors coming back over here tonight so they can go over where to put the gaudy house he'll more than likely start building in two weeks or how much of Gram's cabin they should keep around for firewood.

A frustrated, smothered noise escapes my lips. I press my fingers to the computer keys and type out a message in record time.

Why can't you just tell me now? I demand.

For close to five minutes, Kylie doesn't answer, but I see the little notification in the center of the message box that lets me know she's typing.

"Ugh, this had better be an epic message," I mutter. I'm impatient as I continue to wait, tapping my fingertips on the flat space on either side of the mouse pad and grinding my teeth back and forth, the clicking noise coursing tiny prickles through my body. The teeth gnashing is the worst in the history of awful nervous habits. It's one that I picked up as a kid after my parents dissolved their ill-fated marriage and not even relaxation massages or yoga have been able to control or stop it.

It's a nervous habit that, two years ago, had driven Lucas Wolfe crazy. *"Don't grind your teeth together,"* he'd ordered, as his rough hands explored my body, as I writhed beneath his touch in his king-sized bed. Shutting my eyes, I give in to the memory until the ding indicating a new Facebook message drags me back to the present and into my bedroom.

> **Kylie Martin:** Sorry, I'm only willing to do it in person. If it's not tonight or by tomorrow evening, it will be too late to do anything.

Suddenly, all thoughts of Lucas's hands fly out the window because of his assistant. Kylie's giving me an ultimatum. She's using a limited time frame to coerce me into going out to dinner with her, and it makes me irritated and uncomfortable and more than a little angry. Ever since my sophomore year at college, I've tried hard to avoid people who do this to me because it's too reminiscent of Preston, the boy I dated all through high school, who wanted to control everything I did.

Thinking of Preston makes me grip the computer harder, until parts of the screen change colors beneath my fingertips. I pull my hands away, and tuck them under my thighs.

Preston had had different demands for one thing or another

every other day, and he would change his mind about each of them as soon as I followed through. By the time he ended things with me he swore I was codependent. Looking back at the situation now, I was.

I focus on the screen again, attempting to ignore the bevy of emotions that memories of Preston always seem to bring about. I don't still love him. Tori swears I probably never did and just went out with him because of my parental issues. Still, there's a bitter ping in the center of my chest.

Swallowing back memories, exasperation, and the sense of defeat, I send Kylie a reply.

> I don't like being bullied any more than I enjoy being given an hour to decide something.

Kylie fires back a response seconds later.

> **Kylie Martin:** It's just dinner—it's not like I'm asking you to get pregnant with my blue-haired love child and come live with us in Paris, you know? Like I wrote you before, I know a way you can save your grandmother's house. You just have to . . . trust me. I can't do anything more than that online.

Massaging the bridge of my nose in a slow, circular motion that doesn't do a damn thing for my sudden migraine, I start tapping out a one-handed reply. It's only a few words, but it takes me a couple of minutes and several tries to make sure I don't sound like the blubbering idiot I feel like right now.

Where and what time?

I wonder if she's smiling wherever she is because she immediately writes: *Yay!* About a minute later she adds, *Fondue. Oh God, please tell me you love fondue?* After I respond positively, she types one last comment:

Kylie Martin: Kick-ass. Fondue it is, then. I'll pick you up at your place at seven, and I promise to have you home by midnight. See, I'm a respectful date and won't even try to get to second base. Catch up with you soon!

I send Kylie two or three more messages asking her if she's going for casual or formal dress and whether she can park at the end of the driveway so Gram doesn't see her, but she doesn't answer either of them. It's just dinner, like Kylie pointed out, but I can't help feeling like I have to make a good impression. Like she'll be judging whether or not I'm worthy of receiving the information she has while we eat fondue.

There's a loud boom downstairs—the front door slamming—and I startle. The bookshelf in the corner of my room is still shaking from the impact as I stumble off the bed, nearly breaking my neck on a pair of tall boots I left in the middle of the floor. I race to the window. My grandmother's Land Rover is sitting in the driveway, backed in so that the open trunk is closest to the house.

I heave a sigh of relief.

Tori and I have had way too many people try to break into

our apartment in California for me to be comfortable with doors opening and closing abruptly.

A moment later, Gram yells up the stairs in a noticeably tired voice, "Sienna?"

"I'm here!" I call out. I slip my feet into a pair of green flip-flops and pad out into the hallway.

I reach the foyer as Gram shuffles through the front door, struggling to carry several bags of groceries. Quickly, I scoop them out of her hands, where the plastic has started to make harsh indentations on her thin wrists. She offers me a grateful look.

"I stopped and picked up some food for you, so you won't starve to death while you're here. All your favorites, and I'll even cook them for you," she says, her voice just a touch too bright and cheery.

I can clearly see into the back of her SUV from where I'm standing. There are at least a dozen more bags in the trunk alone, not to mention what's probably being stored in the back-seat. I feel a swell in my rib cage because my grandmother is on the verge of losing her house and having to spend money to relocate somewhere else. We both know she's doesn't have the funds to do things like stock a house with the foods I enjoy.

Instead of pointing this out to Gram, or immediately grilling her about where she's been, I move the bags in my right hand up and around my wrist and give her hand a tiny squeeze.

"Thanks," I say. Then, keeping my tone as light and as teasing as possible, I add "You haven't cooked in, what? A year or two, when Seth was still in high school?"

Gram lets out a throaty chuckle. "You're worth it and more."

But I wonder if she'd feel the same way if she was aware of just how torn I am about the man who now owns her house. How more than half of my thoughts since touching down in Nashville have been focused on Lucas. And not the bad kind.

Good thing Gram will never find out.

"I'll put these away. You go and rest," I insist breathlessly, motioning to the groceries. I keep my face turned away from her. The last thing I want is for her to notice the telltale flush thoughts of Lucas always seem to bring about at the most inconvenient moments.

Gram doesn't give me hell like she usually would, but graciously murmurs, "Thank you, hon. I don't know where I would be if it weren't for you and Seth." Then she goes willingly into the living room down the hallway, so obviously dead tired. I move about the kitchen as quietly as possible so I won't bother her while she rests.

Unloading the bags is a monotonous task that reminds me of my time bagging groceries at the store up the street when I was in high school. I'm grinning by the time I finish because I have images of cart-racing with my coworkers and an even more vivid picture of racing wardrobe racks on the set of *Echo Falls* with Vickie, the other wardrobe assistant. If I ever got the nerve to do something like that, Tomas would shit a few bricks.

As I store the final item in a low cabinet, the digital clock on the stove catches my eye: 5:45 p.m. I'll be with Kylie soon, and there's a chance—albeit not a very strong one—that I'll know what to do to make sure this house stays in Gram's possession.

Speed walking into the living room, I say, "Hey, I'm going to—" But I stop short. My grandmother is asleep on the couch, snoring softly, her chest rising and falling. "Head out with a friend," I whisper.

As I turn to leave, my eyes land on a wadded-up piece of paper in the corner of the doorway. I stoop down and pick it up, carefully unraveling it and smoothing out the wrinkles as I return to the kitchen. When I set it on the counter and lean close to examine it, a painful frown comes over my face. It's the grocery receipt from Gram's massive shopping expedition. And it's not the amount of money she has spent that makes my heart beat faster. It's the city and state the groceries were purchased in.

Bowling Green, Kentucky, which is an hour's drive from Nashville.

It's the halfway point between here and the prison in Lexington that houses my mother.

More than anything, I want to feel denial or shock or even anger. Hell, I've experienced all three emotions and often at once when it comes to Mom in the past. But as I fold the receipt into tiny, even squares, the only thing I feel is a sharp pang in the middle of my chest.

Kylie arrives early—a quarter 'til seven—in the giant silver Cadillac SUV and I hurry to finish up the last touches of my makeup. Lucas's assistant must not have gotten my message because she parks halfway up the drive and jumps out of the car. As she practically skips toward the house, and into the path of the motion detection lights, I decide she looks like the Stay Puft Marshmallow Man in her blindingly white parka with her short black and blue hair poking out from beneath a slouchy white crocheted hat. Tennessee's not *that* cold.

Kylie pauses in the circular walkway, tilts her head up until her dark eyes connect with mine, and then smiles and waves. Feeling myself flush from head to toe at being caught, I wiggle my fingers back at her. Why the hell is she so friendly when she hardly knows me? A moment later, she stops flapping her hand and disappears under the covered wraparound porch. The doorbell rings.

"Ah, shit," I mutter. "Gram . . ."

Feeling a wave of nausea pass through me at the thought of my grandmother answering the door and having to face down Lucas's assistant, I speed down the stairs. I'm too late. My feet hit the final step just in time to hear Kylie complimenting Gram on how beautiful the house is. My grandmother's not giving her dark looks or asking her to leave, so I'm caught off guard. Then I realize that Kylie wasn't in court yesterday. Gram probably has never had the chance to meet her, but now that she has, she's utterly charmed. Kylie's praise is making her blush hard-core.

Lucas's assistant's sugary act is really starting to freak me out.

"Um, Gram, this is Kylie, she's—" There's no way I can introduce her as Lucas's assistant without screwing myself over and having to answer a million questions. I shoot Kylie a pleading look.

"A friend from high school," she effortlessly adds, sliding a short blue strand behind her ear. When Gram looks away for a split second, Kylie winks one of her brown eyes at me. It's heavily lined in a blue liner that matches her hair. "I'm in town before heading off for vacation in a couple of days and hooked up with Sienna online."

My grandmother's eyebrows draw together as she tries to place whether she's ever met Kylie before. I can read the emotions on Gram's face as she thinks back to graduation and homecoming dances and piano competitions. Coming up with nothing, she lifts her shoulders slightly and shakes her head, her gray hair springing around her face.

"That's so wonderful you stopped by for Sienna," Gram tells Kylie. Then she darts her blue eyes up to me, where I'm still standing on the last step, giving me a questioning look. "Did you want me to cook or—" she begins, but I shake my head quickly.

There's a massive lump forming in my throat. I know I shouldn't but as my grandmother stares at me, I'm thinking of the Bowling Green, Kentucky, receipt that I've folded until there are hundreds of tiny creases lining it. It's upstairs, tucked under the magazine on my nightstand. I shouldn't keep it. I *should've* dropped it where I found it.

Because now I feel like a spy and the only thing I'll do when I see the slip of paper or Gram mentions cooking for me is wonder whether or not she was actually with my mom this afternoon. It's going to eat away at me until I have the chance to talk to her about it.

No, I'll have to confront her in an interventionlike scenario because my grandmother always clams up when it comes to talking about Mom.

My mother tends to evoke that type of response from everyone.

"You've been busy all day, so you should get some rest," I finally force myself to say, despite the constriction in my throat. "Plus, Kylie's got this outrageously unlimited expense account for her job and she's taking me out to dinner to catch up. Isn't that right, Ky?"

Biting her lip—either to avoid laughing aloud at the emphasis I placed on the word *unlimited* or to keep from telling me to shut the hell up and that her name's not "Ky"—she gives us a thumbs-up, and replies, "Sienna's right. My boss lets me splurge, and I take every advantage of it." She flicks her brown eyes down to her wristwatch before giving me a tiny shrug. "And we'd better get going because I'm starving and we have a reservation."

"I'm ready if you are," I murmur, hobbling off the last step.

Then Kylie takes Gram's hands in between her gloved ones and offers her a genuine smile. Once again I'm struck, curious as to why she's being so nice to the old woman her boss wants to evict. "It was so great to meet you, Ms. Previn, and thanks for letting me borrow Sienna for a while. I promise I'll take the best care of her."

I'm pretty sure that's exactly what my ex-boyfriend said when he picked me up for junior prom, the night he talked me into giving up my virginity.

I fidget with the short hem of my chocolate-colored boatneck dress.

Gram's nose wrinkles. She crosses her arms over her chest as if she's in deep thought, as if there's something she desperately wants to say but she's too afraid to come out with it. At long last, she says, "You girls have a good time. And absolutely no drinking and driving!"

It isn't until I'm buckling my seatbelt in the Escalade, which smells like cigarettes and too much pine-scented air freshener, that I realize why my grandmother had such a strange expression on her face just before Kylie and I walked out the door.

Gram and I have different last names—hers is Previn and mine is Jensen, my dad's last name and Mom's former married name. Not once had Gram mentioned her name to Kylie.

The Tuesday night crowd at the costly fondue restaurant on Second Avenue is scant. Kylie and I are seated in a dimly lit, horseshoe-shaped booth. She removes her coat, revealing an oversized sweater with bespectacled owls covering it and a pair of stretchy pants. I'm not one for bold colors or prints like Kylie—I mean, I've played with the idea of dying my hair for years because it's *that* red—but the way she dresses suits her.

As she rolls her coat into a tight cylinder shape and slips it between us, she asks, "You're not dissecting my outfit, are you?"

I feel my ears turn red. "Of course not. Why would I do something like that?"

She makes a weird face, curling her upper lip up so it almost touches the tip of her nose, and rubs her chin with her index finger and thumb. "Hmmm, I don't know. Maybe because it's your job. I mean, I find myself doing my job even when I'm off the clock and critiquing every little piece of music I hear. For example, the music here"—she moves closer, as if she's about to share an intimate secret, so I do the same—"is really, really shitty. But just so you know, I don't mind if you're taking creepy wardrobe-person notes about my clothes. I happen to like the way I dress."

I almost want to tell her I'm taking notes on how off-the-wall she is in general, but instead, I take a giant sip of my water to clear my throat before getting directly to the point. "You said you know a way to save my grandmother's home, Kylie. That's the only reason I agreed to come out tonight. So . . . what *is* it?" I drop my voice to a hush, adding, "What do you know about Lucas?"

Kylie flips open the tall menu and begins skimming over it, glancing over the edge every few moments to watch me. "You know what I've been wondering? Just how in the hell did you manage to keep a body like that growing up in a place with such amazing food?" she asks. "They deep-fry *everything*. I've been here literally a month and had to have Lucas advance me my clothing allowance for next season to buy looser-fitting jeans."

She's evading my questions, but I can play this game, too. For a little while, at least. "Where are you from?" I ask in a carefully controlled voice.

She grimaces, clenching her hands around the menu, bending the laminated paper into an odd angle, before cheerfully replying, "Oh, just Atlanta."

Oh, just Atlanta? The city where butter and bacon and pecans are more of a household necessity than they are here in Nashville. For some reason, I'm not exactly buying her bullshit comment about the amazing food here, even if she has been living in Los Angeles for a while.

Changing the subject, Kylie asks me about my childhood, about the school I went to, and what I did for fun. I answer each question politely, taking the utmost care not to mention my mother. I feel myself growing more and more frazzled because every second that passes seems to crawl by at a snail's pace.

By the time our first course arrives, and Kylie's questions have moved on to my current job working for Tomas, I've had just about all I can take of her elusiveness. I mean, there are only so many questions I can handle regarding my opinion of the *Echo Falls* cast, whom she says (and I agree) suck. I place my palms flat on the table and clear my throat. She drags her gaze up to mine, her dark eyes as enormous as the owls on her shirt. "Kylie," I say as patiently as possible, "why did you want to bring me here?"

Dipping a broccoli spear into the pot of scalding cheese that sits in the center of the table, she frowns. I watch as she swirls the vegetable around until it disintegrates, each second making my heart thud louder, making me feel like she's hiding something.

"Lucas wants you," she says and then shrugs before blowing on what's left of the broccoli.

I already know Lucas desires me, but then a reason I didn't think of this afternoon for her wanting to see me hits me hard. I come to terms with a frightening possibility and drop the piece of bread I'm gripping onto my plate.

"Oh God, you're not going to try to scald my face off with fondue or pour it in my lap because you're in love with your boss, are you?" I ask in a shrill voice.

Her head pops up from the cheese and she stares at me blankly. I'm already making quick, jerky movements, straining to get myself out of the narrow booth and away from this situation. To just leave her sitting here alone before drama ensues.

Then she starts to laugh hysterically.

That's it. First thing in the morning, I'll find a way to contact Lucas so I can tell him to keep Kylie the hell away from me.

Blinking back tears, Kylie grabs my hand and pulls me back down. My knees lock up, making it impossible for me to move another inch. Left with no other choice, I sit. I'm wheezing like I've just run a half marathon when she finally manages to squeeze words past her amusement. "No, don't go, it's just that what you said— *Dude*, so gross. I mean, I love Lucas, but that's because I'm forced to. Our parents would have my ass if I didn't."

Their parents?

"Wait—what?"

She smiles. "Yep, guilty. I'm Lucas's kid sister but only by a couple of years."

My hands automatically fly to my face to cover my embarrassment. "I thought you were . . . your last name is Martin," I mumble slowly because there's a sludgelike thickness building up in my throat.

She holds up her left hand, placing it close to my face so that I'm able to see the thin tattoo circling her ring finger. She twists her hand, back and forth, so I can read the Old English text that clearly says MARTIN.

"Eight years ago, the day I turned eighteen. His name was Bradley Martin and my marriage lasted about as long as the sex we had on my wedding night and was just as goddamn awful. Sorry, babe, you're going to have to reevaluate your opinion of me because I'm not one of *those* assistants."

How did I fail to notice what Kylie is to Lucas? Even though I've witnessed very few of their interactions with one another, it's not like I've ever seen him treat her like anything other than his assistant.

I feel wretched for jumping to conclusions about her. "Kylie, I'm so, so sorry that I—" I begin, but she waves it away, grinning broadly.

"Are you kidding me? Trust me, you're totally fine." When I give her a skeptical look, she sighs, rolling her eyes. "Look, you want to see real psycho assumptions, go and check out some of Lucas's fan message boards. These people are *devout* fans, know exactly who I am, and still bash the shit out of me."

I swallow hard. "Anything else I should know about?"

Gradually, her grin gives way to a worried look. I've always hated looks like this because it almost never indicates something pleasant. Kylie drops her head, rearranging the silverware in front of her.

"I hate fondue. Like really, really loathe it," she says in a high-pitched voice.

"Then why did you ask me to come here? We could've gone somewhere else. I'm not picky. I'm not . . ." But I *am* sweaty and nervous. I'm not so naïve that I believe her shame face stems from a hatred of melted chocolate and cheese. No, Kylie's with-holding something else. Something that's bound to completely ruin this night for both of us.

"Because you wouldn't have come for him," she whispers, pointing. With my heart pounding so violently I swear I can hear it, I turn my head, following her outstretched finger across the restaurant to a smaller booth.

Lucas is sitting there.

My stomach pitches, and I cross my arms over it.

Why is he in this restaurant infecting the place with his . . . *ugh,* rock-star charm? Why can't I think or move or speak right now? The only thing I'm able to do besides hold my stomach and wish myself smaller or invisible is observe. Lucas beckons a pretty brunette waitress over to him and whispers something into her ear. When she pulls away from him, she smiles down seductively, nods her head, and swishes her hair over her shoul-der as she goes over to do his bidding.

He doesn't spare her a second glance.

Now, he's standing, walking toward *my* table. A scarlet haze stretches from the back of my skull and wriggles its way to the front of my face, making me unable to see straight for several seconds. That's just how pissed I am at having been set up by Kylie and Lucas.

I'm still speechless, but now absolutely seething, when he comes back into focus.

He towers over me, his intense hazel eyes blazing into mine as a cocky grin stretches across his handsome face.

"I'm going to have dinner with you, Sienna," Lucas says confidently.

5

There is no way in hell I want to share a meal with Lucas Wolfe, not after what happened the last time I agreed to eat dinner with him, so as soon as feeling reenters my lower body, I bolt up out of the booth. Since I'm so tall, my knees bump hard alongside the table. Wincing in pain and bowing over in humiliation, my vision pings back and forth between Lucas and his sister. Kylie's face is still downturned, and she's not able to see the glare I'm casting her way, but Lucas—

He's standing a mere foot away from me, looking directly into my eyes as he blocks my path out of the booth. He's calm and gorgeous, amused and completely animal. Right now, he embodies everything I want and everything I fear.

I will be so much safer if I forget ever wanting him and, once I arrive home, this whole night altogether.

"Please, take me back to my grandmother's place," I say to Kylie, accentuating every word. I'm livid that she tricked me into coming out with her just so Lucas could invade our dinner. Just so he could more than likely try to convince me to go to bed with him afterward. But most importantly, I'm furious at myself for falling for it and being optimistic enough to hope that she really did have a solution to saving Gram's house.

I feel like a complete fool.

"Kylie, please?" I whisper.

A few people sitting in the tables around us have pretty much given up on their meals and conversations. Now, they're leaning in toward us, hoping to get a glimpse of what's going on, and I can only imagine the thoughts filtering through their minds. *A lover's quarrel, perhaps? Or a man who's come to convince his girlfriend to come home because he thinks she's spent too much time with her friend?*

Or worse.

I try to tell myself I don't care what these people think of the situation because I'll never see them again, but I only succeed in making myself more ashamed. My hands are flushed as I clench them together, and I wish it was Lucas's neck between them, though it's not very likely that will ever happen.

I have better luck getting my wish that the floor will open up and swallow me whole.

"Sit down, Sienna," Lucas orders me in a low tone. Shaking my head stubbornly, I drag in a deep inhale through my nose. I grip the leather back of the booth in one hand and the edge of the table in the other.

"Please move so I can leave," I say, earning a dangerous look from him.

"Not until you hear what I've got to say."

"I've heard plenty from you, Lucas, so move out of my way," I say through clenched teeth.

He bends his head down to mine, so near to me that I can feel his breath fanning my ear and smell spearmint from the gum he must have chewed earlier. "For once, do as you're told before you shoot yourself in the foot."

I gawk at Kylie, who's as flushed as I am and staring down at her phone. Maybe she feels awful for luring me here, but then I shake that notion out of my head. If she's anything like her brother, she's more concerned about the scene we're making and the people who are pretending not to watch us than about hurting my pride. I shouldn't have fallen for her act with Gram either, but I've always been too quick to give people the benefit of the doubt.

"Sit down, Sienna," Lucas repeats.

Quietly, I lower myself until my bottom hits my seat, staring daggers at him all the while. He croons something in a pleased voice that sounds suspiciously like "that's my girl," and then slides in next to me. The farther I slip into the curved booth, the closer he comes. Finally, I just stop moving because there's no use trying to put any more space between the two of us. I'm unreasonably close to sitting right on top of Kylie.

Lucas has me right where he wants me, with the length of his body hot and hard and extremely noticeable against my side.

If I just listen to what he has to say, then I'll be able to leave and forget this night ever happened, I tell myself.

Right after he fucks with my head a little. Right after he tries to convince me to fuck *him*.

My skin prickles all over.

"You'll be across the street?" Lucas questions Kylie. When she says she will, I glance over to see her getting up. My mouth falls open and I shake my head in protest. Even though she sold me out, I don't want her to leave. She's the one who got me into this mess to begin with, so what gives her the right to skip out?

"You can't go," I say, my voice deep.

But she gives me a guilty, almost sad, smile.

"Sorry, Sienna, but this one's between the two of you. I'll be the one to take you home, though." She reaches out to give my hand an encouraging pat, but I knock her fingers away. The sharp edge of one of the bronze skull rings she's wearing nicks the tip of my thumb. I press my finger between my teeth.

"Thanks," I say to Kylie, the word muffled. Not that it matters because I don't mean it.

Lucas clears his throat, and she ducks her head, shimmying out of the booth. "I'm so sorry," she murmurs. She glances back once, before she disappears from sight, but I pretend not to see her. I know it's childish but being an adult has gotten me nowhere in this situation.

Lucas clears his throat, drawing my attention back to him. He drags my injured thumb from my mouth and kisses it. "God, you look like sin," he growls.

There's an edge to his voice—a desperation to the way his lips touch my skin—that sends a cold thrill racing through me, from the toes of my black pumps to the top of my head, where I'd styled my long red hair into a messy updo. My eyes flutter shut and silently, I count down from twenty.

It won't take much to walk away. No, it won't take *anything*. I can call a cab, or God forbid, Seth. I shouldn't stay here with Lucas because he's about as bad for my mental health and my family's life as anything.

Seventeen, sixteen, fifteen . . .

But if I just leave without hearing him out, I'll seem weak. He'll know I can't take being around him. He'll figure out how big the part of me that can't resist him *really* is. And I want to *think* that he can't use that against me, but he can. Lucas is the type who will exploit any weakness to get what he wants.

Seven, six, five . . .

No, I won't leave. Not until I find out—

His fingertips tangle into my hair, sending hairpins flying to the tabletop and onto the seat in a quick, gentle motion. Red strands spill onto my face, around my shoulders, and both of us suck in our breaths at the same time.

"Your fucking hair . . ." he murmurs against my thumb. His tongue teases my skin every other syllable, and it feels so deliciously good.

"What do want from me?"

"All of you," he whispers, dropping my hand. Touching his lips to my temple, he inhales the scent of me, and I listen to the sound of his breathing, letting the warmth from his body send waves of heat and pleasure through me. I moan. He lets out a growl. Finally, he speaks, sounding intoxicated. "But for now . . . I want you to work for me."

He draws back and puts a—dare I say—professional amount of room between our bodies. I'm stunned when I realize that the cheese and vegetables have been cleared away and now there's a salad sitting in front of us. I was so wrapped up in the moment with Lucas that I hadn't noticed the server's return.

Damn this man for driving me to distraction over and over and over again.

And fuck myself for letting him. Why do I do this to myself?

Lucas spears a fork into his salad and takes a bite. I study the way he chews—slow, deliberate movements. Tiny flicks of his tongue that cause my body to burn as I think of how it felt on my fingertip a minute ago. He turns eating, something that is so basic, into a seductive art. I catch myself sinking my teeth into my own lip as I imagine him drawing it in between his teeth.

"I'm offering you Ms. Previn's home in exchange for your . . . services. Ten days. My rules. All you have to do is cater to my every need. Then I'll personally sign over the deed to your grandma's house."

I let his words sink into my brain sluggishly, like spoiled milk. Let the shame wash over me until it replaces every bit of hazy desire I felt just moments ago. "I'm not like that," I whisper, turning my face away from him so he doesn't see the tears threatening to spill down my cheeks and ruin the makeup I so carefully applied.

Lucas catches my chin between his thumb and forefinger, forcing me to look at him. To face him. He gives me a sarcastic, pouty expression and I dig my fingers into the fabric of my dress so I don't try to smack it right off. "I never said you were. Just took you for the type who likes to work for the things she wants."

What he's just said—it takes every cruel comment Preston

ever made to me when we were dating, adds them together, and multiplies them by a million. "I'm not going to fuck you for money, Lucas."

He doesn't try to stop me as I stiffly maneuver my way out of the booth.

I'm three steps away from the table, and struggling with the bitter urge to just break down bawling, when he says, "There's no fucking involved." His voice is so soft and cold, it makes me shiver, like a gust of wind has just swept through the room.

Warily, I take a peek over my right shoulder. He's pushed his salad away, and has his arm draped over the back of the booth, expecting me to sit back down. But what's surprising is his face. The sardonic look is gone, and is replaced by one that's apologetic. And earnest.

"What?"

He motions a finger to the spot I just left. "Sit and we'll talk."

Another order, but he has my attention. He knows there's no way in hell I'm exiting this restaurant tonight without finishing this conversation. Quietly, I climb into the booth, sitting in a way so that we're facing each other. I can feel his eyes blistering into me as I play with my fork, twirling it between my fingers as I wait for him to explain himself.

Lucas lets me sweat for a couple of minutes—allows me to think of so many scenarios that I'm left squirming in my seat. I tap the toe of my shoes on the hard floor, beating out a staccato rhythm. He takes a breath and then, at last, he speaks.

"Kylie's going on vacation to New Orleans and I need a personal assistant while she's away."

"A personal assistant," I repeat, and he bows his head, smiling at me so politely I'm sure it hurts his face. Polite on Lucas Wolfe is about the same as aggressive on me. Outright fucking awkward.

"Mmm-hmm, and naturally I want someone I already know. You."

Me—the same wardrobe girl who was banned from ever working on the set of a Your Toxic Sequel *anything* ever again. The same girl who'd shot him down after he tried to convince her to be bound to his bed.

The same woman he still so obviously wants to bind.

"You want me to work for you because you just want to have sex with me," I snarl. Blowing out a noisy breath, I continue, "You can call me a personal assistant all you want, but this is because of sex. So why not just ask me to screw you?"

He smiles that unsettling smile that makes me question my sanity for still being near him. It's that same smile that also makes me wonder why I'm not throwing my body into his arms right this instant. *Because of what he'll do to you,* the broken little voice in the back of my head warns me. *He'll take everything and won't give a damn thing in return.*

"I told you already," he says. "This is work of the nonfucking variety."

"And where does my grandma's house come into play?"

"Isn't it obvious? It'll be your paycheck. You play my game for ten days, I give you the house."

The sip of water I've just taken goes down my throat the wrong way, and I choke on it, clutching at my chest. He moves closer, his face wrinkled with concern. Gasping, I manage to assure him that I'm fine. Then I squeeze the bridge of my burning nose as I try to give his words a chance to fully register.

He wants me to work for him for ten days. In exchange for Gram's house.

Ho-ly fuck.

"Are you smoking crack?" I demand, in a rough voice I've never even heard myself use before. His eyebrows arch, and the corners of his lips quirk up. "That's not even— Is that even plausible? That would have to be the most idiotic business decision ever."

Chuckling, he places his elbows on the table and links his fingers together so that he can lean his chin against his hands. The sleeves of his gray and black henley roll up just slightly, drawing my gaze to the tattoo on his left wrist. An ornate skeleton key surrounded by barbs, which is very different from the stars on his right arm.

"It's just a house," he says. I flinch—a slight jerk of my body that I hope he doesn't notice. But inside, I feel like he's reeled back and slapped me across my face with every ounce of force he's capable of. What's merely a house for him is something else entirely to my grandmother, to me and Seth.

"Just a house," I repeat.

He shrugs his broad shoulders nonchalantly and his unruly hair brushes his neck. Even now, when I'm so pissed at him, I want to reach out and rake my hands through it. "It's just money."

"A lot of it," I hiss. "It's a whole lot of money."

"And I've got it to spend. I've blown what I spent on your grandma's house on parties and strippers and booze in a month."

For some reason, I'm not at all surprised, if not more than a little disgusted. Shaking the thought of him raining enough money to buy a home on a spray-tanned pole dancer named Candi, I say in an even tone, "But what do you have to gain by this? If you don't want me to have sex with you, why make this kind of offer?"

"Do you know what I realized about you?" he asks, seemingly changing the subject. When I don't answer, he keeps talking, "You are infuriatingly compliant to everyone around you . . . except me."

And it hits me. The reason why he kicked me out of his house two years ago, why he wants me right now. I am a challenge to Lucas Wolfe. "You want me to submit to you," I whisper, and I'm not sure if I'm offended or turned on.

"I want you to do it willingly, yes," he says.

With my heart pounding erratically, my defenses shattered, I don't tell him off when Lucas slides around so that we're touching again. He catches my fingers in his hands, rubbing the pads of his thumbs against the inside of my wrists. "Why?" I whisper. "Why *me* when you can . . ."

"You want honesty?" he demands, filling the silence, taking me back to a moment in his dressing room a couple of years ago when he'd asked me the exact same thing. Slowly I nod my head, and he smiles, dips his head until his warm lips tease my ear. "I've wanted to own every part of you since I first met you. I want to hear you beg me to keep you."

It's an effort, but I manage to keep my breath steady, leaning back so that we're eye to eye. "And if I say no?"

He lets go of my wrists but doesn't bother to move away from me. "Then you finish your dinner, and leave, no strings attached."

"Except I won't get the house."

He ignores my statement, offering the servers who bring our next course—shrimp and steak—a crowd-winning smile. From the way they're looking at him, they've got to know who he is and that he's using this restaurant as a setting for shady business deals. By the way they keep their eyes down and say very little, I don't think they're about to put up a complaint about what he's doing. He probably autographed napkins for them and paid them well for minimal interruption.

I push my food around the plate with my fork. I've lost my appetite. All I want to do is finish this so I can go home and take a shower. Yet, I hear myself ask, "You won't make me have sex with you?"

God, why am I even questioning him? I should be running away, not continuing this conversation. Everything about what we've discussed tonight just screams "escort."

Lucas's lips curl into a sneer. "I don't have to pay girls to fuck me, Sienna, and I'm not going to start with you. I just want you with me, for ten days, answering to my every need. My band's coming so we can record the last couple of songs for the new album, and I'm doing a documentary with a film crew. I've also got a party to go to for a close friend in Atlanta where I'll perform. I *need* someone to keep me organized."

"And that person is me because you want to make me your little—"

He leans forward, pressing one finger over my mouth. Instinct kicks in and I try to lick my lips, grazing his flesh instead. "Assistant," he says. "And yes, it is you. It's always been you. You do this for me, I hand you the deed to the house and your grandmother doesn't get evicted. I'll go back to California and everyone will be happy."

"And no making me do sexual favors?" I ask one final time.

He grants me a hungry smile, and I know there's a caveat. "Oh, we'll fuck, Sienna. Believe me, it's been bound to happen since I first laid eyes on you. But this time it's going to be because you beg me, not the other way around. And when you do, it'll be because you're ready to completely give yourself to me."

Squaring my shoulders, I sit back stiffly on my side of the booth, glaring down at my plate full of food. "I see."

He slides a folded square of paper across the table. I open it to see his name, a phone number, and a time written in precise handwriting.

9:00 p.m.

"The offer's on the table until tomorrow night," Lucas says.

6

There's not much else to discuss after Lucas gives me his ultimatum, so once again I ask to be taken home. This time he doesn't argue with me about my decision to leave. I watch him cautiously as he pulls his phone out of his pocket. His fingers fly across the smooth screen, and when he lays the iPhone facedown, he gives me a tight, harsh stare. "Sent Kylie a text, she'll be around sooner or later."

True to Lucas's word, his sister comes back to the fondue restaurant ten minutes later to drive me back to Gram's house. Kylie chats nervously to me as she steers the Escalade through the stop-and-go traffic on West End Avenue, but I'm hesitant to talk. She'll only turn around and snitch to Lucas. Anything I say to her—every word that comes out of my mouth—will be filed into the mental folder he's keeping on me.

That's the last thing I need right now.

Releasing an exasperated moan, Kylie punches a button on

the radio, cutting the rock song that's blasting through the SUV off in the middle of the guitar solo. "Would you just say something? Cuss me out and call me a vicious bitch if you want, but don't ignore me." I hear the flick of a lighter followed by the smoky, menthol scent of a lit cigarette. I exaggerate a cough, even though I grew up around smokers and had gone through my Marlboro stage in high school. "My ex-husband used to do that ignoring shit, and it sucks. Bad," Kylie tells me, sniffling.

Apparently, we have something in common because Preston used the same tactics on me when we dated. It's still not enough to change my resolve. I press the side of my face to the cold window, sliding my teeth together.

"You don't understand how Lucas gets when he wants something like he wants you," she continues once she realizes I have no intention of talking to her.

So it's her job to go out and herd the redhead in for her big brother? Wonderful. Doesn't she understand that I'm not some object that Lucas can simply click his fingers for and have? That it's wrong for him to even make me an offer like the one he's just given me because he's dangling something that I hold dear over my head?

That she's just as screwed up as he is for helping?

At last, Kylie turns the SUV onto the private drive to get to my grandmother's home. Instead of parking the Escalade halfway down the driveway, as she did at the beginning of this evening, she drops me off right at the door.

Before I get out, she grabs my wrist. I try to tug away but she tightens her grip. What was with their family and the unwelcome touching? She flips on the interior lights, and I turn halfway in the leather seat to look at her. Kylie's gorgeous—in an untraditional way—but right now her face looks twenty years older with the way her features are all bunched up in distress.

Maybe I shouldn't have ignored her.

Then I admonish myself for thinking that. This is the second time this evening I've felt bad for offending Kylie, and if this time is anything like the first, she's about to punch me square in the vagina.

"Just hear me out," she says, her voice determined. The hardness doesn't reach her brown eyes.

"Fine, I'm listening."

"There shouldn't even be a question of whether or not you'll do this. Luke can be a jerk—I'll be the first to admit that—but he's offering you an *assload* of money to spend ten days with him. I don't know the specific terms of the deal he offered you for working for him, and God, I don't ever want to know, but it has to be worth all this."

She releases my hand, then gestures up at the house.

"I'm not a whore," I blurt out. "Nothing's worth feeling like that."

She scoffs, shaking her head from side to side. "You're only what you make yourself. And just so you know, if you were *that,* my brother wouldn't waste his time pursuing you. He's got more class than people give him credit for."

Her words bother me. My hand flutters up to my neck where my fingertips rub anxiously over the soft flesh. My thumb still stings from cutting it on her ring—still tingles from Lucas's lips touching it—but it's nothing compared to the sting in my throat. Reluctantly, she dips her head toward the passenger door.

"You know how to get in touch with me if you've got questions, okay?"

"I've got your number," I assure her.

I step out of the car, letting the crisp February air kiss my skin. I breathe in the scent of exhaust and chimney smoke—my grandmother must have started a fire. "Thanks for bringing me home, Kylie," I say, shutting the car door. I don't look back at her again, but I hear the Escalade backing away and the angry pulse of heavy metal that'll probably burst her eardrums before she reaches the main road.

I'm so not ready to go inside, so I rest my forehead on the wooden front door, letting a few tears fall as I attempt to gather my thoughts.

What the fuck just happened?

I almost feel like I've witnessed this entire night outside of my body. Almost like I'll awaken tomorrow morning to discover that I'm still in Los Angeles and it's time for me to get my ass to work before Tomas goes into convulsions.

But then I hear the strains of the television from inside the house—Gram's watching her favorite reality show. I feel a gust of air hit the spot on my leg where I nicked myself with a razor a couple of days ago. I rub my thumb and index finger together, shivering as I worry the skin there.

This is all very real.

Sighing, I let myself into the cabin and lock the door behind me.

"I'm home," I say enthusiastically, poking my head into the family room.

"You sound like you used to when you came home from a date in high school," Gram teases, grinning at me. She's in her recliner on the far side of the room. I'm trying my hardest to make myself look happy, but if she were any closer or wearing her glasses, I'd be royally screwed. "Did you have a good time with Tori?"

I force out a laugh. "Tori's the roommate, Gram. I went out with Kylie. Look, I'm pretty tired from getting up so early this morning, so I'm going to head up to shower and read for a bit. Do you need anything before I go to bed?"

Clearing her throat, her smile fades away and the gleam in her blue eyes seems to go right along with it. "Seth spoke to me earlier this evening."

"Oh," I manage to say. Had he said anything to her about what he and I talked about early today? It's just like Seth to change his mind about a confrontation and try to wheedle a confession out of Gram anyway.

She nods. "He wants the three of us to go house-hunting tomorrow," she replies, and I mouth an inaudible "Oh." She takes in a tremulous lungful of air, and stares down at her hands. "I've told him I'll go as long as I have you two with me."

"Always, Gram," I say. My feet automatically carry me to her, and I squat down to give her a long hug. Then I kiss her cheek, being cautious not to look her in the eyes. I don't want her to see I've been crying. "I love you and I'll be with you through whatever."

"You, too," she whispers, smoothing down strands of my red hair.

As I climb the stairs, it feels like I'm dragging a hundred pounds right along with me. I sit in the shower with my arms wrapped securely around my knees, allowing the hot water to serve as a diversion from thinking about and wanting Lucas. Even after everything that happened in the fondue restaurant and how confused he made me feel, just hearing his name in my head causes the pit of my belly to tighten.

I don't stop the water until I'm coughing, choking, from the steam. Then I simply remain where I am, resting, listening to the shrill ping of water dripping from the faucet and onto the porcelain.

I'm shivering by the time I crawl into bed, but my body is on fire.

From need. Desire. From words left unsaid and actions left unfinished between me and Lucas. From feeling something I've never felt before with anyone else.

And sleep—it doesn't come because that momentary distraction I sought when getting into the shower is gone. Now I'm left breathless and aching for a man who sees me as nothing other than an object he can win.

I wake up the next morning to multiple messages from Tori. My best friend is worried because I haven't called or texted and she's afraid I've fallen prey to Lucas's charms. Groaning at just how close her assumption is to being true, I compose a reassuring e-mail letting her know that I'm okay. I say nothing about Lucas or Kylie or last night because even though she's two thousand miles away from me, Tori's got this insane ability of picking up on a shitty situation.

Once I'm happy with the message, I hit send. Almost immediately I receive a new message notification, this one from Kylie Martin. Her message is simple and only one line:

> Sienna, I'm so sorry for putting you through that.
> K

It takes me twice as long to figure out what to say to her. I'm still angry—correction, I'm furious at the stunt Kylie pulled—but at the same time I don't want her to know that what happened last night is still bothering me. Because if she knows, there's a 99.9 percent chance Lucas will be made aware. Finally, I send her a short, but pleasant, message that reads:

> Don't sweat it, I'm fine. Please thank Lucas for dinner
> for me.

Shutting my laptop before Kylie has a chance to respond, I change into a pair of skinny jeans and an oversized dolman sweater. I grab my boots from the middle of the floor and walk barefoot downstairs. Gram is already eating breakfast—cereal and turkey bacon—and Seth's with her.

"Good . . . morning?" Considering my brother is here, I have to double-check the time on my cell phone; it's 8:45 a.m. I wasn't aware that Seth even knew there were hours between two in the morning and noon, but I guess he's proven me wrong. "You're up early."

"You don't look happy to see me," he pouts through giant bites of Rice Krispies. He's wearing a baseball cap and a faded Abercrombie & Fitch polo shirt, and I'm instantly reminded of the frat boys in college who wore tiny shorts and boat shoes year-round.

"Of course I am." I sit down in a chair at the middle of the table, flicking my eyes back and forth between Gram and my brother. I spend a good minute trying to come up with reasons why Seth is here. Then I remember what my grandmother said last night before I sulked up to my room, and I thunk myself in the forehead with the palm of my hand.

"House-hunting?" I question.

They nod in unison.

"You hungover, Si?" Seth asks mockingly as I scoot the chair I'm sitting in out so that I can put my boots on. I cast a glare at him. He holds his hands up in front of him, defensively.

"I don't drink," I say darkly, jerking one of my leather riding boots onto my foot, then the other. I consider calling him out for the empty Jose Cuervo bottle I found in his center console, but Gram gives us both pleading looks, and I squash the urge. There's no need to upset her just because I want to head-butt Seth square in the teeth.

Of course, my little brother is not at all the driving force behind my bad mood.

As much as I dislike admitting it, I'm still fuming and bothered by Lucas. He effortlessly managed to make me come undone after one meal together. I don't want to imagine what he's capable of doing to my head, heart, and body in the course of ten days, like he's proposing.

It wouldn't be good for me.

"We're ready if you are," Seth says, standing and brushing crumbs off the front of his shirt.

I suppress the urge to roll my eyes, giving him a sweet smile instead. "Then let's go."

If seeing my brother out of bed early was a surprise, my heart almost stops when he reveals that he's already taken the initiative to set up appointments at available places throughout the city. He insists we take his truck. He's cleaned it out since the last time I was in it a few days ago, but it smells damp and suspiciously like spiced rum, McDonald's, and vomit.

Gross.

Gram notices it, too, because she sniffs a few times but doesn't say anything.

As we drive to the first location, I try to keep our conversation on Seth's school schedule—it's boring—and away from my brother delving into what Gram does on Tuesdays. He catches my gaze in the rearview mirror, giving me an angry, questioning look after I change the subject yet again to the Tennessee Titans. He knows I'm not a football fan.

"Stop it," I mouth at him. Today is going to be hard enough for Gram as it is, so I don't want him adding any more stress by bringing up Mom.

But sooner or later, before I return to California, I'll speak to her about it.

Alone.

When we arrive at the first house, we're greeted by the owner, a woman named Tiffany Bernard who has a megawatt smile that's locked into a wrinkle- and emotion-free face. She extends her French-manicured hand to Gram the moment we exit Seth's Dodge Ram truck.

Mrs. Bernard gets five minutes into her pitch—and it's a good one because the house is amazing with hardwood floors, a great neighborhood, and is only one story—and then she asks about rental and ownership history.

Ashamed, Gram looks down at a dark spot of tile. "My home was recently foreclosed," she says in a shaky voice.

Mrs. Bernard's smile doesn't change, but I can tell that the pleasant atmosphere has shifted. She speeds through the rest of the showing, giving us barely enough time to look at each room. At the end of the tour, I thank her and ask for a copy of the rental agreement. Despite the owner's frosty attitude, Gram really seems to like the house and if I have to, I can place the rental contract under my name. The only thing I've ever bought using credit was a used 2004 Mercury sedan that I paid off late last year.

But Mrs. Bernard gives me her creepy Botox smile. "It's available on our Web site, dear," she says sweetly and I realize that it doesn't matter if we put the rental contract under the governor's name. This woman wants nothing to do with us.

Gram thanks her and says we'll be in touch. On the way to the truck, I lag behind to walk with Seth. "Did you find this place on a Web site?" I hiss.

"Craigslist," he says in a gravelly voice.

The next two rental properties are just as disastrous. One property manager completely overlooks Gram, reaching past her to shake my hand instead and finally looking at her like a nuisance when I point out that I'm not the one searching for a place to live. The final property is an overpriced town house that smells so strongly like animal urine, Seth steps in and right back out, shaking his head.

"Fuck no," he says under his breath. My grandmother is too upset to admonish him for cursing.

My brother and I pool our resources—well, I offer some money and I guess he donates some of my cash, too, considering he owes me—and take Gram to lunch at a fancy restaurant in Franklin, one of the suburbs a half hour outside of the Nashville city limits. Gram points out that the last time she came here was before our grandfather passed away nearly two years ago, but she doesn't so much as smile. Throughout the entire meal, there's a heavy silence that bears down on all of us.

"John built that house for me as a gift for having"—she swallows, as if it hurts her to say the name that follows—"Rebecca. We had offers from country music stars and celebrities for that house because it was truly his best work, but it was our home. Our life."

"Gram . . ." I begin, but the rest of the words catch in the back of my throat.

She forces a bright smile and nibbles on an oversized roll. "Now that he's gone, she's gone, I'm not sure at all if it even matters anymore."

But it does matter, and it always will. I feel miserable that she has to go through this. I feel like I should be doing everything I can to prevent her from having to suffer, just like she's done so much to protect me.

Upon our return to the cabin and after Seth leaves, Gram claims exhaustion again. My eyes follow her as she disappears upstairs, and I flinch when the door to her bedroom creaks closed. Almost as clear as day, I hear Kylie's comment to me from yesterday evening echoing in my head.

"The deal . . . it has to be worth all this."

Before I can chicken out and change my mind, I fish the sheet of paper, the one that Lucas had given me last night, from the bottom of my bag and walk outside so that Gram won't be able to hear a word of what I say during this phone call. Pacing the driveway, I anxiously grate my teeth together as I dial Lucas's number.

As I listen to his pretentious ringback tone—one of Your Toxic Sequel's dirtier songs—there's a part of me that hopes he doesn't answer, or that he refuses to acknowledge my call.

At least then I'll be able to say I gave it my best shot.

But then the song abruptly stops playing, and Lucas comes on the line. "You changed your mind," he says in a whispery, sexy voice that makes me feel as if he's right in front of me, kissing me, making me come.

Suddenly, I'm light-headed.

"Ten days?" I ask, stopping in front of one of Gram's steel outdoor benches. I slide myself down on it because I don't trust my legs at the moment—I'm *that* nervous, *that* worked up.

"Yes," he confirms. "Ten days, my rules."

I shiver, despite the giant dolman sweater I'm wearing, and hug my arms around my body. "How soon do I start?"

Lucas takes a long pause before he answers me, and I almost think that he's thought better of the whole offer and decided to take it off the table. I'm grinding my teeth together when he responds, "Kylie's leaving first thing in the morning, so it would probably be best if you come tomorrow. I'll have my attorney fix up the contract."

"So you don't try to fuck me over on the house?"

He chuckles, a ferocious sound that caresses my body with heat. I squeeze myself even tighter. "Shitty for business to do it any other way."

"Right," I hear myself say.

"Message Kylie your e-mail address so I can send you training instructions tonight. I'm guitar shopping at Gibson right now."

As if to prove his location to me or to taunt me because he remembers just how he was able to drive my body, my senses, to a breaking point with only his guitar and voice two years ago, he strums out the opening of—and I kid you not—a Britney Spears song.

It's the same song that had been playing when I changed the radio in his car, the night I went home with him. He'd humored me for a minute or two, and then rolled his eyes, jabbing a button on the steering wheel to switch the station back to rock.

"You into pop?" he'd asked, giving me a sideways glance. When I nodded, he said, "Figures. Come on, I'll play you all the bubblegum shit you could ever dream of." And he had—my own private show as we sat on the granite countertops in his spacious kitchen. He only stopped playing every so often to pop a strawberry into my mouth or his own or to trail his lips, his teeth, up my thighs.

And then later . . . well, shortly after he was through playing for me, I found myself in the backseat of a taxi, furious at him and myself and crying like a fool.

"You're sending me training?" I finally ask, thrusting the memory of the near-sex experience with Lucas out of my head. When he stops strumming the guitar abruptly, murmuring to someone with him in the Gibson store, it makes keeping my thoughts in the here and now that much simpler. I begin to ask him if Kylie's job is really that intense to need specific instructions, but then I recall all the events and traveling that he's got to do over the next ten days. And how our deal is contingent upon one major aspect: I have to be obedient, doing exactly as he says, for the duration of the week and a half.

"I am," he confirms. There's a smile in his voice. "So you're mine?"

Fighting back fear and pride and something else that causes my heart to beat erratically, I tremble all over and say, "Yes, I'm all yours."

7

Lucas doesn't wait until the evening to send his list of training instructions to me. The e-mail shows up in my inbox rapidly, less than a couple of hours after I give Kylie my e-mail address. He has personally sent it himself, along with a short note that makes my breasts tingle and my nipples harden with excitement.

Sienna,

As promised, I've attached the training instructions. Look over them. Learn them. Don't forget the deal you're making.

Can't say I'm not looking forward to the next several days. I've already got this vivid idea of how you'll taste after you've said the words. How you'll feel when I'm inside of you. Have you imagined it yet?

—Lucas

Without thinking, I reply and ask him if workplace sexual harassment laws apply to being employed by a cocky rock star. He responds while I'm opening the training instruction attachment.

Why? Do you feel intimidated by me?

No, not in the way he's referring to. I am drawn to Lucas—I always have been. And I know without a doubt that I shouldn't allow myself to give in to my attraction to him because it's one of those things where there's no possibility of a happy ending. Even if we wanted to be together for something more than sex, it's impossible. His career and the steady influx of women he comes in contact with would make certain of that.

That's what's so damn intimidating and frightening about him.

I'm shocked to discover that Lucas's "list" is in reality a multiple-page Word document that contains more black writing than empty white space. Sighing, I tote my laptop downstairs, grab a bottle of water and an apple from the kitchen, and set up shop in the family room. I place my computer on the coffee table and open the document. Reading every word carefully, I study the instructions laid out for me. As I read, my skin grows more and more flushed, until it's hot to the touch.

When Lucas said he wants me to submit to him, he wasn't shitting me.

"'You will report to me at eight a.m. sharp on Thursday morning. You will live with me in the residence of my choosing for approximately ten days, which includes, but is not limited to, my current rental and hotels, etc., during out-of-town business,'" I read aloud in a soft whisper. "'You will be provided your own room.'"

My chest clenches up because I realize that I'll have to say a temporary good-bye to Gram. *Hello will be so incredible when I return, though,* I remind myself, picturing her face when I slide the deed to the house into her hands and tell her she doesn't have to worry about having to move.

"'You will consent to carry an electronic tablet for the purpose of note-taking and a cell phone provided to you by myself and reply to any calls or messages in a timely manner. You are not to give this number out to personal acquaintances.'" A special cell phone and tablet? Just . . . *wow.* I shake my head incredulously. "'While you are in my service, you will awaken no later than seven a.m. unless otherwise discussed.'"

Farther down the page, there's information on my public uniform—yes, a fucking uniform. I'm to wear all black, along with dark underwear, though I'm not sure why that even matters since Lucas has sworn he has no intention of stripping me down to them unless I beg him to. Below that, he lays out the rules for private and public protocol. I'm to call him Mr. Wolfe or . . .

I scroll to the next page and my heart beats a little faster as I whisper, "Sir."

On the final page, the fourth page, the training is broken down into categories and what's expected of me: physically, mentally, and verbally.

Personal appearance and concentration and speech restriction: Under no circumstances am I to speak to the press or pa-parazzi, though I've never seen a paparazzo in Nashville and the last thing I want to do is seek them out.

The next categories are "Punishment and Discipline," but there's not a single instruction to be found beneath the headings save for three words that send a trill of excitement through me: "To be discussed."

"You are *so* not spanking me, *sir*," I murmur.

The two final categories are "Sexual Training" and "Emo-tional Training." There are double strikethroughs through both, but I wish he'd simply removed them from the docu-ment all together because they give me thoughts that I'm not quite sure I dislike. Thoughts that make me wet and con-fused.

As I send Lucas an e-mail, informing him that I've read over the instructions and will follow them to the best of my ability, I realize something that would almost make me giggle if the situ-ation were any different.

On the last Your Toxic Sequel album, the final song on the CD was called "Your Master." I remember the first time I lis-tened to it, on the way to work one morning on a radio sta-tion that censored a quarter of the lyrics, and how Lucas's every other word made me fidget in my seat.

Now, I can vividly picture *Mr. Wolfe* going through this list of instructions and changing every reference to himself from "Your Master" to what's currently in front of me.

Because most of what's on my screen is in that song, leaving me to wonder whom the hell he wrote it about in the first place.

When my grandmother wakes up two hours later, I lie to her about where I'm going for the next ten days.

It's the third time during this trip that I've deliberately lied to her, the third time I've let something dealing with Lucas make me be dishonest with the one person I've always been upfront with, and I feel like shit when I do. I convince myself that I'm doing this for my grandmother's own good, and it's better to let her believe something else entirely than to misinterpret the truth.

I'm taking the same approach with Tori. After I first agreed to go along with Lucas's deal, I immediately picked up the phone to call her. As soon as she picked up, though, I froze. She's been warning me since I arrived in Tennessee to avoid Lucas like the plague and sure enough, one of the first things she asked was if "shithead" had been in touch again.

I told her he hasn't, but made a promise to myself that I'll fill her in on everything that's happened during this trip the moment I step foot off my flight home to California. At least then I'll be able to explain the motives behind my decision face-to-face instead of over a bad connection.

"And you're sure your boss needs you back already?" Gram asks me, breaking my thoughts. She gazes across the narrow trail at me with expectant blue eyes.

I take a few more steps forward so I don't have to meet her stare and let the cold wind slap me in the face before I continue with my lie. "Just a little over a week. The other wardrobe girl

EMILY SNOW

has gotten ridiculously sick and it's important for me to go back so nobody ends up jobless."

It took me a half hour to come up with a story that made sense and couldn't be easily ripped to shreds if Seth decided to stop being lazy and do some research. Once I had my lie prepared, it had taken me an additional forty-five minutes of practicing in front of my mirror so that I could sound convincing. As soon as I was prepared, I persuaded Gram to take an early evening walk with me.

"That's a shame they don't have someone who's willing to take both your places for a little while."

I rush to reassure her. "It's totally fine, Gram—it's just that wardrobe is such a picky business and my boss is . . . Well, he's Tomas. Don't worry about a thing, okay? I'll be back to help you here before anything else is done to this place."

Mouthing a silent "Ah," she nods her head understandingly. "You do so much for everyone else, Sienna."

God, I wish she wouldn't say things like that when I'm lying to her face!

"And this is coming from the most selfless person I know," I point out, pulling my bobble cap down farther onto my ears, trying to hide myself.

Gram flushes, the sullen expression she's been wearing for the past couple of days slowly giving way to a look that's both shy and pleased. "Do you need me to drive you to the airport in the mor—"

"No!" When her blue eyes expand, I squeeze my hands together and reply in a more collected voice. "It's an early flight, so it's probably best I just call a taxi."

98

"But it's so expensive to call a cab, I really don't mind."

"Don't worry, my boss is *totally* covering the expenses back,"
I say. Yet another lie because I'm *totally* full of them today. Gram
easily accepts each one and as she does, I feel more awful, more
helpless, and more doomed.

I pray with all my might that in spite of the fact I'll be working for Lucas Wolfe, rock star extraordinaire and asshat, Gram
will never find out any of the details surrounding this charade
that's less than twenty-four hours from going down.

While my grandmother and I are eating an extremely late dinner—I invited Seth but of course he texted at the last minute to
back out—Kylie stops by unannounced. To be honest, I'm grateful
for the interruption. I prepared the meal of baked chicken breast
and steamed vegetables and I'm the lousiest cook I've ever met.

Kylie comes bearing a gift for Gram, an oversized Valentine's
Day Edible Arrangement, and a bottle of French champagne for
me. "Told you my boss gives me free rein with his credit card,"
Kylie says, flashing a hopeful look that's brimming with apology.
I respond with a brisk bob of my head. To Gram, she smiles
sweetly and asks, "Do you mind if I speak to Sienna for a few
minutes? I swear I won't keep her for too long."

Gram's more interested in the chocolate-dipped strawberries, so when she shoos us away, I usher Kylie out to the front
porch. She lights a cigarette, inhaling deeply as if it's her very
last one and she's expecting the apocalypse to happen at any
moment.

"God, this view is amazing," she says, sighing as she gazes out into the night.

I send a bitter smile in her direction. "Yeah, it is. Must be why your brother wanted it so damn badly." *Even though he's willing to give it all up to have me right where he wants me.* When Kylie cringes, I add in what I hope is a teasing voice, "You think you can smoke that thing any faster?"

"I'm giving them up next week—hence, the vacation to New Orleans," she explains, firing up a second cigarette. "You don't even want to know what my friend Heidi's sacrificing this year. Don't judge me."

"Wouldn't think of it."

Kylie slows her roll on the cigarette she's presently smoking, slides one of her palms in the back pocket of her paint-splashed jeans, and says self-consciously, hopefully, "I'm guessing I'm not on your shit list anymore. Or maybe I've been upgraded to your mini shit list."

"Don't hold grudges for too long," I say. Of course, that's a lie, but I don't feel at all bad about hiding things from Kylie. The *truth* is, I still hold a grudge against my mom for the things she did to my grandparents and to Seth and me a few years ago, and it probably won't ever be void, even when Lucas hands me the deed to this house. And damn, I still have to have the talk with Gram about her seeing Mom.

When I'm done with Lucas, I promise myself. *I'll talk to her when I'm done earning back the house, and if I have to, I'll drive myself to the prison and talk to Mom, too.*

Or let her talk down to me, which is probably what my mother is waiting for anyway.

I hug myself to keep from trembling at the thought itself. I haven't seen my mom in a long time because of the way she's able to dig her claws into my self-esteem with only a few words. I already know opening up that corroded relationship again just to try and warn her away from my grandmother is a horrible idea. I mean, I only speak to my dad once or twice a month and he's my *normal* parent.

"You're worried," Kylie says.

Pushing myself away from the toxic thoughts that have started to rot my mood, I look across the porch at her. She's staring at me attentively as she takes slow drags of her menthol cigarette. "Why do you say that?"

"You're grinding your teeth."

I hadn't even realized I was doing it this time. Running my tongue along the smooth surface of my teeth, I manage a lame, "Oh."

"You're going to ruin them," she says emphatically. "And Lucas will probably make you buy a mouth guard." As soon as the sentence leaves her mouth, her cheeks turn the color of my hair and she polishes off the cigarette in two elongated puffs.

If she hadn't blushed, I wouldn't think anything of what she's said, but now . . .

"Why does he want to do it?" I ask, referring to his need to possess me.

Kylie leans against a wooden post, her face drawn together as if she's deep in thought. After a while she says, "I don't question anything he does with his girlfriends or—"

"I'm not his girlfriend; I'll only be his personal assistant," I say. I want to add *just like you* but even I know that my role is the complete opposite of what Kylie's is.

He's already sworn my role will eventually transcend that of his personal assistant, and that I'll be the one begging for it to happen.

"Yeah, I know. Look, if you're wondering about his vices, ask him about it. Nobody is going to tell you better than Luke himself. Of course, Lucas's personal life is one of those squick things for me. I'm sure you understand."

I think of digging through Seth's center console, and I find myself wrinkling my nose and bobbing my head back and forth. "So why'd you come here tonight?" I ask, suddenly desperate to change the subject.

"A few reasons, actually. First, I wanted to wish you good luck and tell you I'm so glad you're doing this. Every time you think of quitting . . . just think of how happy you'll make *her*." She pauses for a moment, either for dramatic effect or to give me time to sort out what she's said or perhaps both. I don't want to process her words because then all I'll do is stress over why she's warning me already not to give up on the job.

"Second, I wanted to tell you to watch out for the band. Because you *will* meet them again. And they will act like man-sluts. I don't give a shit what any of them tell you, if they make you feel weird or uncomfortable, send me a message."

And now Kylie's succeeded in making me feel like I'm going on my first date and my mom is telling me not to let the horny boy touch my boobs. Wonderful. I give her a smile that I just know looks lopsided and awkward.

"But most of all I came to give you this" She slides a stiff white card with an address written on it in loopy handwriting into my hand. I wasn't even aware anyone still used cursive. "So you know where to go tomorrow. And so I could apologize in person for last night." She motions her chin toward the house. "And I brought you a peace offering, though I'm sure your grandma is in there getting sloshed right now. That champagne is *that* good. Hell, I buy it for my parents and they're youth ministers."

Lucas and Kylie's folks. Ministers. *Wow.*

"Courtesy of your expense account?" I ask, trying to hide my disbelief at what she's just told me. She nods, her short black and blue hair swinging around her face. "And let me guess, the trip to New Orleans is a company-paid vacation."

"Oh, hell yes."

I find myself laughing right along with Kylie, the ministers' daughter, and Lucas's younger sister—the same blue-haired woman who deceived me last night all for the sake of helping him obtain what he wants. I can't hold a grudge against her.

Lucas is just . . . a *force* that not many people can reckon with, least of all either of us.

"Well, thanks. For, you know, making me feel like an eighth grader. And for the offering, of course." This time, I mean it. I fully intend on getting a little sloshed myself on the champagne she brought me.

Because starting to tomorrow, while Mr. Wolfe is taking pleasure in training me as his assistant, I will begin counting down the days until the deed is in my hands.

And I'll be doing my hardest to resist him.

8

I don't sleep well. I'm fitful and nervous about the coming days so it takes no physical effort at all to leave the comfort of my bed behind at 5:00 a.m. The force holding me back is mental, *emotional,* and I take my time carefully making the bed, running my fingertips over the worn pink and orange comforter as I smooth it out over the sheets.

"Jesus Christ, Jensen, pull your shit together," I mutter to myself, clenching a large chunk of fabric in either hand and then retucking it. By the way I'm acting, you'd think it was the last time I'll ever see Gram's house and not going only six miles up the road.

To a house where I'm expected to do as I'm told, but still.

While I stream some music over Pandora, I flip my suitcase open and set about the tedious task of pulling my clothes down from the hangers and neatly storing them into the bag. As I work, I set as many of my black items of clothing aside.

Black drop-waist dress that I've only worn once.

Ankle pants and a tight black cardigan, a lace-edged camisole.

The flutter-sleeve top I wore when I first came here and the four-inch pumps that Tori swears make my legs look amazing but I've always been skeptical about because they boost me up to well over six feet. The tweed pencil skirt, too, which is charcoal gray, but I doubt Lucas will even notice.

The music coming from my laptop switches to another song—an older Your Toxic Sequel sex ballad called "Crave It." Automatically, the corners of my lips drag up into a nervous smile because of the irony of it all.

"I'll hold out 'til you crave it," Lucas Wolfe sings. I hum along with him, and a tingling sensation that borders pain and pleasure streaks through me, from my nipples to between my legs.

"Ten days," I moan. "I can hold out on your ass for ten days."

I pad into the bathroom, shrugging out of the spaghetti-strap tank top and shorts I wore to bed last night. The tips of my thumbs skim over the dampness in the skimpy pink shorts, and I shiver. "I mean, I've worked for Tomas for more than ten months."

Of course, Tomas is a short, balding guy prone to temper tantrums and breaking things. Lucas Wolfe is a rock god with the ability to inspire spontaneous wetness just by listening to him over the radio. Lucas Wolfe is a gorgeous and infuriating and unavoidable man prone to . . .

Possessive behavior.

Pressing my forehead against the shower wall, I support myself with my forearm and let the downpour of water beat upon me, first icy cold and then so hot my skin screams. Neither really bothers me at all. My mind focuses on Lucas, on whether today and the nine following it will work well in my favor.

I'm still thinking of Lucas when my fingertips push past my damp folds, seeking out my swollen clit. My breath catches in my throat as I draw the sensitive flesh between my fingertips, carefully rubbing my fingers in a back and forth motion. Slip and slide. Forward and back. My knees buckle, and I whimper.

Trailing my fingers away from my clit, I slip two inside of me, moving against them. My hip bone beats against the tile wall, but I imagine it's Lucas's body touching me, his hands digging roughly into my hips as he guides me down, plunging his cock into my tightness.

I sink my teeth into the wrist of the arm supporting me to hold back a sob. When I think of his face hovering above mine—and his sweat-dampened hair clinging to my wet skin—I pick up the rhythm, gliding my fingers back and forth urgently inside of myself.

When I come, it's quick and hard. I'm nowhere near satisfied.

Slumping, I reach up and grab the shower bar for support. I tell myself that by getting this over now I won't want him. I won't let myself be sucked in by the inevitable scenario that he swears by.

But damn me, he's still on my mind as I send Tori a message, a brand-new lie for yet another person I care about.

Hey, I'm still alive. Still immune to Lucas's charms.
Still . . . well, you get the picture. I'll call you when I get
the chance—things are busy around here what with
everything going on. Miss you.

I dress in the ankle pants, the cardigan, and the camisole—
all black, just as he's requested.

But I wear red underwear beneath my clothes.

My grandmother insists on preparing breakfast for me, though
to be honest, I'm not the least bit hungry. I feel nervous about
lying to her. And sick to my stomach whenever I think about the
next week and a half. There are millions of tiny butterflies in
the pit of my stomach, swarming around, making me more and
more nauseous as the time seems to zoom by.

6:02 a.m.

"I've left some clothes in the closet, for when I return. Please
don't give them to Goodwill, okay?" It's my best attempt to
lighten the dark mood that hovers over the dining room table
and a poor attempt at that.

Gram smiles, genuinely, and the corners of her blue eyes
crinkle. God, Kylie was right about one thing—there is nothing
that's not worth seeing my grandmother's face light up that way.

"So you'll certainly be back then," she replies, taking a sip of
her black coffee. I can't mistake the relief in her voice or how
her face seems less strained once her smile begins to fade away.

She wants me home, I realize. Not just for a few days, but for good and there's a huge part of me that wishes I could stay after this is all said and done.

I clear my throat. "There's nothing that can stop me. And then we'll fix things."

She laughs. "If determination could win this thing we would be set, sweetheart."

That's something else that I'll have to work on while I'm with Lucas—coming up with what to tell Gram when I suddenly show up with the deed to her house and, quite literally, save the day. I nearly groan out loud because it means I'll have to tell Gram more lies and dig myself deeper into holes I prefer not to sink my shovel into.

6:37 a.m.

"Determination and hope have won wars," I say and Gram just smiles, granting me one of those looks she gave me when I was younger and I came up with wistful dreams. While my mom shot my hopes down, my grandmother nurtured them. Even if she didn't believe something was possible, she never let me know that.

"Yes, I suppose you're right."

More than you'll ever know because I'm winning this one for you.

I check the clock once again—it's 6:45 a.m.

The cabdriver seems skeptical about taking me to an address that's in Green Hills, the ritzy part of the city, especially since Gram comes outside and tells me to have a safe flight right in front of him. I tell him I've got to make a stop to visit a friend, and that they'll take me to the airport, though I don't know why I feel the need to explain myself. When the driver pulls up to the entrance of the palatial corner lot, I frown because the mansion is gated. Luckily, Lucas quickly answers the intercom.

"Sienna," he says in a low voice, and I blush.

"Yeah, it's me," I reply, staring down at a piece of lint on my black pants because the cabdriver gives me a knowing look in the rearview mirror. A second later, the gate buzzes and the driver pulls forward.

The home itself is stunning—three stories and all brick, with a long, high fence enclosing the backyard. I've retained very little information from the days I spent helping my grandfather in the office of his construction business, but I know enough to definitively say this house is Euro style.

And probably worth more than I'll make in my entire life, save for the house Lucas has promised me, but then again that's not really mine.

I'm almost reluctant to let go of the forty dollars the cabdriver collects from me—my bank account is just that pathetic—but I take a deep breath, reassure myself again that it's only money. For some reason, when words like that come from me, they don't have nearly the same effect as when Lucas says them.

It's four minutes past eight when I ring the doorbell. To my surprise, Lucas's attorney opens the door—the male lawyer. I wonder if Boobs McBeal is inside the house, too.

I hope like crazy she's not because I'm not in the mood to

witness her jutting out her breasts toward Lucas first thing this morning.

"I'm Court Holder, and you must be Ms. Jensen," the lawyer says pleasantly, taking my hand into his as soon as he closes and locks the door behind us. As he activates the security system on the wall behind him, I decide that his name has got to be the most kick-ass lawyer's name I've ever heard in my life. "I've heard so much about you."

My body freezes in place. What exactly has Court Holder heard about me? The idea of Lucas revealing details about me to his attorney is enough to make me sweat. I mutter my mantra over and over again in my head to keep from turning around and saying screw this.

It's worth it.

"Nice to know Lucas—I mean, *Mr. Wolfe* talks up all his help," I reply through a clenched smile.

Court chuckles, reaching out to take my suitcase. My fingertips brush across his palms as we make the exchange. His hands are smooth and his fingers are neatly manicured, the opposite of Lucas's callused hands. Placing the old Coach suitcase with its worn brown leather piping at the foot of the stairs, Court tells me that the couple who comes to clean every afternoon will take it into whichever bedroom Lucas designates for me. Then, motioning me to follow him, Court ushers me through the house.

"The contract is ready for your signature," he explains, and I bob my head in understanding. "You will, of course, agree to take over Ms. Wolfe-Martin's duties until she returns and

EMILY SNOW

then I'll assist Lucas in initiating the transaction to return Mrs. Previn's home. The contract is extremely . . . simple." But another word hangs in the air, and silently, I mutter it.

Generous.

Extremely generous.

I wonder if the contract I'm about to sign mentions anything specific from the instruction list Lucas sent to me yesterday evening. My agreement to obey, to willingly meet his every demand in exchange for my grandmother's house? Our mutual agreement about emotions and sex that guarantees that unless I ask for it, I'm safe from Lucas's affections?

Judging by the polite, yet somewhat curious, look Court has trained on the side of my face, the contract states none of the above. Relief trickles through me.

As Court and I navigate our way toward the very back of the house, I take in the place I'll be living in over the next couple of days, at the very least. There are photos and awards lining the walls of several of the rooms, and when we pass through the living room, I notice a giant image of a short man in a suit along with the members of Your Toxic Sequel and the lead singer of Wicked Lambs, Cilla Craig. She and Lucas have their arms around each other.

It's not the first time I've seen photos of the two of them together, but it doesn't stop my stomach from hardening.

"Their record producer?" I ask Court, pausing in front of the photo. I choose to ignore the stab of jealousy I felt a second ago.

Jutting his square chin out, Court corrects me. "The *executive* of the record company. It's his house, and I'm his personal

112

attorney, of course." He sounds incredibly proud of himself for being able to handle everything from carrying out eviction proceedings to acting as an entertainment attorney.

I consider patting him on the back, or at the very least giving him a golf clap, but I stop myself, locking my fingers in an uncomfortable angle by my side. This attorney will be handling the transfer of property once I've fulfilled my agreement with Lucas. The last thing I want to do is piss him off thanks to some sudden burst of rebellion and cause a delay in the whole freaking process.

Smiling sweetly, I say, "It's a beautiful house."

"I live right up the block," he tells me in a condescending tone. "In the Tudor."

Lucas is waiting for us in an office that's twice as big as any I've ever seen with a polished bamboo floor and a high ceiling. He looks every bit the kick-ass rock star with his shaggy dark hair tousled about, distressed jeans, and a vintage Pink Floyd T-shirt, but he's so much more than that.

Seated behind the L-shaped desk with his hands clasped together, he doesn't seem the least bit out of place. He's all in control.

And suddenly, I'm tingling all over, wishing his hands were clutched around me instead.

"It's eight ten," Lucas points out, standing up. "You agreed to be here at eight a.m."

I take a tentative step forward. Then another until I'm on the other side of the desk with my thighs pressed against the hardwood. I stare up into Lucas's eyes and say, "Sorry, Lu—Mr.

Wolfe, my taxi was late picking me up from my grandmother's place."

His hazel eyes seem to go from green to toxic brown in a matter of seconds. "Do you make excuses like this to Tomas Costa?" he asks me, his voice dark. Oh God, he knows my boss's full name? Has he contacted Tomas? What else has he discovered about me? "I play music but I've got the same expectations as any other employer you've had. Probably more. Got it?"

I nod. "Yes," I whisper, and when his eyebrow shoots up, I quietly add, "Mr. Wolfe."

He gives me a smile as if he wants nothing more than to eat me, and then motions Court—who's lagged cautiously behind and is staring between the two of us with the blankest face he can manage—forward. "We're ready to sign," Lucas says.

Court produces three copies of the document from the expensive Italian leather briefcase that's sitting beside the plush black couch across from the desk. Hobbling over to us, he hands one copy to Lucas and another to me. Then he goes over the terms of the agreement, explaining all the technical words in detail. Lucas pays close attention to everything Court says, even though he's probably already read over this a hundred times.

Thankfully, the contract is only a couple of pages long and, as I figured, there's very little reference to the instructions I've received except for a one-line blurb. Still, I heave a relaxed sigh, pleased that Court Holder has no idea just how significant the words like *rules* and *obey* are to this agreement.

I start to scribble my name across the section for my signature on my copy of the contract but I stop after I've written the

A at the end of my first name. I glance up at Court and Lucas. Lucas gazes down at me expectantly, but Court's face creases into a frown.

"Is there something wrong with the language in the—"

Shaking my head fiercely to each side, I wave my hand in protest. "No, no, nothing like that, it's just that . . ." I roll my tongue back and forth in my mouth to get rid of the sudden case of dry mouth and drop my eyes back down to the papers on the desk. "I want to make sure none of this will be mentioned to my grandmother."

"Maybe it would help if you looked up when you're talking," Lucas says in a voice that's sympathetic and strong. Commanding.

Slowly, I drag my eyes back up. Lucas is leaning back, his body at ease, his hazel eyes taking in my every movement. "I want your word that nothing about this agreement will get back to my grandma or her attorney, Richard Nielson," I say in an assertive voice that brings a satisfied grin to Lucas's face.

Court begins stuttering, so Lucas confidently takes the reins to answer my question. "Although Court is bound by attorney–client privilege, I've gone ahead and had him sign another agreement. Trust me, if he wants to keep his practice and all his cash cows, he fucking knows better."

Court laughs—a nervous, cough-ridden sound—and I finish scrawling my name on the contract. I complete the other two copies and afterward, he and Lucas do the same. Neither of them seems to notice when I slink away to sit down in the center of the couch. They speak in hushed tones for another couple minutes and then Court claims he needs to go. "Client meeting in an hour," he explains as he backs up toward the double doors.

Lucas smiles at him dismissively, waving him off.

Feeling a little overwhelmed, a little wary, and incredibly conscious of hazel eyes burning into the side of my face, I turn my attention away from the doors Court just closed behind him and to Lucas, who's leaned against the front of the desk. He clears his throat. "Looks like you're mine," he says, his gaze drinking me in. Then he cocks his head to the side and shrugs. "For the next ten days, that is."

"You don't have to look at me like . . ." I lick my lips, trying to come up with the best word to describe how he's making me feel at this very moment.

Lucas crosses the room slowly, confidently, not stopping until he stands right over me, peering down into my blue eyes. "How am I looking at you?" he demands. He reaches out to me, causing the air to rush out of my body as I wait for our skin to collide and the unavoidable spark to flare up just like it does every time we touch.

I wait and wait, but nothing happens because his hand never actually touches my face.

"Tell me what you were going to say," Lucas presses.

I glower at him. "Like you did two years ago when you said you wanted to devour me."

He stuffs both hands into his pockets and takes a step away from me. He licks his lips, sending a pang from my chest to my stomach. "You're wrong, Sienna," he replies. I raise an eyebrow, prompting him to continue. "I said I needed to devour you and I still do. Except now I have every intention of following through. Now, I want you more than ever." Then, as if he didn't just say something so outright sexy it left my head reeling, he goes to the doors. "Come on, I want to show you where you'll sleep while you're here."

9

The downstairs bedroom that I'm given—conveniently located a few rooms over from the office—is nearly twice the size of my bedroom across town at Gram's house. Just like most of the rest of this place, it has wall-to-wall bamboo flooring and smells like lemon cleaner. Unlike the remainder of the house, there's a high cathedral ceiling with skylights. Lucas explains that this is the record executive's college-aged daughter's room as he slides my bags inside the closet. He'd insisted on going to the front of the house and grabbing them for me, telling me how he prefers to bother the housekeepers with as little as possible. When I argued with him that I was capable of carrying my own shit, he gave me a frigid, piercing look.

I'd lunged for the suitcase anyway.

"You're not even halfway through day one, Sienna," he'd said, plucking the bag from my hands and stalking toward my bedroom. If I hadn't followed closely behind him, I wouldn't have

heard him add, "And I already want to punish you for not showing up on time, so don't fucking push me."

Drawing my mind away from how the authority in his voice
had made my face tingle, how I wasn't sure if it was from nervousness, excitement, or irritation, I clear my throat and say, "If
you're staying in their house, where are *they*?"

He sits down on the sofa at the foot of the bed. "Artie Mor-
gan, the owner, and his new wife are vacationing in Ireland, and
his daughter's at school. Vanderbilt student," he says. I'm not sure
I like the fact that I'm holing up in a room that belongs to someone who may potentially know my little brother. I make a move
to sit down, but Lucas shakes his head slowly to each side. "Not
a chance. You've got work to do, Sienna. No sitting on your ass."

Seething, I return with him to the plush office a few doors
over. "Stand there," Lucas orders, pointing to an area in front of
the desk. He seems pleased that I comply without so much as a
whimper. "You read the instructions, right?" he asks, digging in
one of the desk drawers in search of something. His unkempt
hair flops over his face. It gives him an almost vulnerable look,
and my fingers ache to touch the part of his forehead and the
cheek that it brushes.

I'll save wants like this, ideas like wanting him, for when I go
to sleep and keep them far away from my reality.

"From cover to cover," I answer.

"Good," Lucas says. "These are yours." He hands me a small
Best Buy bag, and I reach out and take it. Our fingertips skim,
causing the hair on my arms and nape of my neck to stand on
end.

I focus all my attention on the contents of the bag—a cell phone and a Samsung tablet—so I don't spend too much time dwelling on his easy effect on my body. "Mine to keep?"

He deadpans. "I'm giving you a house. Don't push your luck."

"What do you want me to do now?" I ask.

His mouth draws up into a grin. Oh, he's got me right where he wants me and he's abso-fucking-lutely loving it. I curse at myself for ever showing my timid nature around him two years ago, yell at myself for showing balls long enough to go on his radar. When I return his look—an expression that makes my face hurt—his smile fades. He gestures his head toward the leather couch.

"Sit down, and take those fucking chopsticks out of your hair."

I slam my bottom down on the couch and drag the pretty silver hair accessories from my red locks, letting the tangled strands fall in a mess around my shoulders. Lucas is by my side, standing over me, in a matter of seconds. His hand hovers by my face just like it had earlier, as if he wants to run his fingers through my long hair, to tug on it, but then he clenches his fingers.

"I'm not going to touch you," he promises. "I'm not going to have any physical contact until you beg me to."

"Maybe I won't," I challenge. "Maybe I'll get through all ten days without giving in to you."

And, though I know it's cruel, I find myself swishing my hair over my shoulders, and running my fingers through it in an effort to comb out the tangles. I sense when his body goes stiff.

He mutters something to himself. I make out a couple of words like *ass* and *red*.

I can only imagine that the word *spank* was somewhere in between them.

Feeling a surge of bravery, I continue, "You said that I'm obedient to everyone but you, so maybe—"

"There's no maybe to it," he growls between bared teeth. "By the time you leave me—if I send you away—you'll grow a damn backbone and the only person you'll ever answer to will be me."

What does he mean by *if* he sends me away? I want to ask him, but he begins talking, taking long strides back and forth while he explains in detail everything we're going to do over the course of the next ten days. There's a photo shoot tomorrow for a magazine spread. Then a film crew is coming in from Los Angeles the day after tomorrow. They'll be filming him, outside of his personal space, for a documentary that's being released for a movie about the future of rock and roll. That's on Saturday, day four. On Sunday—

Wait—day four?

When I stop him to ask if he has his days mixed up he shakes his head to each side. "Don't interrupt." I bite the inside of my cheek, and he gives me a look that's almost tender. "But to answer your question, since you accepted my offer early yesterday, I've decided to be nice and give you credit for it."

Well, this is unexpected. I clack my teeth together, side to side, so I don't show how surprised I am that he's taken time off my . . . work schedule. I'm ridiculously grateful, because what

DEVOURED

he's decided to do will give me an extra day with Gram once I'm able to return to her cabin.

"I'm not a total douchebag, Sienna. I do give a shit what happens to you—whether you're happy or not. I always will."

There's a lump in my throat, and I choke out a thank-you.

Then his mood changes and he raises an eyebrow almost mockingly, saying, "Now, no more interruptions or I really will punish you." I open my mouth, but he holds out a finger in front of him, stopping me from speaking. "God, when will you listen? No, I'm not going to physically punish you because that requires . . ."

When he nods his head, giving me permission to speak, I whisper, "Touch."

"And the only way I'll do that is if . . ."

"I beg."

He grants me a smile and then continues giving me a play-by-play of the schedule for each day after Sunday. Day nine will be a recap of everything I've learned and on the final day, ten, he'll conduct a small assessment. Of what, I'm not sure. "Nothing fucked up or"—he raises his eyebrow wickedly—"too strenuous."

Yeah, right.

"Now, tell me what I've just told you," he says.

I make it to day four, knowing that I've left out important details, and then I completely falter. "I-I don't remember."

"Verbal training," he reminds me, and I flush.

"Sorry, Lucas."

I've not called him Mr. Wolfe or sir like he's asked me to, but instead of pointing this out or correcting me, he seems to shrug off the mistake. Maybe today counts as an orientation.

"Let's try this again, this time"—he pulls a long strip of dark fabric from the same desk drawer he found the Best Buy bag in—"let's do this." He hands it to me, making sure our skin doesn't touch.

"A blindfold?"

"Yes, a blindfold."

"I won't be able to see. And then—"

"You don't have to see anything to listen or speak, do you?"

I feel like an idiot for even trying to protest because he has a point. I don't need my eyes for any of those things. Sifting the cloth back and forth between my hands, I ask, "And you want me to put it on right now?"

"Why else would I give it to you?" Lucas demands in a husky voice, wiggling his index finger to let me know he's ready for me to follow through with his request. Hesitantly, I press the fabric to my face, over my eyes, shivering at how soft it feels, how very dangerous.

As I sit in darkness, I listen carefully, intently, as he repeats our schedule to me. When he finishes, asking me what we're doing on day seven, I don't miss a beat. "Wednesday: A tour of your childhood neighborhood and an interview with your parents with the documentary crew in Atlanta."

He quizzes me a little more, and I ace each question. The entire time he speaks to me, I feel hyperaware of everything around me. At every move he makes, every sound. It gets to the point where I have to dig my fingernails into my knees because my nerve endings are prickling so fiercely. By the time I answer Lucas's final question, my voice is trembling.

He's quiet for a long time, but I feel how close his body is to mine as he paces the floor in front of me. Smell the mind-altering scent of his Polo cologne. My skin flushes.

"Take off the mask, Sienna," Lucas says in a strange voice. A moment later, after I've slid the blindfold down so that it hangs around my neck like a supple cloth necklace, I raise my blue eyes up. He's touching the base of his neck and his eyebrows are drawn together. When I stare into his hazel eyes, I see something there that makes my belly twist into an even tighter knot:

Hunger mixed in with a heavy dose of longing.

The entire mood in the room shifts after I realize Lucas wants me at this very moment. "Sienna?" he whispers.

My eyes close and my back arches. "Yes . . . sir."

"You have a license, right?"

"Why do you—"

"One word," he says. "It's a single-word answer."

"Yes."

"Good. Now you won't have to spend the rest of your day at the DMV. Those places are a pain in the ass."

"Oh," I say, opening my eyes. I push my hair back from my face with damp palms. I know there's more that he wants to say to me. With my body still humming from the experience with the blindfold, now would probably be the best time for him to get it off his chest.

Instead, a few seconds later, Lucas decides to send me away.

I've done a lot of work—all through high school and college and, most recently, my job with Tomas—and this is the first time someone has actually uttered the words: "You're dismissed."

"Dismissed?"

"Do I need to have you pull the blindfold back over your eyes and repeat it for you? Leave."

I'm shaken and suddenly a little light-headed at the way his tone has hardened. Gone is the almost teasing voice he'd taken on while he was admonishing me over my lack of listening skills and drilling his schedule into my head. Now, he just sounds . . . like I'm the biggest nuisance he's ever met.

"No, sir, no blindfold," I say, a sarcastic edge creeping its way into my voice as I stand up stiffly, and walk past him toward the French doors. When he shuffles his feet, clears his throat just slightly, I know he's watching me leave.

He stops me before I step over the threshold, back into the sitting room outside the office. "Kylie's left a list of her own for you in the smaller office on the bottom floor."

This time, I simply nod. There's a massive lump in my throat and I don't think I could possibly call him sir again without my voice breaking apart and giving away my disappointment. Gripping the Best Buy bag, I clench my teeth and do as he's asked. I don't even know why I'm upset to begin with.

I grab my laptop from my bedroom and take it along with the new phone and tablet Lucas has given me. I find the stairs that lead to the lower section of the house in the kitchen and head down there. It's cooler in this part of the house, like purposely colder, and my nipples harden under my thin cardigan.

This whole floor was probably a basement at some point, but the contractor who did the conversion managed to make it look as elegant as the rest of the house. When I pass by a piano room, my letdown from the Lucas debacle momentarily disappears and I creep inside.

I was never the pianist my mom had been when she was a kid—she had wanted to perform before she met and married my dad—but I took years of lessons. One of my few good memories of Mom was sitting at the Steinway my grandfather had bought for her when she was a child. She had guided my fingers to the correct keys, teaching me to play some cheesy eighties song, "Take On Me." Of course, twenty minutes later she was yelling at me for tapping a flat instead of a sharp, and my dad was forbidding she ever try to teach me anything ever again, but it had been fun while it lasted.

I'm suddenly aware that I'm quietly playing that eighties tune, and I drag my fingers from the keys. Rub my hands down the front of my black pants.

Leaving the piano room behind, I find the office Kylie's been using. She's left me a long list of things I should be aware of, such as the e-mail address and password for answering Lucas's fan mail along with a credit card paper-clipped to a note that reads:

Spend to your heart's content (I'm not even kidding)!

After I've collected Kylie's folder, I find myself standing in the doorway to the piano room, staring inside. That Steinway piano that had belonged to my family—it was one of the many things Gram had been forced to sell to help pay for Mom's legal fees.

10

"There's something ridiculously sexy about how fucking slow you drive," Lucas drawls, causing me to bite the inside of my cheek.

Usually, driving is a therapeutic experience for me. I've never taken the Metro in Los Angeles because no matter how long and unpredictable my daily commute is, it gives me time to gather my thoughts, flush out any anger from the day. Sometimes, it's the one chance I have where I feel like I'm in complete control of my life.

Driving Lucas from point A to point B the next afternoon, though, is almost painful.

"Would you prefer I speed?" I question, keeping my eyes straight ahead.

"What I want is for you to stop grinding your teeth, Sienna," he says, his low voice weaving up from the third row—where he insisted on riding so that he could write music in "peace"—up to the driver's seat to irritate me.

"It's stop-and-go traffic. It's nerve-racking," I hiss. Then, reluctantly, I add, *"Mr. Wolfe."* I won't mention that Kylie's notes explicitly said that a car would be sent to take him to the photo shoot today. That I *heard* him canceling said vehicle earlier this morning while I was making myself a cup of coffee. Or that the only reason I *personally* think he's having me escort him around is so that he can screw with my head.

Make me fail.

Tempt me.

Reluctantly, I drag my gaze up to the rearview mirror, locking it with the hazel eyes that had consumed my dreams all last night. Today they're frustrated, tired. "Well?" I ask.

Lucas lets out a growl. "Just stop with the teeth."

Before what? You discipline me? I take a breath, ready to verbalize the taunts, but then I decide better of it and remind myself that Lucas is holding something important over my head. Plus, despite his promise not to touch me unless I ask, I know he doesn't have to lay a hand on my body to punish me. He's proven that to me more times than I'd like to remember. Wetting my lips, I tighten my grip on the steering wheel to stop my hands from shaking.

For the rest of the ride, I slide my tongue back and forth between my teeth to keep from grinding them together.

When we reach the location for the shoot—a historic diner in the heart of downtown Nashville that's been rented out for the entire day—Lucas clears his throat, stopping me before I open my door. I turn around in my seat so that I'm facing him.

He runs long fingers through his dark, disheveled hair and

offers me a soft smile that immediately weakens my defenses, causing my pulse to pick up speed. "Look, I don't . . . do very well with this kind of thing with other people around."

Shyness is not something I expect from Lucas Wolfe, and I'm taken aback. This man performs in front of thousands of people and he's telling me he can't take pictures in front of me? Strange. "Meaning you want me to stay outside," I say.

The tender look drops from his face, suddenly replaced by a sarcastic grin. "Don't sound so fucking dejected, Sienna. You've got the business credit card Kylie left, right?"

"Yes," I say.

"There's seven more days after this. You have a tendency to dress like a first-grade teacher and since you're a direct reflection of me— Well, do something about it."

"I'm a wardrobe girl."

"Who dresses like a twenty-three-year-old teacher."

"I *am* twenty-three."

"And you're my assistant who's agreed to do as I say. Right now I'm telling you to buy clothes that fit the role. Don't tell me you can't because I know you're incredible at what you do," he says. Then, lifting his eyebrows suggestively, he leans forward and places his elbows on his knees. "Because as it stands, the only thing I want to do when I look at you is take a ruler, bend you across a desk, and—"

I cover my ears. "I'll do it!" I cry out, squeezing my eyes shut to flush out the imagery that's just thrust itself into my brain. Every time I think I'm making a little progress of not thinking about sex and Lucas, he stomps all over it by giving me looks that confuse me and saying things that send trills of unneeded excitement hurtling through my body.

Hesitantly, I pull my hands from my ears and open my blue eyes. "How long do you think this'll take?"

He shrugs. "A couple of hours, maybe more."

"Fun," I say in a dry voice.

If he notices that I've not referred to him as Mr. Wolfe or sir once during this exchange, he doesn't say anything. He sits in the same position, staring at me expectantly until I realize at last that he's waiting for me to let him out.

Seven days. After today, that is.

I walk around the car to let him out, and he winks at me, stepping out of the Cadillac. As he slides past me, his body brushes mine. It's just the tiniest of touches, the back of his wrist against my belly button, his shoulder skimming the top of my head so that strands of my red hair cling to his V-neck tee, but it's enough to make us both pause.

Tentatively, I shift forward. The muscles jump under his cheeks, and he reaches up, past me, to close the SUV door. He keeps his eyes off of my face as he says, "When you're shopping . . . remember you're dressing a rocker's personal assistant, and remember we've got a semiformal birthday party to go to while in Atlanta. And if I so much as see one lame-ass cardigan covering your perfect body, I swear I'll burn it."

He stalks past me and into the diner. Instead of following him with my gaze, I sag back against the door he just touched, closing my eyes.

I fantasize about what would've happened if our lips had met.

Feel parts of me that I shut down two years ago wake up once again.

As I shop at the trendy boutiques and vintage stores for which downtown Nashville is popular for, my mind pings back and forth between Lucas, my duty to finish up today, and the next seven days and getting the house back.

And my life in California.

I can't resist wondering if I had given in to Lucas when we almost spent the night together a couple of years back, would things be different now? Would I be different? My attraction to him had been immediate, one of those things that took my breath away, numbing my senses and making me ache all at once. I was drawn to his music, the way his voice had a way of tearing away my layers and digging to my very core, even when he was singing about strippers and partying and one-night stands.

Apparently, Lucas was drawn to me because I had a hard time saying no on set.

Except to him, and he was too infatuated to realize that fact, until it was too late.

The back of my neck tingles, and I tilt my head to each side to stretch it. I've got to quit letting the past mess with my head. I just need to forget Lucas Wolfe and all this and move on. I just need—

"Sienna?" a female voice calls my name.

I glance up from the pair of black skinny jeans I'm clutching to face a girl with short, spiky turquoise and pink hair and snakebite piercings. I squint for a second, trying to place her. As she comes closer, her face unblurs, and I mentally take away the facial piercings and picture her with blond Jennifer Aniston–esque layers and a pink Polo shirt. I feel my lips automatically curl into a grin. Ashley rushes forward to hug me.

Drawing back, she squeals. "Dude, I haven't seen you in—what?—four or five years? What are you now, a teac—?"

"Wardrobe assistant for *Echo Falls*," I say before she has the chance to call me a teacher. What was with that anyway? Self-consciously, I tug at the hem of my flutter-sleeve top. Guess it does its job of making me look professional. To the point that my boss wants to spank me with a ruler and an old friend assumes I spend my days drilling addition into first-graders' brains.

Nice.

"No shit," she says. She drapes the armful of clothes she's carrying across a mannequin's arm, despite the nasty look the salesgirl working the floor gives her, and Ashley rolls her eyes. "I fucking hate that show."

"Me, too," I say, and she grins.

"How long you here for?"

Glancing down at a rack, I shrug. "Just another couple of weeks. I'm doing a favor for a . . . um . . . a friend and helping my grandma with a few things."

"How's she doing?" When I tell her that Gram is well, she tilts her head to the side, nodding. "And your mama?"

That familiar buzz of humiliation makes me bow my head a little, but I fight back the urge to flinch. When my mom and her husband had gone down for selling and trafficking prescription drugs, they'd taken Ashley's uncle with them. Ashley never seemed too hurt about it—she never actually liked the guy and she's not mentioning it right now—but I still hate that she's asked about my mother.

Trust me, if your mom went to prison for one of the biggest drug busts in state history and snitches on every dealer within twenty miles, you'd be afraid and embarrassed when someone asks about her, too.

"She's fine," I say stiffly.

Ashley murmurs something inaudible in a sympathetic voice.

"Your parents still run that bar?" I ask and she theatrically blows strands of multicolored hair out of her eyes.

"I thought it would be awesome getting all the free booze, but yeah. My dad's a fucking slave driver." As if on cue, her phone beeps and she drags it out of the pocket of her tight fuchsia jeans. "And as usual, work calls—I swear Dad's like a freaking psychic or something. Look, I've gotta pay for these and run, but if you're not busy tonight . . ."

She digs in her messenger bag and hands me a red and black flyer. It's an advertisement for a Your Toxic Sequel cover band performing at her parents' Broadway Avenue bar. I nearly choke on my own saliva.

She squeals, clapping her hands together. "Ahh, a YTS fan, I see? I adore them. My boyfriend's in the band and they're amazeballs—almost better than the real thing. Come out if you can. See you around," she says, plucking her clothes off the mannequin. "And find me on Facebook if I don't see you tonight!" she yells as she walks away.

I pay for my own selections soon after. Then I ball the black and red piece of paper up and throw it in the bottom of the shopping bag.

"I have all the Your Toxic Sequel that I can take at the moment," I mutter aloud. A front-row ticket and courtesy backstage pass to the most complex rock star I'll probably ever meet.

An hour later, Lucas has that look of worshipped star as I drive him back to the house on Green Hills, so he doesn't complain about how the ride back is twice as long, or how I nearly run into the back of a minivan that boasts about a hundred of those kid and animal stickers on its rear window.

"You'd think they give blow jobs with photo shoots," I say under my breath.

"What was that?" he asks.

"Nothing at all, Mr. Wolfe."

Of course he demands to see the clothes that I've purchased the moment we enter the house. My head hurts from the long day spent out, so I gesture toward my room, and he follows behind me.

I toss the shopping bags on my bed, and sit on the edge. "You're not going to turn all Richard Gere on me and make me try them on, are you?"

"No fucking idea what movie you're talking about, Sienna," he says with a grin, pushing away from where he's standing at the door to make his way over to me. Glancing down at the shopping bags, he makes a face. "This it?"

I nod.

"For someone who plays with clothes all day, you didn't buy much."

My face and the muscles in my neck tighten painfully at the insult. "I don't play with clothes all day, Lucas. I . . . work with them." But my voice falters as if I'm unsure of myself.

He raises his hands up in front of himself apologetically. "Hey, I didn't mean anything by it. I think it's . . ." He pauses and bends his knees a little so his face is closer to mine. "Are you crying?"

I swallow hard. "No."

He lets out a long exhale, his spearmint-scented breath blowing on my slightly damp face. "I huff and puff and yell and you say nothing. I make a joke about your job and you cry?" he asks in a gentle voice.

Well, at least he acknowledges that he's a bully. Crossing my arms over my chest, I shrug and he sits on the arm of the couch at the end of the bed, facing me. He stares at me expectantly, and after several seconds under his scrutiny, a shaky sound comes from the very back of my throat.

"I just—" I begin, but he cuts me off.

"Don't lie to me either," he says in a stern voice, but I shake my head.

When he's looking at me like he is right now, with serious hazel eyes that make me feel as if I can say anything to him and he'd give a fuck, it's impossible to lie to him.

"My mom used to call it 'playing with clothes.' Hell, she probably still calls it that, that's all." I say. Shrugging my shoulders, I add in a harsh voice, "I've got a few mommy issues."

Tilting his head to one side, Lucas says, "I bet." I furrow my eyebrows, and he continues, "My mom's never been the biggest fan of what I do. I mean, she jokes about it at Thanksgiving and her friends think me and Kylie are demon worshippers, but she's never made me feel like what I love isn't important. If she did . . . well, I don't think I'd want much to do with her, no matter how much I love her."

I want him to elaborate because this is one of the first times he's given me insight into his life outside of music and fame, but he nods his head down toward the bags strewn out across my temporary bed. "Now, show me what you've bought for yourself." His voice is soft now, encouraging. Another reminder of just how puzzling Lucas really is. His mood switches at the drop of a hat, and it's suicidal to be attracted to someone I can't predict.

I slide the rest of my body onto the bed so that I'm close to the sofa. He hisses in a deep breath of air, and my head pops up, red hair flying everywhere. He's frozen in place, his face just inches from mine and drawn. His full lips are parted, as if he's seconds away from pulling me to him—to saying screw the promise he'd made me—and taking control of my own mouth.

"What?" I whisper, feeling every part of myself involuntarily move closer to him.

Lucas stands up, putting space between us and to my shock, there's a look of disappointment on his gorgeous face. "Don't do things like that, that's what," he growls.

I drag both my hands through my hair, knotting it and letting it fall loose around my shoulders. "You're incredibly uptight." But I sound just as frustrated as he did a moment ago because whether I like it or not, I want his hands, and his lips, all over me.

"Try living with someone who's hard to resist," he answers, walking around to the side of the bed to watch me. "You going to show me what you bought?"

Painfully aware of his every move, his every inhale and exhale, I show him the clothes. He murmurs appreciatively at the piles of rocker-friendly gear, leaning down to rub his fingertips over edgy T-shirts and vintage lace tops and the leather jacket I'd picked out. As he touches each piece of clothing, handling them with care, I imagine his fingers are stroking my body. Dipping beneath my waistband and inside of my black panties. Spreading my legs apart and kissing my thighs with his lips, his fingertips.

By the way he's staring at me, I can tell he's thinking the same thing.

I look away from him and set about the task of folding the clothes into neat piles. I'm on the second pair of jeans when I hear something crinkling.

The red and black flyer for the Your Toxic Sequel cover band is in Lucas's hand, held between his index and middle finger. When I make a move toward it, he backs up, shooing me away. I watch with my heart in my throat as he slowly unfolds the paper. He reads it carefully, a shit-eating grin growing wider and wider as his eyes scan the page.

After smoothing out the wrinkles and folding the flyer into neat creases, Lucas drops it on top of the clothes I've just folded. "You're going to be my DD tonight, Sienna."

I groan and he cocks an eyebrow at me. Plastering on a smile, I grind out, "Absolutely not, Mr. Wolfe."

"That's not a request." Then Lucas winks at me, as if to remind me of the contract I signed for him just yesterday, before adding, "So yeah, you are."

11

When he turns to leave my bedroom a few seconds later, I'm right on his heels, with my arms wrapped tightly around my body. "Why not just stay here?" I demand, walking into the office. He throws himself down on the plush sofa.

"You're flushed," he points out, staring me down with laughing hazel eyes, and I swallow hard.

"Don't change the subject," I say hotly, sliding down onto the floor where I press my back up against the couch. Glancing over my shoulder at him, I ask, "Why would someone like you want to go see a cover band? Why not just stay in and, I don't know, watch videos of yourself on YouTube?"

Lucas smiles, a disarmingly sexy look, and I realize that one of his hands is an inch away from grazing my shoulders, from touching my hair. I hold my breath. "Maybe I need fresh air," he says, but I shake my head.

"You look exhausted. I mean, you're lying down *right* now."

"We're going," he tells me. Then his eyes narrow, though the grin never drops from his face. "Unless there's another reason you want to spend the night here. One that involves my tongue—"

"Lucas . . ." I say warningly, and he bites his lower lip, drawing my attention to it.

He sits up, swings his long legs over the side of the sofa, and peers down at me. "Let's compromise. Go pick up some dinner for us, and when you come back we'll figure out what we're going to do. Whether or not I get to bury my—"

"Going now," I say in a breathy voice, shoving myself to my feet. I leave the office quickly, before Lucas has a chance to give me a play-by-play of everything he'd do to my body if I just said the word tonight.

By the time I return with dinner nearly a half hour later, Lucas is already dressed to go out to Ashley's parents' bar.

I've got to give him credit—he's managed to perfect his disguise. And I have a feeling that's all thanks to the fact that in Los Angeles he doesn't get to enjoy the peace he's found in Nashville. During the video shoot for "All Over You" there were daily incidents of fangirls (and fanboys) finding ways to sneak themselves on set to try and hook up with members of the band, not to mention the diehard Your Toxic Sequel fans who'd camped outside the studio every day to get a glimpse of Lucas and the rest of the guys.

Tonight, Lucas is wearing his usual jeans, but instead of boots, he's got on old-school Converse shoes. A black and white henley covers every last one of his tattoos, and his messy hair is covered by an oversized black beanie. And he's wearing . . . glasses. Nerdy ones, at that.

I stand at the door to his office for a moment, taking in the sight of him. No man should look that sexy in nerd glasses.

"Borrowed from wardrobe?" I ask, making his head jerk up toward me. He grins and, instinctively, I smile, too. "The glasses, I mean."

He beckons me to come into the office and I comply, setting the Styrofoam platter of food on the desk. Up close to him, I realize that those glasses have to be—hands down—the hottest thing I've ever seen him wear.

He laughs. "Not borrowed. A nearsighted bitch."

"You look . . . rocker geek."

Tilting his head to one side, he considers what I said for a moment, then bites the tip of his tongue to suppress another grin. "You're not going to take pics and send them to the paparazzi, are you?" he teases.

"Only if you're doing this to humiliate my friend's boyfriend," I say. "You're not, are you?"

He's on his feet and towering over me an instant later, his eyes unreadable. "I'd never hurt my fans. They're the reason I'm here and not in Atlanta strung out on something. But to answer your question . . . I've got a soft spot for cover bands."

"Why?" I ask.

"Google's your friend," he says, winking at me. He steps aside and sweeps an arm out toward the double doors. "Now go get dressed—your clothes are on your bed."

I move to go and do what he's asked me to, but then ice

travels down my body, freezing me. What am I *doing*? This is the first time he's issued a command and my mind automatically compelled me to follow it, and that's a realization that frightens me.

"You want to get me dressed, too, Mr. Wolfe?" I demand, forcing a sugary smile when I say his name.

He rakes his teeth over his bottom lip, and then blows a stray strand of hair away from my neck. "God, if only. You're thinking about it, aren't you? We're only three days in, and you already want to give in to me."

Despite his words, there's not the slightest hint of mockery behind his voice. It's teasing—yes—but so full of promise. I back up until the desk hits my bottom. My fingers curl around the wood and my back arches.

"If I am?" I whisper breathlessly.

He thinks for a moment and then grants me a look that's so delicious it sends heat spiraling through me. "At this point I'm not sure if I'd fuck you or spank you with one of those." He motions to a set of signed drumsticks on the opposite end of the desk. "Maybe both. Maybe just tie you to a chair and taste you 'til you can't move or think or breathe."

"And after?"

"There are seven more days," he reminds me. "There's so much I can teach you, so much we can do, and after that . . ."

I roll my eyes, but I can't deny that he's affected me by what he's said and the way he's looking at me. It should be illegal for any man to have such a magnetic, irresistible effect. "I'm good," I say.

"For now."

"No, for—" In twenty years if you ask me who initiated the kiss, I still wouldn't be able to tell you. It's that sudden, that breathtaking, and all-consuming. Lucas's tongue glides across my lips, tracing the outline of them—once, twice, a third time and then once more. I cry out and my backside slumps onto the desk behind me because my legs are trembling so violently. He makes a noise that's part curse, part moan, and enough to send me over the edge. I splay my hands out on either side of his chest, digging my fingertips into the soft fabric of shirt, into his skin, and pulling him to my body.

His hands are locked behind his head because he's so determined to make me beg before he uses them on me.

My lips part easily the moment his tongue probes the space between them. I'm wet. Wet and moaning and rubbing my body against his. Yet he still doesn't move his hands.

Touch me. Touch me. Dammit, Lucas, just touch *me.* But I can't bring myself to say the words to him. Not yet.

When he drags his mouth away from mine, I catch his lower lip gently between my teeth. He winces as my teeth rake over the tender flesh before releasing it. Then a sexy smile creeps across his face. "You a biter, Red? Would have never guessed it."

He knows I hate it when he calls me Red, just like he knows he's gotten me too flustered to complain at the moment. "Lucas?" I murmur against the side of his mouth. Suddenly brave, I kiss his upper lip, his strong chin. I draw his lower lip between my own and suck gently.

"Mmm-hmm?"

I lean back and gaze up into his hazel eyes. "Is it really inescapable—this . . . *us*?" I challenge, running my hands down the front of his chest. He trembles.

"Since the day I met you."

Our mouths meet one last time. I can't fight the temptation to skim the tip of my tongue across my lips after he pulls away. "Get dressed—no shower, leave your hair down. *Don't* even think about touching yourself," he says.

"I won't," I promise, even though there's nothing I want more than to go to my bedroom and finish what Lucas has started or even better, ask him to take me there and do it himself.

I turn to leave the office and go to my bedroom, but a thought occurs to me. Glancing over my shoulder, I speak again, my voice so low I can barely even hear myself. "Why'd you remember me? Why when you've slept with so many of the others?"

"Because you're the one I didn't."

A few minutes later, when I'm in my bedroom shrugging on my clothes and staring into the bathroom at the bathtub I've been forbidden to use, I decide I'm satisfied with his response.

Before I leave the bedroom, I let my hair fall loose.

Ashley's parents' bar—a little dive called The Beacon—is filled to capacity when Lucas and I show up. I'm ready to turn around and head back to the Cadillac when the big, red-bearded doorman tells us we'll have to wait, but Lucas shakes his head. "Get us in now," he says.

Of course that's an easy order for him to give. All he's done since we stepped out of the vehicle is shove his hands into the back pockets of his jeans and look down at the ground so as not to be noticed. He was right when he swore up and down that nobody would recognize him, though. He exudes shyness, the complete opposite of the Lucas I know, and irritatingly similar to myself.

"You should be in movies," I hiss as I stalk back toward the door with him in tow. "*Mr.—*"

He stops me with a promise I'm certain he'll actually keep. "Say it and I swear the second you do I'll take you back to the car and spank your perfect little ass."

Tossing my hair over one shoulder I gaze back at him, grinning. "*Sir.*"

"If only you were this sarcastic and infuriatingly confident with everyone you meet," he points out, as we come back up to the doorman again. Red Beard rolls his eyes and tilts his chin to one side. Mimicking my best Lucas impression, I place my hands on my hips. There's not enough lighting out here for him to be able to see how my fingers are nervously working the thick fabric of my black skinny jeans.

"I've got a personal invitation from—" Then I see Ashley's small body grinding on the dance floor several feet away, and I take in a deep breath. Screw it. "Ash! Hey, over here!" I yell at the top of my lungs. Several people passing by turn to cock eyebrows at me, but the shouting works. Ashley pushes her way through the throng of people in the bar and pokes her head out the door.

She gives the doorman a pouty face that doubles as a lethal

look of warning thanks to her snakebite piercings. "You're not being a dick, are you, Nicky? She's with me."

Begrudgingly, Nicky stamps our hands and moves his giant body aside so we can go inside. I almost want to give him a triumphant smile but even a small victory isn't enough for me to press my luck.

Hundreds of Your Toxic Sequel fans surround us—their hips swaying and their sweaty bodies grinding together. I glance up at Lucas. His eyes are still downcast, but his face says it all. He's in heaven right now, witnessing all these people who've come out to pay homage to his band.

"Ugh, don't feed your rock star after nine p.m.," I hiss under my breath so that only he can hear the *Gremlins* reference, and his grin widens.

Ashley finds the only empty table in the whole place, toward the back of the bar, and leads us to it. "Sit here and I'll go and get you—"

"I'm good," I say, and she gives me a skeptical look. "I'm DD."

"Sam Adams," Lucas says in an incredibly deep voice that sounds so ridiculously forced, I can't help but release a tiny snort. He shoots me a dark glare.

"Nice choice," Ashley says, grinning. She bows her back a little and tilts her head trying to get a good view of his face. When he tucks his chin closer to his chest, she purses her lips and stalks off.

"This isn't going to work," I warn him and he glances up at me.

"Well, no. It typically never does."

Feeling my temperature rise, I study him. He's so full of contradictions. One minute he's talking about wanting peace and quiet and the next he's craving the adoration that comes with his world, his fame. It's enough to make my head dizzy. When I gather up the courage and say this to him, he grins.

"I just wanted enough peace to finish my solo project and I've—" His voice breaks off and he traces a heart that someone has carved into the table. When I examine it closely, I see that the words LOVE HURTS are written in the center of it.

"You've what?" I question.

Snapping his hazel eyes up, he tells me in a barely controlled voice, "I've written enough goddamn material in the past few days for two or three albums."

"Ah . . . I see."

Lucas continues to trace the heart on the table. "No, I don't think you do."

Suddenly irritated and tired of playing a game of words with him, I change the subject back to his reasons for wanting to come here tonight. "So why risk being noticed and groped by your fangirls just to see a cover band?"

"You never Googled it, did you?"

I shake my head. "It wasn't a direct order, sir."

His face breaks out into a smile and he tilts his head back and laughs. It's one of those full-bodied expressions that sends warmth pouring into my belly. "Jesus, Sienna, you're so frustrating. It's fucking with my head." He regains control, slumping down in his chair and getting an unfocused look in his eyes. "There's not much of a story. Just that when I was in high school, me and Sinjin Fields and Wyatt McCrae had this god-awful cover band. It was how we were discovered eventually. Us and Cilla."

Cilla. Why do I feel a pang of jealousy every time I hear or see her name? It's ridiculous because I've never met her—all I know is that she and Lucas are friends. What exactly the word *friend* entails, I'm not sure, nor do I think I ever want to find out.

"So you're here to discover Ashley's boyfriend?" I question.

He shrugs, and corrects me, "I'm here because I appreciate them." Then his eyebrows knot together. "But I've got to admit, they're really fucking good and I don't mind dropping their name to a few of my contacts."

Lucas's drink slides across the table and he looks up, meeting Ashley's curious stare. "I knew it was you," she whispers excitedly. She plops down in the chair beside me, directly across from him. I watch, fascinated, because she's on the verge of salivating and her eyes are practically glittering under the dim lights.

"Before or after you eavesdropped on the last minute of what we were saying?" he demands, taking a giant swig of his beer.

Ashley's naturally tan skin flushes but then she quickly regains composure. "Sorry about that, but . . . dude, you're Lucas-*fucking*-Wolfe. You're in my parents' bar and sitting at a table with me, and I'm about to freak the hell out." The way she says his name, whispering it reverently, brings out his panty-slaying smile. Turning to me, Ashley says in an accusing voice, "You didn't tell me you know him."

"He's my boss," I explain lamely.

"Your work involves going out to bars with him at ten at night. Ugh . . . I need to become a wardrobe person. I'm in the wrong field, I—" Then she bites her bottom lip and glances over at Lucas. "You're going to play, right?"

"Wait, he's—" I start but Lucas gives me a warning stare.

"Fuck yeah, I'll play," he says.

I've got no other choice but to follow them as they weave their way through the crowd toward the front of the bar where the cover band is rocking out to "Lucky You're Wasted." Ashley bounces on the balls of her feet as she waits impatiently for them to finish up. When they're through, she waves the bass guitarist over to her. He bends his head, attempting to brush his lips across her mouth, but she shakes her head, too excited to deal with her boyfriend. I watch as her lips move rapidly and she gestures over to me and Lucas.

His eyes widen—and I swear to this—at least three sizes. After he gets over the momentary disbelief, he nods and crosses the stage to have a powwow with the rest of the band. At some point, I can clearly hear one of them say "Holy fucking yes."

The crowd's going crazy at this point, wondering what's up, if the band is calling it quits early, but then the lead singer saunters back up to the microphone. He's grinning and his voice is shaking as he gives Lucas the only introduction someone like him needs: "Welcome the real Lucas-fucking-Wolfe, people!"

For a moment, everyone in the audience is utterly unclear of what's going on and they're hushed, murmuring amongst themselves. But as Lucas strides across the stage, taking the lead's guitar and bowing his head graciously, the silence turns from confused to stunned. Lucas calls out "All Over You" and then the hell-raising guitar intro begins.

Nicky, the giant grumpy doorman, and another bouncer, who Ashley says keeps watch over the bar, make their way to the stage, but none of Lucas's fans try to bum-rush him or anything. Everyone's too entranced by the music, myself included.

I'm so spellbound that it takes me a moment to realize that at certain lines of the song, Lucas's eyes drag to the far left of the stage, seeking me out. Making me feel like I'm the only person in this crowded bar. When I grind my teeth together in frustration, Lucas's eyes narrow a fraction and he shakes his head slowly to each side.

Drawing in a deep breath, I do the only other thing I can do. I sing along with the rest of the crowd—lyrics that are all too familiar about a one-night stand he's got no plan to stop seeing. I ignore the wetness that has built up in the lacy black panties I'm wearing.

Panties that Lucas himself had touched and laid out for me to put on.

12

When I wake up the next morning at 7:00 a.m. on the dot, there are at least twenty YouTube videos of Lucas's performance circulating the Internet. There are already—and I shit you not—death threats about the "redheaded cunt" Lucas was serenading on a forum belonging to a Web site that claims to be the official Your Toxic Sequel fan page.

And I find out about all of this because Tori has sent me links, e-mails, and enough text messages to make me want to deactivate my Facebook account and change my phone number, at least until I return to Los Angeles.

My phone rings again, the sound of one of Taylor Swift's breakup songs filling my bedroom, and I groan, scrunching my face into a tense frown. I start to mute the volume, but then I decide to just suck it the hell up and answer.

Tori should still be in bed—I mean, it's 5:30 a.m. in California—so I feel bad about hitting the ignore button over and over again to avoid speaking to her. "Hey," I say as calmly as possible.

"Sienna . . . there are pictures of you with Lucas Wolfe online," she says in a monotone voice. "Why are there pictures of you with Lucas Wolfe on the Internet?"

"I-I . . ." Well, there goes my plan to stay calm. My gaze lowers to my laptop screen, at the muted video of Lucas performing, and suddenly, I wonder who else has seen these videos besides every rabid Lucas Wolfe fan with an Internet connection and an anonymous online profile to hide behind. For once I feel fortunate that Tomas, my boss, is such a media snob and refuses to read gossip magazines. I don't need this getting back to him—not when I'm supposed to be here in Nashville taking care of my gram.

"Are you messing around with him?" Tori asks.

"No, I—"

But I have a sinking feeling in my chest, and I ball my hand into a fist, massaging it over my heart. What if my grandmother sees this and wonders the same thing that Tori just asked? It would literally break her heart.

"Sienna, talk to me," Tori says pleadingly.

"I . . . I work for him," I admit.

And just as I expect, my best friend starts freaking out. She starts doing the exact thing that made me avoid telling her about my deal with Lucas in the first place. "Since when? Why? Sienna . . . he's trying to take your grandmother's goddamn house away. How could you work for him? Why *would* you work for hi—"

"For the love of God, shut up for just one second so I can

think," I snap. I hear a sharp gasp for air on the other end, and I immediately feel horrible for barking at her. In all the time that I've known Tori, I've never once raised my voice at her.

I've never spoken to *anyone* like that besides Lucas Wolfe.

"Tori . . . I'm sorry," I whisper.

She sounds dazed when she speaks. "I'm actually hovering somewhere between really fucking irritated you told me to shut up and being impressed. Sienna, what's *really* going on? Please . . . I'm your best friend."

Tears trickle down my cheeks as I tell her, though I can't exactly pinpoint why I'm crying—whether it's because of the photos and videos online or because being so close to Lucas has been such a battle, one that I'll have to repeat for six more days. I leave nothing out except for Lucas's sexual habits, and when I'm done all Tori's able to say is "Wow" repetitively until I tell her that she's giving me a headache.

"You've got to be the most . . . selfless and ridiculously awesome person I know. To be doing something like *that* with someone like *him*."

I don't like the way her tone suggests that he's a bad person. Hell, I don't like the way I'm so willing to jump to his defense, but I do it anyway. "He's not all bad," I say, my voice sounding totally convincing.

"Oh. My. God."

Thinking that there's been a new article put out about me and Lucas, I frantically refresh the Google news search I have open on my screen. "What? What?"

"You're falling in love with *him*."

The second those words come out of her mouth, sounding like an accusation and a curse and a crime all at once, I wish she had said there was a new set of rumors instead. I'm not in love with Lucas. Completely in lust, yes, but not in love.

Definitely not in love.

"That's ridiculous. I don't know him well enough to love him."

"Then he's got to have the biggest freaking di—" Tori's words are cut off midsentence by the sound of my cell phone beeping. I pull it from my ear and my heart launches into my throat, gagging me, when I see that it's Seth.

God, this can't be a good thing.

"Hey, Seth's calling so I'm going to have to call you back," I say, my voice unsteady, and Tori releases an irritated groan.

"You'd better or I'll fly to Nashville tonight. That's right, I will spend all our rent money, and leave us homeless, just so I can check on your ass," she warns.

I laugh, but it sounds forced. "I promise." Then, sighing, I click over to accept my brother's call. He's already cursing, seething, before I get a chance to say hello.

"You lied to Gram so you could go fuck the douchebag who bought her house?"

"Seth, I—"

But he doesn't want to let me get a word in.

"You're disgusting. Guess you're more like *Mom* than you let on, huh? Don't worry . . . what you're doing won't ever be big enough news to reach Gram and I sure as hell won't tell her. Maybe if you're lucky he'll—"

My heartbeat picks up wildly when long fingers pluck my

phone out of my hand. When I drag my gaze to meet Lucas's, I flinch. Though his face is unreadable, he embodies anger, just from the tense way he holds his body.

I jolt up from the bed as he raises my phone to his ear, but he shakes his head curtly, motioning for me to sit down. I comply, balling my hands up by my side.

"You got something to say to me, you come to me with it, not her," he tells my brother in a low, dangerous voice. I can hear Seth trying to get a word in, but Lucas refuses to let it happen. "I don't give a fuck who you are. You treat her like shit, talk to her like that, and you're screwing with me, too."

My mouth drops open as Lucas jabs the end button and hands the phone back to me. "You didn't have to do that," I whisper, but there's a painful burn deep in my chest.

He is trying to protect me.

Lucas Wolfe had just come to my defense.

"You didn't have to sit there and let him talk to you like that," Lucas growls, pacing back and forth. "That's your brother, right? The skinny little prick with the big mouth from court?"

I never realized Seth had ever said anything to Lucas, and I glance down at my lap, at my hands. "He was angry," I whisper.

"That's no excuse for him treating you like shit."

"We're all over the Internet," I argue. "You and I are everywhere because of last night."

I look up at him to gauge his reaction. There's no emotion on his handsome face, and his hazel eyes are unreadable. But when he shrugs his shoulders, I can tell that this gets to him, too. That he regrets ever looking at me while he sang.

"It's not a big deal," he murmurs. "And stop changing the subject. We're talking about your brother speaking to you like you're nothing."

"He'll—" I want to say that Seth will get over it, but I don't even know how to defend him to someone like Lucas. My brother hadn't even said very much to me but somehow managed to take a pair of sharp scissors to my self-esteem.

Lucas kneels down in front of me, on his knees, and places his forearms on either side of my body so that they're almost brushing my hips. He bends his head toward my lap and a primal ache stretches across my belly. I bury my fingertips into the bedspread because I want to dig them into the hard muscles in his back.

And I want his fingers buried into my skin, too, though I can't tell him that.

"Call him back and stand up for yourself," he says.

I shake my head, my long hair sweeping back and forth over his face when he looks up at me. "No," I whisper.

His eyes narrow. "You're going to have to one of these days. Stand up to your brother and your mom. You don't have to take shit from people. You don't have to try and explain yourself."

He climbs to his feet, looking down at me with almost sad hazel eyes. "Today's the first day of filming for the documentary and I've got some studio work that needs to be done. Take the day off."

"Bu—"

"Take the day off," he orders. "I can't—you can't expect me to be able to be around you like this when I want you so bad. When you're not willing to let me have you."

And now—now I think I fully understand why he's encouraging this. Because Lucas Wolfe thinks that if I take on the things and people that I always back down to, I'll allow him to conquer me.

The sad part is, I'm beginning to think that maybe he's right.

As promised, Lucas is gone all day, so I spend my time answering his fan mail. But I find myself missing him, even when I spend an hour talking to an extremely drunk and obnoxiously cheerful Tori. A few minutes short of midnight, I drag myself to bed. I want to immerse myself in the delicious dreamland where I don't have to beg Lucas to take me.

Where he uses my body—and I use his—without so much as a single word exchanged between the two of us. In my dreams, there are only appreciative moans. Only the rushed sound of our breathing and our hearts beating wildly.

It turns out my fantasies will have to wait. The sound of the Steinway piano downstairs awakens me a little after 1:00 a.m. After I slide a short cotton robe over my T-shirt, I follow the noise down to the lowest level of the house. Once I hit the bottom step, I let the scent of what Lucas is smoking guide me. I've always hated the smell of pot because it reminds me of Preston, of the people who used to hang around my mom's house when I was a teenager, and I automatically wrinkle my nose.

Lucas doesn't look up when I open the door to the piano room, but I know he's aware that I'm in here because his back straightens and his shoulders tense up. I sag against the door frame, listening to him, drinking this moment in. He's shirtless, wearing nothing but a pair of jeans that ride low on his hips. Lucas Wolfe is all muscles and tattoos and sexiness, but it's his music that has a way of getting to me. It strips me down.

Then it devours me.

And I let it. The only difference is that now, it's in person and once it's over I'll have to face the real Lucas Wolfe and not the poor excuse I keep in my nightstand drawer or my own fingers.

Lucas's shoulders relax a little as he pushes out the last few chords. He scribbles something into a tattered blue notebook, reading over his notes a few times before he lifts sleepy, hazel eyes to mine. Locks of his messy, dark hair spill into one of them, teasing me to come forward and touch him.

"I didn't call for you," he says huskily. "What do you want?"

"I-I didn't realize you played," I whisper. God, where is my voice? My nerve? Why the fuck do I always come apart into hundreds of pieces when I'm around this man?

"Google is your friend."

I feel my body ignite, but when I turn to leave, he says softly, "Stay. I don't want to . . ." And while there's a part of me that wants to take advantage of the vulnerability in his voice, there is another part that reminds me of the deal that I made with Lucas. I'm at his beck and call for the next five days.

And now, he wants me with him.

Tentatively, I walk forward. The tile is cold under my bare feet, and I wish I'd never gotten out of bed. I stand next to the piano and cross my arms over my chest. "How long do you need me for?" I question.

He's writing in his notebook again—shorthand lyrics from the look of things—but his lips move into a slow grin that makes those uncomfortable flutters start in the pit of my stomach. Does he realize how much these little gestures screw with my resolve?

Of course he does.

"Long as it takes," he says.

"For what?"

Lifting an eyebrow, he tilts his head to one side and studies me for a good minute before starting to play again. It's the same song from before, but now he's changed the key, slowed it down. Now it's haunting and unnerving. He sings along in some spots. The lyrics aren't whole enough to fully make sense, but paired with his voice, they're the sexiest I've ever heard. He sings about keeping the lights on and fucking right now and I feel like it's an invitation meant only for me. All of a sudden, my throat is dry.

He glances up at me when he's done. "Well?"

I flick the tip of my tongue over my lips, and the muscles in his toned back tense up. "The end is wrong," I murmur. "Too happy. It should be"—I move forward, lean down, and play several chords—"this."

"You play?"

"Google is your friend, Wolfe."

He stands abruptly, slides the bench to the wall and gestures almost sarcastically to the piano. "Play it again."

I don't argue. I'm too tired and too worked up and all I want is to go back upstairs and climb in bed. All I want are my dreams where there are no questions, but I stand behind the keyboard and repeat the chords.

"Again. Slower. And this time, close your eyes."

I do what he asks. The moment I smell his Polo cologne, though, I miss a key. "This is when you tell me to have sex with you and then make me run out for Cheetos to cure your munchies, right?" I ask, my voice high-pitched and strained.

He laughs. I swear I feel his mouth on my skin, even though he's not touching me. "Cheetos suck. And you know what you have to do for me to have sex with you," he reminds me.

Gritting my teeth, I slam my palms down on the piano, causing the keys to make a horrible screeching noise. I glance over my shoulder into Lucas's hazel eyes. "Since you don't need me, can I go to bed, Mr. Wolfe?"

"Abso-fucking-lutely not. Look, Sienna . . . all you've got to do is say the words."

"And what would those be?"

He dips his face down, bringing his mouth so close to mine we're only a breath away from kissing. From tearing each other down. From the inevitable he's mentioned so many times before. "Take me all the way, Lucas," he drawls in his best impersonation of my accent. "And that's what you're going to say the first time we fuck. My name. Just Lucas."

But the thing is, the last—and only—time I was weak enough to avoid the inevitable with this man, he sent me away from him. I won't let him do that to me again. "Fuck you, Lucas."

My words don't faze him. He's boasting that cocky look that always makes me want to karate chop him in the throat. Instead—like an idiot—I rise up on my toes and crush my mouth to his. His tongue parts my lips. He still refuses to touch me, so

I whisper, "Please . . . your hands . . . I want your hands touching me from now on."

I'm safe as long as I'm in control.

Keep telling yourself that.

He doesn't cup my face or touch my hair or anything romantic like that. He roams his hands down my body, squeezing my breasts hard before trailing them over the curve of my hips. Gripping my waist with one hand, he slips the other between my legs, nudging them apart to touch his palm against my panties. He draws his mouth away from mine. "Fuck me, you're wet," he says. "I want to take you all the way, and I know you want me inside of you. Say the words."

"No."

His fingertips stroke my wetness through my thin cotton underwear, and I moan, feeling my legs start to tremble. He's right. He's so right about what I want, it physically hurts right now, but I won't give in.

I can't.

"Are you sure?" he asks, and when I nod, he orders, "Turn around, and play. Same as before and don't stop."

I expect him to take his hands away from my body the moment my fingers make contact with the keys, but he doesn't. I'm one chord in when he slides my panties aside, gliding his fingers beneath the damp fabric so that he can stroke my slick lips. Three measures when he pushes one finger inside me. I gasp and he growls in my ear.

"Don't. Fucking. Stop."

He slips another finger inside of my body, spreading them

apart and back together, over and over in a motion that seems to ignite my very core. I hear myself cry out, and he moves his hand hard and fast. Back and forth. I swear I must be dying or already dead. I have to be, because never in my entire life have I felt like this.

Lucas breathes heavily into my hair when I curve my bottom closer to him, pressing my ass up against his body. He's hard. He's so fucking hard and big that I'm suddenly grinding against his hand. A moment later, when he presses his callused thumb to my swollen clit and glides it around in a circular motion, I come.

I slump against the keyboard on my elbows, my ass in the air. I don't have it in me to play anymore, but I don't think he could give two shits either way. He's staring down at me with his lips pressed into a thin line and all I can think of is how I want them and his tongue on me.

And my mouth on *him*.

"Lucas, I want yo—"

"Go to bed, Sienna."

Carefully, he pulls his long fingers out of my body. I shudder again as yet another ripple of pleasure takes over me. Though my flesh feels like it's scorching, I manage to stand upright. "No," I say.

"Let's try this the way you're familiar with then: Get the fuck out. I need to work and like I've told you before, you're fucking horrible for music."

Something sharp and prickly twists my chest. He knows exactly what to say to piss me off. I want to tell him he's the dumbass who came up with this arrangement in the first place, but I choke back the words. All he'll do is turn it back on me and remind me why I agreed, throw the deed in my face. I keep my face emotionless and my hands clenched by my sides as I say, "Good night, Mr. Wolfe."

As I leave the room, I become aware that my panties are still pushed aside. And that as long as I am around Lucas, he'll keep pushing me away and then pulling me right back to him. Consuming me until there's nothing left.

13

I spend the rest of the night alternating between tossing and turning and hating myself, and wishing Lucas was between the sheets beside me. Or on top of me. When the alarm on my phone goes off at seven, I drag myself out of bed and slink into the bathroom. Stripping down, I climb into the shower, turn the water as hot as it will possibly go, and stand under the stream with my head against the tile. The heat is uncomfortable—in fact, it burns—but it's helping the vomit-inducing headache beating the hell out of my skull. Today, I'll need my brain totally clear to deal with Lucas-*fucking*-Wolfe.

What the hell was I thinking when I asked him to put his hands on me last night? Frustrated, I bang my fist against the shower wall. Pain shoots through my hand, but I ignore it. I'm more concerned with the way I melted in Lucas's hand—literally. And I hate my body for reacting to thoughts of him right now. I'm wet and horny and I feel stupid for letting him fuck with my body and mind.

The water is running cold and the bathroom is a cloud of steam by the time I finally step out of the shower. I'm wrapping a thick towel around my body when I notice my Lucas phone is blinking where I left it sitting on the sink. There's a text message from him. From three o'clock this morning.

Meetings all day. Wake me. 8 sharp.

It's 8:12 right now. Fuck my life. Groaning, I rush into my room and shrug on a pair of shorts and a T-shirt, then speed walk upstairs to the room Lucas has been sleeping in. The door is closed, and I can hear an old Seether and Amy Lee song playing softly on his iPod dock. It's fitting for how torn he makes me feel. How I can barely breathe whenever we're together. Clenching the doorknob, I linger for a moment and try to gather my bearings. I've only got five days left, and three of those will be spent out of town on the go. If I can't hold it together for a week, then I'm screwed all around.

I open the door and step inside.

Every blanket has been pushed to the floor at the foot of the bed, in a black pool of fabric. Lucas is sprawled across the mattress on his stomach and he's naked. Completely naked. Holding my breath, I tiptoe across the room. I'm standing over him like a creeper and his text explicitly said to wake him up nearly half an hour ago, but God, I can't get over how amazing he looks while he's sleeping.

I have a full view of the tattoos covering his back, and my

hands drift over them as I study each one carefully. I decide my favorite is the stopwatch tattoo at the bottom of the piece—inside of the watch is a queen of hearts who's grinning evilly. I've never seen a tattoo like this before, and I decide there must be a story behind it. A dare from a bandmate, maybe, or something to remember a girl who broke up with him.

That'd explain why Lucas is such a dick half the time.

He groans into his pile of pillows and mumbles, "Keep your mouth right there; I'll roll over for you."

Startled, I jolt straight up to a standing position, but he catches my wrists, pulls me onto the bed and on top of him. If I was hot before, I'm on the dangerous verge of spontaneously combusting right now. I'm sitting with his cock pressed against my bottom and it's as hard as it was last night in the piano room. The only difference is that now he's not pushing me away. I feel my pulse in my throat, and my body temperature rising quickly.

"Lie with me," Lucas says, cradling my face between his hands, guiding it down until it's mere inches away from his.

"Why?"

"Because I've wondered what this would be like with you, Sienna."

For what seems like an eternity we stay this way—staring into each other's eyes while I straddle him. Does he realize that I'm a hip grind away from breaking my oath? That now that he's touching me and his fingertips are entwined in my hair and his body is so warm against mine, I can barely function?

I'd be a liar and a coward if I didn't admit to myself how good he feels, how natural his heartbeat feels against my chest.

"I was a shithead last night," he says at last. He traces his fingertips down the right side of my cheek, his touch a feather-soft stroke. He's making the shape of an *L*—like he's branding me.

I roll off of him to my side, so that we're facing. "Is this your way of begging for my forgiveness?"

"No." He groans, racing his large hands from my face, to my shoulders, and finally to the small of my back. This closes the little bit of space left between us, and when he shifts to get comfortable, I gasp. "Ugh, yes. I'm apologizing for being a douchebag. It's just—you fuck with my head, Sienna."

You fuck with my head, says the confusing man. I roll my eyes and start to call bullshit. He pulls my lower lip gently between his teeth.

"The next five days don't have to blow," he points out, cupping my ass cheeks.

I fight back the guttural moan building in my throat. I can think of several ways to keep our week civil and most of them involve us in this position—or similar—except there'd be no clothing between us. Only sweat.

"They will if you're doing *that* to me day in and day out," I murmur, referring to the events from last night. He chuckles. The expression sends a warm vibration through my whole body.

"You could just give in right now."

"Why not just sex? Why does it have to be so complicated?"

He rolls over onto his back and stares up at the ceiling. After a long pause where both of us are completely quiet, Lucas props himself up on his elbows and gazes down at me. Strands of dark hair fall into his hazel eyes, and I automatically reach up to brush them back. He grabs my fingers and kisses them, one by one. "I don't want just sex from you because I need you to submit to me. Completely. I want all of you and I'm determined to have it, Sienna."

"And what'll happen when you get what you want?" I whisper. Lucas is always saying how badly he wants me—how he has to have every part of me—but not once has he told me what happens afterward.

Cocking his head to one side, he gives me a sad smile. His hair falls into his eyes again, but this time I don't bother pushing it back. He looks too heartbreakingly beautiful for me to ruin this moment by doing something like that. He does it for me. "I better get the hell up," he says.

Stiffly, I roll over and climb off the bed, standing with my fists balled up by my sides as I wait for him to tell me what our plans are for the day.

"I've got to be at the studio by ten, so go get dressed."

Another order, but at least I won't be stuck in this house all day answering Lucas's fan mail. Yesterday had been a beast, considering a good majority of his e-mails were frantic demands from fans about the chick he was filmed in the bar with.

Despite the tenderness of the last fifteen minutes, he's grinning like the Cheshire cat. I grit my teeth into a sugary smile. "Right on it, Mr. Wolfe."

"Your teeth," he warns. I stop grinding them. Just as I reach the door, he says, in a voice that has dropped an octave, "That thing you asked about what I plan to do once I have you?"

My heart skips a beat or two, but I manage to look back over my shoulder at him. "Yes?"

"I'll keep you, like I should've done two years ago."

I nod, unsure of what to say or how I should feel about what he's just told me.

As I go back downstairs, I try my hardest to keep Lucas's words out of my head so they won't haunt me for the rest of the day. "I've got to focus," I tell myself as I open the door to the walk-in closet in my bedroom. I'll think about Lucas keeping me later on, when there's not work to be done.

Taking a deep breath, I step into the closet.

Since Lucas didn't specify what we're doing after the studio, I opt for a black vintage-looking fit-and-flare dress. It's cute and when I plucked it off the shelf a couple of days ago, I instantly thought of Kylie. It's definitely more her style than mine, so I snap a photo of myself in the bathroom mirror and send her a picture message. Then I dab on minimal makeup and leave my long red hair loose.

Not because Lucas always tells me to wear my hair down.

Of course not.

While I wait for Lucas to call for me, I check my Facebook page.

There's a message from Tori. Okay, three messages from Tori. They all pretty much say the same thing—*Don't have sex with Lucas*—but the last one makes me laugh. She's gone the extra mile and personalized one of those eCards she sends me whenever Tomas is behaving badly at work. It's a picture of some Edwardian woman being groped by a man with a handlebar mustache. The caption reads:

MAY YOUR ATTEMPTS AT HAVING SEX WITH ME RESULT IN A

172

GUITAR BEING SMASHED OVER YOUR HEAD. WHICH HEAD IS OPEN
FOR DEBATE. . . .

Laughing, I shoot her back a quick message:

> Be nice. Hope you're being good. Miss you like crazy,
> you beautiful girl, and thanks again for listening to me
> yesterday.

I move the mouse up to close out the page, but someone
sends me an instant message. It's Kylie.

Kylie Martin: Loved the dress! I see Lucas made you go
shopping. He treating you well?
Me: Besides bossing me around and being hell-bent on
sleeping with me?

No, on keeping me, I mentally add.

Kylie Martin: . . . I could've lived without knowing half of
that.

I snort. She had asked how her brother was treating me. Did
she really think I'd hold anything back considering she's already
fully aware of all his vices?

Kylie Martin: Look on the bright side—five more days and
I'll be back, your job will be done, AND you'll be able to

give your grandmama the deed to her place back. Easiest mega chunk of change ever made, right?

No, wrong. Very, very wrong. How can anything be easy when being around Lucas makes my emotions feel like they're in a game of extreme tug-of-war? I wonder if Lucas was always so dominating or if it happened once he became famous. Was there ever a point in his life where he wasn't so dynamic? Regardless, I know one thing: Gram is the only person for whom I would put myself out there like this. I wouldn't have even agreed to this arrangement to save my own place because of all the physical and emotional turmoil involved.

And we've got five days left.

Me: Yeah, real simple.
Kylie Martin: Got to run. Tell Lucas I said be nice to you— well, as nice as he's capable of. Text me or call if you need anything! <3

She logs off before I can ask her about Lucas's obsession with consuming all of me, but even if I had asked her, I'm pretty sure she wouldn't answer. Kylie seems to stay as far away from her brother's kinks as I do with my little brother's . . . everything.

I curl my toes at the thought of Seth, at the thought of confronting him after yesterday. I clutch my phone, considering whether or not I should call him. I get three digits in and end up dialing my grandmother instead. Her voicemail picks up.

"Hey, Gram . . . haven't talked to you in a few days. Just wanted to let you know that I'm thinking about you and that I love you. See you soon, okay?"

Staring down at the phone, I sigh. Then there's a knock at my door and Lucas yells, "Let's go, driver."

Because I'm feeling facetious, I return to the eCard message Tori sent me and send it to his personal e-mail address.

Live rock is all dark lights and grit and sweaty bodies slicking against each other, but the moment we reach the music studio, I realize that studio music is the total opposite. The Music Row studio is all ambient lighting and luxurious technology. Lucas is the first of his band members to show, probably because he has an obsession with being on time. He tells the pretty blond-haired assistant that we want to wait in a private room, and then she asks us if we'd like refreshments.

Lucas goes for a bottle of water and I order a Coke. From the way the size-nothing assistant looks at me, I'm almost afraid she's never heard of caloried drinks, but then she nods and sashays off. I hate Lucas's effect on other women just about as much as I hate the way he quickly glances at her butt as she leaves. Reminds me of what a player he probably is.

"Nice," I say. He must hear the bitterness in my voice because he smiles. It's the lopsided one that always gets to me.

"Not really. But I'm a huge fan of your ass. I could write a song about your ass."

"You've never actually seen it unclothed, remember?"

He cocks a dark eyebrow and gives me a wicked look. "Feeling is believing."

I smooth a bunched section of my dress down and ease into one of the plush leather seats. I cross my legs at the ankle. Stuffing his hands into the back pockets of his jeans, he follows my every movement. Every flinch. Every sigh. He's still looking at me like he wants to pull my panties off with his teeth when Size Nothing returns with our drinks. She hands me a Diet Coke and I start to accept it, but Lucas shakes his head.

"Ms. Jensen asked for a Coke," he says.

"But—"

He shakes his head, cutting Size Nothing off. She just stands there obediently, her hands clasped in front of her, waiting for him to speak. To give her an order. "Run to the grocery store if you have to."

She glares down at me like I'm scum under her four-inch pumps and then casts a beaming smile at Lucas. "I'll get it ASAP, Mr. Wolfe." She leaves, but this time, he's not staring at her backside.

"Do you always have to be in control?" I hiss.

"That wasn't controlling, that was—"

"Asserting your dominance?"

"Don't be a sarcastic little shit, Sienna. You asked for a Coke, she brought you Diet."

"I don't need you to speak for me."

"Then learn how to do it for yourself. God, you've had no problem telling me to fuck off from the start, but everyone else . . ."

He turns away from me, and I focus on a tiny piece of lint on the hem of my dress. My heart is beating erratically—faster than it was last night or even this morning. I wait until it slows down and I catch my breath to say, "Because you scare me, Lucas."

More than anything. Because right now, I'm to the point where I don't want to win the losing fight against him.

Lucas's muscular shoulders shake. It takes me a moment to realize he's not trembling with anger. He's laughing at me. "I scare you? Do you realize what you're doing to me, Sienna? What you did to me two years ago?" he asks, turning around so that he can face me. When I shake my head slowly because I don't know how to answer what he's asked me, he comes to me, dragging me to him until my body is flush with his. He shoves my hand against his jeans, where his cock is hard, straining against the rough fabric.

"Oh," I murmur softly. My gaze flicks back and forth between my hand and his eyes, which are so full of want and need I feel my body immediately react—breasts tingling, face flushed, and a primal urge to shove him into a chair. To push his hardness inside of me and take until this want is satisfied. Then I remind myself that Lucas and I are in public, and that I never behave like this.

That even if we do get down to it right here, it won't be enough. I'll need more of Lucas.

I always will.

So, I squeeze my fingers around him a little until a look of pain and desire flashes across his gorgeous features. He pushes me away from him, raking his hands through his dark hair in exasperation.

"Of course you wouldn't realize how dangerous you are for me," he says.

Luckily for me, his band members begin showing up shortly after he says this because there's not much else I can say without completely giving myself away. I follow him into the studio and he instructs me to wait with the sound engineer and the creator of the documentary inside of the control room. Lucas raises his eyebrows like he's waiting for me to argue with this, too, but I don't.

I'm getting a private show from him—this man whose voice turns me on even when it's marred by the static of a bad radio station. There's no place else I'd rather be at the moment. Even if he dismisses me, I don't think I could go.

As Lucas steps through the glass doors leading to the live booth, I hear the drummer, Sinjin, say in a nasty voice, "Snap your fingers and she comes, huh?"

Lucas shoots Sinjin a dark look, jerks his guitar from its stand, and says something icily to the rest of the guys. The engineer flips the sound on in the booth just in time for us to catch the tail end of what Lucas is threatening.

". . . her and I'll break every bone in your fucking fingers."

It's obvious the "her" he is talking about is me and that he's probably warned his band to stay away from me while they're here because there's a ripple of nervous laughter among them. I'm half expecting Lucas to drawl in a thick Southern accent, "Sienna is mine!" but he doesn't.

Apparently, I watch way too much *True Blood*.

Shrugging the strap of his bass guitar onto his shoulder, Wyatt McCrae makes a soft tsking noise. "Not into redheads," he says, meeting my eyes. He's grinning like the damn cat that ate the canary and his head is tilted to one side. Suddenly, it feels like the entire band—minus Lucas—along with the sound guy and the documentary maker are staring at me.

Waiting with bated breath for me to snap under the pressure and admit that I want to rip Lucas's clothes off.

I do, but none of them needs to know that. Especially not Lucas himself.

Not yet.

"But your assistant is cute," Wyatt says to Lucas. Then he winks at me.

Digging my fingernails into my palms, I decide I should go ahead and nip any snide remarks from the band in the bud right here and right now. Being around these guys is awkward enough as it is without them making me feel like I'm just one of Lucas's fuck buddies.

"Instead of trying to get a rise out of me, maybe you should focus on the music. After all, Mr. Wolfe's schedule is very, very busy."

Lucas smirks, and glances sideways at Wyatt. "Dude, I think Red just told you to fuck off. You heard her, let's do this."

"Kylie's taught her well," Wyatt murmurs, earning yet another irritated look from Lucas.

The sound engineer asks if they're ready to begin. Lucas bobs his head, and the documentary cameraman who's inside the booth with them gives him a thumbs-up. Holding my breath, I watch as Lucas becomes the person I'd fallen all over myself for two years ago. Confident and talented and dominating, but in a way that doesn't frighten me like it once had.

He grins at me, constricting my chest and stomach a little, before gazing into the camera and saying, "This is Lucas Wolfe and Your Toxic Sequel, and you're getting an exclusive first look at music from our fourth studio album. This is 'Handcuffs.'"

And this is when I feel my body go numb. Maybe it's pretentious and silly of me, but I'm about 99 percent sure this song is about me, specifically the night I almost spent with Lucas. It's not rude and he's not saying anything fucked up, but I feel completely naked right now.

And from the way his eyes occasionally seek me out, still full of the desire I saw when we were in the private room, I know he wants me bare.

"Did you hear me, Ms. Jensen?" I hear a voice ask. Slowly, I tilt my face up toward it. The documentary maker's pockmarked face comes into focus. He's looking at me expectantly. "Would you like to comment on your relationship with Lucas?"

"I don't have a relationship with Lucas," I say. Then I think better of it, and add, "I'm standing in for his assistant while she's on vacation."

The man gives me a smile that reminds me of the ones my mother gave me when she was tolerating something I had to say when I was a child. It grates on my nerves. "I'm talking about your romantic relationship."

"There is no romantic relationship," I argue.

Another you-poor-stupid-girl smile. He points to an iPad sitting on a table. "I just looked at your digital résumé. You worked the video shoot for 'All Over You' in 2010, right? And you're currently working on the set of *Echo Falls*, correct?"

When I nod my head carefully, he wrinkles his nose. I decide I hate this guy because everything he does reminds me of my mom.

"You'd skip out of work and come all the way out here to substitute for his assistant?" he questions.

"I—"

"You know, the people who are watching this movie would probably kill to get the inside scoop of how your romance with Lucas went down."

I look toward the sound booth, but Lucas is still performing. His words from earlier haunt me, though. *"Learn how to speak up for yourself,"* he'd said. Squaring my shoulders, I give the documentary guy the steeliest look I can muster.

"I'm from Nashville. Kylie Martin is a personal friend. And Lucas is paying me to work for him. If you can't figure out the correlation between those three, then maybe you're in the wrong profession. If you want something for the people watching your movie, here it is: Lucas Wolfe is not my type. You think you can handle that?"

It's not until I excuse myself shortly thereafter, exiting the control room so I can go outside the building and into the brisk cold, that I break into a nervous sweat.

14

I shuffle back inside the studio ten minutes later, once my face is numb from the brisk February air blowing against it and my fingers are so stiff I can hardly bend them to turn the door-knob. When I slip into the control room and take my seat, Lucas glances up from the conversation he's having with Wyatt and Cal and gives me a look that makes me forget my cold face and hands. It's the same look he'd given me this morning in his bed-room, and instantly my thoughts wander back to what he'd said to me then.

"I'll keep you, like I should've done two years ago."

I flush all over, growing even warmer when a rough, confi-dent grin forms on Lucas's face and I realize he knows exactly what I'm thinking about. If there wasn't a thick sheet of glass separating us at this very moment, he'd probably be making some frustratingly sensual comment that would leave me once again questioning why I haven't given in to him yet.

"We're getting back to it as soon as Sin comes back," the sound engineer announces behind me, reminding me that I'm not alone in the control room.

"Sounds good," I say, dropping my gaze to my lap.

Sinjin staggers in a few minutes later, plops down behind his drums and says he's ready to go. As the band records "Handcuffs" once more, I play a game on my phone, slinging pissed-off birds at grinning pigs as I try to ignore the fact that the documentary maker is staring a hole into the side of my face.

The guy hasn't said a single word to me since I came back in—no doubt he thinks I'm a massive bitch now—but I know he wants to probe me for more information about me and Lucas.

I'm relieved that his attention wavers back to the band a couple of minutes later, when Lucas abruptly stops the song in the middle of the second verse. Gripping his guitar tightly, he faces the control room and rakes a hand through his messy brown hair. "This is shit. This sounds like shit."

The sound engineer rolls his eyes, but I don't think Lucas notices—he's too busy sending dangerous looks at Sinjin, causing me to wonder what the hell is going on with Your Toxic Sequel.

"Let's do another take," the engineer suggests, flipping several buttons on the electronics panel in front of him as soon as Lucas agrees.

The band performs four takes before they finally nail the song. I flinch when Wyatt all but slams his guitar against the wall and says loudly, "I'm getting the fuck out of here before I rip these walls down." Then he disappears, storming out of the booth and the studio, slamming doors loudly behind himself.

Both the sound engineer and the documentary maker head into the booth to speak to the rest of the band, so I take this opportunity to check my personal cell phone. There's a missed call from Seth and one from Gram. Even though I called her earlier, fear slices through my body as I gaze down at her call information on the screen. Does she know where I am? Has Seth told her what was on the Internet yesterday morning?

Slightly disoriented, I leave the control room yet again and call my voicemail as I pace the hallways. Seth's message is short and, surprisingly, sort of sweet.

"You can't ignore me forever, Si. I was wrong. I'm a shithead. Let's talk, okay? You and Gram are all I've got, so call me back."

I listen to my grandmother's message next—she's just returning my call and wants me to dial her back when my work isn't so crazy. "And I'm so happy you're coming home soon," she says before ending the message. She doesn't say anything about Lucas or the videos or pictures of us that ended up online and I feel a weight lift off my shoulders.

For now.

I start to call Seth back but then decide against it. When I call my little brother, I want to have plenty of time to get some things off my chest, and I don't want to do it in a studio where pieces of my conversation may end up in some movie about the future of rock bands. I pass by the private room that Lucas and I were in earlier, pausing when I hear the sound of someone moaning on the other side. I move forward, but a rough hand closes around my upper arm.

Startled, I jump and spin around to face Sinjin. He lets go of

185

his grip on me, holds up his hands, and wiggles them around as if to show me he's not armed. Then he grins. "Spying is rude," he tells me. "Though if you want to join Wyatt and the little blonde with the tits, I'm sure he'd let you, red hair or not."

Size Nothing and Wyatt are in there. I don't want to be surprised at learning this but I am, especially after the way she'd eyed Lucas earlier. That private room must be the sex mecca of this studio.

I take a step away from the room Wyatt's in, and another to put some space between myself and Sinjin. "I'm good, thanks," I say, starting to walk off. He plunks his hand down on the smooth wall next to my face to stop me. Feeling my muscles tighten, I shove it away and continue toward the exit of the building. He follows.

"You look really familiar, you know."

I hold back the urge to cringe, clenching my hands and teeth instead. "I'm sure you meet a lot of girls in your profession, even redheads." If my grandmother could hear the coolness in my voice right now, she'd pop me in the mouth for being so rude. I can't help it. There's something about Sinjin that rubs me the wrong way, but then again, it always has.

When I worked the "All Over You" video shoot, I had tried my hardest to stay as far away from Sin as much as possible, but of course he'd been unavoidable. I'd hated the way he looked at me, sneering and regarding me with harsh eyes every time I delivered a costume change to his dressing room. He'd freaked me out back then, but today the urge to shake him off me is twice as powerful.

I push open the exit doors, dragging in a deep breath of fresh air. Sinjin is right on my heels, cocking his head to one side and sizing me up. When he doesn't speak, I hug my arms around myself.

"I'm sure you've met a million girls who look like me," I say, unsure of why I feel the need to explain myself to this man.

Sinjin shakes his head to each side, smirking. "No, I don't think that's what it is at all. Did we fuck? Or did you fuck one of the others before you started up with Lucas? I mean, I know I don't remember you from him because he doesn't hold on to 'em for very long, if you know what I mean?"

"Actually I don't," I hiss. Now, my voice is hard. "I was under the impression that he's had the same personal assistant for years."

"Is that what he says you are—his personal assistant? Whatever keeps your mouth around his dick, right?"

He's just trying to get a response out of me, but God, he sure is going for a big one. When I say nothing, he begins to laugh. Loud, boisterous laughter that makes a woman in the next parking lot glance over at us with her eyebrow lifted.

Turning his body in her direction, he yells out, "What are you looking at, you fat bitch?"

Even from several feet away I hear her gasp as her face turns scarlet from embarrassment. She rushes into her car and speeds off, fidgeting anxiously with the steering wheel.

"You're a dickhead," I say, twisting away from Sinjin to go back inside, but he murmurs something in a quiet voice, making me pause. I turn my body slightly and frown when I realize that he's shaking with laughter, dragging his tattooed hands through his short blond hair and singing.

Badly and off-key.

No, he isn't just a dickhead. There is something seriously wrong with this guy, and every voice of warning in my head is screaming for me to get the hell away from him, to get myself back to Lucas. Calmly, I close the distance between myself and the studio door, knocking on it hard so that the guard will let me in.

When I turn around, pressing my back up to the door to keep an eye on him until security lets me in, I'm stunned to see tears streaming down Sinjin's cheeks. Now, instead of laughing like he was just moments ago, he's sobbing violently. Something—pity or maybe even stupidity—compels me forward a few steps, and I finally notice the beads of perspiration on his upper lip, the way his shivering has absolutely nothing to do with the weather.

He's messed up, completely obliterated. I haven't been around drug addicts for so long that it's taken me a while to notice it.

"Don't touch me, you slut," he hisses, pulling at clumps of his hair.

I've got no plans to. I'm still a safe distance away from him, by the door, and once again I bang on the metal. I clear my throat, attempting to get rid of some of the dryness before I whisper, "Do you need me to go—"

Sinjin lunges toward me, and out of reflex or watching too many UFC fights with Tori and our friend Micah, I ram my elbow back into his nose and bring my knee up to strike him in the stomach. He stumbles backward, glaring down at the blood on one of his hands and holding his belly tight with the other. Then he vomits all over himself and the asphalt.

Finally, the door behind us buzzes open.

The next half hour is frightening, chaotic, with Cal and Wyatt finally managing to convince Sinjin to lie down in the back of the studio as Lucas makes a bunch of phone calls. After a while, I slink outside to the Cadillac, and drink a cup of burned coffee that I purchase from a convenience store around the corner.

I'm deep in thought, wondering what's going to happen to Sinjin, when someone knocks on the SUV window, nearly causing me to choke on the sip of coffee I've just swallowed. I shift around to face Lucas's grim expression, and he motions for me to get out of the Escalade.

The moment my feet hit the ground, he jerks me close to him, resting his chin on top of my head and inhaling the scent of the apple-scented body spray that I've been using for what seems like forever. This is so unlike him, and so comforting, that I melt against his hard body, curling my fingers into the soft fabric of his T-shirt.

"Sienna, I need you to go back to the house in Green Hills and wait for me," he says in a low voice, his hands running up and down the center of my back.

"Are you sure?"

I feel him nod his head, strands of his hair brushing the top of my forehead. "I've got things I need to handle for Sin."

A cold rush explodes through my body at the way he says the word *things*, but I don't argue, despite having a million questions and even more concerns. "I'll go," I say.

Then he leans back a few inches, cupping my face between rough fingers as he touches his lips to my temple. He lingers there for a long time before he breaks away, gently nudging me into the Escalade. When our eyes meet, the fear in his is enough to paralyze me.

He's terrified for his friend.

I'm still shaken after I enter the house and activate the alarm system, but I call Seth. After seeing Sinjin fall apart and realizing how many similar things Seth had seen as a kid, I know it's the perfect time to speak to my brother. Plus, Lucas is right. There's so much I need to say to Seth, and until I do, I won't ever be able to do anything else.

Seth sounds anguished from the moment he answers. "Sienna, I'm—"

"No, you listen for once," I say. "You can't just take out your frustrations on people you care about without even giving them a chance to explain themselves. And by the way, I don't have to explain myself to you, the same way you don't want to prove yourself to me. You ripped into me without knowing a goddamn thing about what was going on. If you had only asked me, I probably would have just told you what you wanted to know."

"Look, I—"

I cut him off again. "I'm not finished. If you ever talk to me like you did yesterday again, I will kick you in the balls, Seth. You're so pissed at what Mom did to you, the people she brought around you, and yet you act just like them." And here I am, the total opposite of Seth. Wincing every time someone so much as breathes at me.

"I'm sorry, Sienna."

"Seth, I don't want to be the fucked-up people they've made us," I whisper. I don't want to be the person who throws the people I love under a bus just because it's easier. My mom had done that—to Seth and Gram and me—and we're all still suffering for it several years after the fact.

We're all still broken.

Seth inhales and exhales heavily for what seems like minutes, hours, but in reality is only seconds. "Me neither."

"So what do we do?" I ask.

"God, I wish I could tell you. But I swear I feel like shit for what I said. I shouldn't have ever spoken to you like that. I-I love you."

"Holy shit, are we having a creepy Hallmark card moment?" I ask, and he laughs.

When he finally stops, his tone of voice turns serious. "Can you tell me what you're doing with Wolfe? *Please?*"

"It's best I don't," I say honestly.

"Well then, let me ask you this: Does it have something to do with the house?"

"Yes."

And no. It started out as having everything to do with the house, and now . . . I'm not entirely positive what it is anymore.

The only thing I do know is that no matter how happy I pretend I am in five days, I'll be dying inside because I'll have to let this go.

I'll have to let Lucas go.

I'm sure my brother's mind has gone to the worst possible assumptions, but after he clears his throat a couple of times, he says, "Then I'm sure you've got a good-ass reason for what you're doing."

It's the closest thing to an acceptance that I'm probably going to get from my brother, but for now it works. I have a feeling that in order for Seth and me to really get all our feelings out on the table, we're going to have to do it in front of our mother.

And when that happens, we'll go ahead and take Gram along for the ride, too. That way Mom can finally explain to us why she convinced Gram to take out a six-figure loan on her house to bail her out of jail just to turn around and skip town. Why she ever tried to convince Seth to say he was the one selling drugs, not her.

It will be a good old family reunion, complete with tears and a lot of hatred.

Lucas comes home looking absolutely exhausted while I'm answering his fan mail. I feel awkward asking him anything about Sinjin, so I don't keep him in the little downstairs office for long. An hour after he arrives, though, he messages me to come upstairs to the main office.

I'm at a genuine loss for words as I linger by the door, my

fingers gripping the elaborate molding as I wait for him to say something, anything at all.

He stands, coming around to the front of the desk, and motions me forward. I go to him but leave a foot of space between us. "Sin's agreed to go back to rehab," he says.

I close my eyes, picturing the wild look in Sinjin's when he came after me. Honestly, I don't think he was sober enough to hit his mark, but it's still terrifying to think about him being high enough to try and hurt me. "I'm so glad. D-do you think . . . he'll be all right?" I whisper.

Leaning his tall body against the desk, Lucas shrugs, frustrated. "He's been before. Every time we gear up for a tour or an album. And it's prescription now, so who the fuck knows."

My chest clenches painfully, and I bring my hands up to my mouth. "God, Lucas. I'm so very sorry," I say. And this is why I hate drugs and the people who dole them out like Skittles. They tear families into a million pieces, and Sinjin is like a brother to Lucas. They've been making music together for ten years, since they were eighteen, and were friends long before that.

I don't want this to be the end of their relationship.

"I'm the one who should be sorry, Sienna. For whatever he said to you. For putting you in such a fucked-up situation to begin with. Kylie warned me he was back on the pills but I didn't want to listen because he said he was fine."

"He's your best friend," I point out. "And he needs a lot of help."

Tentatively, as if he's still unsure of whether or not he should still take my invitation to touch me to heart, he lifts my hands up, pressing them between his. Closing his eyes, he touches my fingers to his lips and kisses them softly.

"He is. He's my oldest friend, but I wanted to rip him to fucking shreds when I found out he was out there with you alone," he says, his voice possessive and hard.

"Really, he didn't say anything that bothered me," I lie. "And besides, I'm us—"

"If you say that you're used to people treating you like that I swear to God I'll bend you over this desk and keep my promise with the drumsticks."

My breath catches, and he squeezes my hands a little harder, a little more desperately. "I called my brother earlier," I murmur, dragging my hands away from his and sliding them down the front of his body.

"Stop," he warns as he grabs my wrists. His lips are inches away from my mouth. I stretch my neck up to touch them but he moves his head a fraction.

"I told him I wasn't going to put up with him treating me like shit. I told him—"

Groaning, he very gently pushes me away from him and slides his hands up and down his face. I watch him carefully. What is he thinking? I'd give anything to be inside of his complicated head for just a moment.

"Unbelievable. I come in from, literally, one of the shittiest days of my life and you're being obedient and—"

His cock is hard. I can see its outline straining against his jeans and he's not making a move to hide it. "Do you want me to go away, *sir*?" I murmur.

"Come back over here, Sienna," he growls. I obey, moving closer to him until I can practically feel static electricity thrumming from our bodies. "Get down on your knees."

I know where this is going to go. I know that if I do this I'm only a few steps away from uttering those words he's challenged me to say since even before day one began. Nevertheless, I'm at the point where I want to see this through. Where I have to have him, even if I have to come to terms with giving myself over in the process.

Where I know that the chemistry between the two of us really is inevitable.

Carefully, I slide down to the floor, one knee meeting the bamboo floor at a time. I don't miss the way he shudders when I lock my eyes with his, waiting for the rest of his instructions.

He traces his fingertips around the outline of my face, gently stroking my temples, my cheeks, my lips. Tucking his fingers under my chin, he draws my face up until my head is tilted all the way back and my hair sways against my bottom.

"You are so fucking beautiful," he whispers, before bending over to claim my lips. He drags my tongue into his mouth, teasing it in a desperate game of cat and mouse—wolf and sheep—with his own.

I lift my hands to touch his face but he barks out a rough command for me to keep them behind my back. I clasp them together, linking my fingers together. He moves his hands to my breasts, testing their weight before rolling and pinching my nipples between his fingers.

My breath comes out in sharp, pleading gasps as he alternates between sliding his tongue into my mouth and sucking on my top lip, between squeezing my sensitive nipples and pushing my dress aside to probe the wetness between my legs. He nudges my slit with his knuckles, never moving my panties.

Whimpering, I squeeze my eyes together. I feel like I'll come at the slightest provocation, at the slightest glance from him, and I grind my teeth. To punish me, he takes his hands and mouth away from my body. I convulse anyway, my body hot and trembling. Slowly, I open my eyes. His cock springs forward and rubs against my cheek. Despite not having received directions from him, I flick my tongue out, taking the head into my mouth.

He tangles his hands into the hair at the nape of my neck, pulling my mouth away from his body. "You're so amazing. So good," he says, stroking my back. "You're going to learn, Sienna."

I nod my head, ready.

Willing.

Craving.

He teaches me slowly. The way to take my mouth down his length until he moans and twists his hands into my long hair. The way he likes it when I use my teeth, placing just the tiniest bit of pressure on him. How he goes frantic when I squeeze my lips together, swiveling my tongue around his cock until he climaxes in my mouth.

Afterward, when I move to sit down on my bottom, he shakes his head and says roughly, "Stay exactly like that."

He sinks down to his own knees, going around my body in careful, animalistic circles as he drags my panties down to my knees with his mouth. I'm shivering, dying for his touch. His hands are warm and gentle yet rough as they guide my thighs apart. Then he parts my wet slit with the hard tip of his tongue.

"God, you taste so fucking sweet," he groans in appreciation, his mouth causing a vibration that sings through my body. A hoarse sound of pleasure escapes my throat.

And as I remain there, with the flooring hard beneath my weak knees and my fingernails raking my hands behind my back—as I remain there with him making me shudder and threatening to spank me if I so much as move my hands or body—I know that I'm ready to learn everything about his world.

Even at the risk of losing my heart.

15

Day six begins in what can only be described as a manic frenzy. I'm awoken at six thirty in the morning when I receive a text on the phone Lucas has given me. My body is still deliciously sore from him making me come over and over again with his mouth and hands last night. I flip over onto my side and grab the phone from my nightstand, expecting to find some type of sexy tease.

But the message isn't from Lucas. It's from his sister.

> Hey, babe, what e-mail address did you send Luke's confirmation for the flight to Atlanta to? Don't see it in the regular e-mail and was worried.

I should be irritated that she's checking up on me, but I'm more concerned with the fact that I have no earthly idea what she's talking about. I shoot her a quick text message back, asking her what's going on. Fifteen seconds later, the phone vibrates in my hand.

"Okay, please tell me you're just kidding me and you sent the confirmation to your personal inbox. You did, right?" Kylie pleads. She sounds half asleep. As if to confirm my suspicions, she yawns rudely into the receiver.

Tossing the warm blankets away from my body, I swing my legs over the side of the bed and stretch my toes. It's too early for any of this. Since the next few days will be so busy, I had planned to make the most of my sleep, and yet here I am talking to Kylie about flight confirmations.

"No, I didn't. How was I supposed to know the reservations needed to be made in the first place?" Although, when I say it out loud, it seems like it would have been a good idea for me to check up on that sort of thing. I have to be the worst assistant ever because the only thing I've been able to focus on for the last five days was how sexually drawn I am to my boss.

At some point, I've even lost sight of the objective that made me say yes to working for Lucas in the first place. Getting Gram's house back.

Kylie releases a tiny yelp. I hear her headboard thud against the wall, and a low male voice murmurs something. "Go back to sleep," she whispers, doing a horrible job at muffling the receiver. To me she says, "Sorry about that, errr—"

"Housekeeping?" I suggest, stifling a snort.

"Right, housekeeping. Sienna . . . this is bad. I could've sworn that I left instructions for you to make the reservation on the list of—"

I glance down at her page of instructions that I keep on my nightstand and quickly skim over it. There's nothing about the flight to Atlanta.

"You didn't," I say confidently.

She groans as if she's in despair, and I can imagine her raking her hands through her mess of black and blue hair. "I had an awful dream about this, you know? Like I woke up in a cold sweat and freaking out, it was that awful. What are we going to do?"

The solution seems simple, but after I start up my computer and pull up several tabs to search for available flights, I see why Kylie has contacted me on the verge of a major meltdown. This is one of those messed-up instances where the universe is laughing at me because I discover there are absolutely no flights left for the day.

"I'll have to drive him, then," I say. There's no other way around it. I cringe at the idea of making the five-hour drive from Nashville to Atlanta with Lucas staring at me, making me nervous. He'll probably do everything in his power to get me hot, *wet,* and distracted while I'm driving, which in his case, won't be too hard.

She groans, and the sleepy guy—*housekeeper*—beside her moans. The bed squeaks again, but I pretend like I don't hear it.

"He's not going to be happy," she whispers. I hear her shuffling about and a moment later, the sound of a horn honking and sirens somewhere in the background. Then I hear her inhaling—she's smoking. "I mean, after what happened with Sinjin yesterday . . ."

I swallow hard. Wyatt and Cal, Your Toxic Sequel's lead guitarist, had come by late last night for evening drinks. None of them seemed like they were in a drinking mood, but they took down shot after shot of stinky dark liquor as if the world were coming to an end. I stayed out of their way, pretending to do work in the other room, until Lucas called for me to drive Wyatt and Cal to a strip club to meet up with some of their friends. It wasn't until I dropped them off and Cal disappeared inside that Wyatt had pulled me aside.

"The way Lucas looks at you . . . don't fuck him over, okay? You fuck with him and it messes with our music. I might not hit girls but I know chicks that'll beat your ass for me."

I guess he knew very little about the solo album Lucas was planning to release or if he did, he didn't say anything about it. I came as close as I could to smiling without breaking down.

"Really? You're threatening to have some girl beat me up over something you're imagining. You rockers are so sensitive," I'd said, squinting at him in the dark.

"And very protective of our careers," Wyatt confirmed as he fished his ID out of his wallet and approached the door to the club. Turning on his heel for a second, he says, "Have fun in Atlanta."

"Sienna? Hey, Sienna? Are you listening to a word I'm saying?" Kylie demands, drawing my attention back to the present.

"Yeah, I'm here. Hey, I'm going to make some calls directly to the airport. I'll get back to you in a few, okay? Bye," I say in one breath. I hang up before she has a chance to start fretting again.

But in the end, before Lucas is up two hours later, it's Kylie who saves the day. She sends me the confirmation for a private jet she's managed to charter to my personal e-mail, CCing Lucas. When I see the cost of the flight, I'm left wheezing. It's enough for Tori and I to pay all our expenses for a good three or four months.

Lucas doesn't seem fazed by the change of plans or the amount of money Kylie has spent when he calls me in to eat breakfast with him. I sit across from him in the kitchen, drinking coffee. He eats fresh fruit, his eyes locked intensely on me. I slump down in my seat, touching my hand to my face.

"Why are you looking at me like that, Mr. Wolfe?" I ask. My voice is tiny, whispery.

He slides a chunk of cantaloupe between his lips, leaving them wet and sweet and sticky. I cross my long legs to try and squeeze the want away. "Remember that time I ate strawberries with you on them?" he asks.

A flush spreads down my body, and I bring my coffee to my mouth, taking a giant sip. The hot liquid rushes down my throat and I rub my tongue back and forth between my teeth. Why is he teasing me like this now? Why when we have to leave for Atlanta shortly?

"I plan on making you sit perfectly still," he continues, his hazel eyes gleaming with desire and power. "Dipping my fingers, and fruit, inside of your delicious body. Tasting you. I've grown addicted to the way you taste, Red."

I feel the throb deep inside of me, and I shift in my seat.

"And let me guess, you don't plan to do any of that until I say the word, right?"

"You're so fucking smart, Sienna."

Lucas is broody the entire flight to Georgia—which, really, is over before it even begins because Nashville is so close to Atlanta. He sits sideways, taking up two seats and writing intently in his notebook. Every once in a while he glances up at me, tilting his head to one side, reading me.

I find myself wanting to know exactly what it is he's over there writing—if it's about me or us. I want to know what thoughts creep through his mind every time his eyes settle on me. There's so much I want to know about Lucas Wolfe that it's dizzying and I'm left with a racing heart.

I play a game on my phone to pass the time; some monotonous brick-breaking application that I continue to lose on the first level because I'm so preoccupied by Lucas.

He finally acknowledges my presence when the jet lands, as we prepare to disembark. Towering over me, he cups my face with one hand, pushing hair away from my temple. I reach up and pull the tips of my fingers through his floppy brown hair. He trails his lips down my face, pausing for a moment to claim my mouth.

"This is going to be so hard," he groans.

"What?"

"Being around you, knowing you're so close to becoming

mine, and not being able to fuck or taste or have you whenever I please because the next few days are so hectic."

His finger—fingers—slide between my lips. He slips them back and forth, and I gently bare my teeth down the way he's taught me to do on his cock.

"There's always our hotel," I say, stroking my hand against his erection.

He releases a muffled noise, grabbing my fingers away from his body and trapping my arms over my head. "You're right . . . there's always that. You are mine, Sienna."

Despite the fact that I've yet to come right out and completely seal the deal between us, I hear myself say in a soft voice, "Yes."

When we step off the jet, a limousine—the first one I've ridden inside of since my senior prom more than five years ago—is there to take Lucas and me to the hotel, the Four Seasons Atlanta. Even though I've been able to witness Lucas's fans' reaction to him in Los Angeles and at The Beacon bar in Nashville, it's nothing like the reaction he gets in his hometown.

"You do realize you're probably going to have to get a bodyguard while we're here, right?" I ask, staring across the limo at him.

He pulls one of my legs onto his lap, massaging my calf through the long black boots I'm wearing. I bite the inside of my cheek to keep from grinding my teeth, and he gives me a little grin that sends butterflies racing through my stomach.

"I can take care of us both," he swears. Even though I completely believe him, I still cock an eyebrow. "But if it makes you feel any better, the hotel has amped up security. You know *A-List Exclusive?*"

Of course I do—it's one of the most notorious gossip magazines in the country, one I've been guilty of purchasing for myself every now and then. I nod, and he continues, "They leaked that I'm in town."

I'd bet money they're probably the same magazine that first released the video of us online when he sang at The Beacon. When I ask him, he laughs.

Shrugging, he says, "There's an editor at that one that I used to . . . frequently meet up with. Needless to say she loves all things Lucas Wolfe, especially when those things involve making my life fucking difficult."

Ugh . . . why *wouldn't* there be a distraught ex–sex buddy of his on the staff at *A-List Exclusive?*

When we arrive at the Four Seasons he stops me before I exit the car, pulling me back down to straddle his hips. He yanks one of his oversized beanies over my head. Sliding a set of ridiculous hot pink shades over my face, he says gently, "Wouldn't want more gossip about you and us finding itself on the Web." He tucks my hair underneath the knit cap, making sure every red strand is hidden out of sight. The gesture is so intimate it makes my breath wobbly. "Do not talk to the press," he commands.

"Yes, Mr. Wolfe."

"Say my name one more time."

"Mr. Wolfe."

"No, my name."

"Lucas," I whisper.

Then he kisses me with a hunger that makes me want to rip both our clothes off right here and now. "God, I could write songs about the way you say that."

"Just like you'll write songs about my ass?" I tease.

"Every part of you," he says in a voice that tugs at my heart. Squeezing my breast hard one final time, he taps on the window, indicating to the driver that he's ready to face his fans.

Our room is on the top floor, in the presidential suite, and my breath catches the moment we step inside. It's stunning, with marble floors and lush furnishings. I sink down onto the massive pullout sofa that's positioned in front of the flat-screen television and give Lucas a wide, lazy grin.

"Holy shit, I don't think I could ever get used to all this," I tease.

He bends down, rummaging around inside the minibar. Once he finds what he's looking for, a giant can of Red Bull, he stands up and leans against the nearby desk. "You will eventually. Might take a few months, but hell, by the time we go on tour later this year you'll be a pro."

I don't know how to react to what he's just insinuated, so I blurt out the first thing that comes to mind. "Your Toxic Sequel is going on tour this year?"

He pops the tab of his energy drink and chugs half of it before lifting the corners of his mouth. "Yeah, we are." He finishes the last of the Red Bull, staring at me the entire time, waiting for me to form a coherent response to what he said about going on tour with him. Finally, he crunches the empty can into a ball and tosses it at the wastebasket by the door. "You and I are talking when I get back."

I frown, leaning forward to press my palms down flat on the coffee table. "You're leaving?"

He nods and drags his T-shirt over his head. I reach up to catch it when he tosses it at me, letting the faint scent of perspiration mixed with Polo cologne fill my senses. By habit, I pull the soft fabric into my lap and fold it neatly before draping it across the arm of the couch. I glance up to find Lucas staring down at his phone, a blank expression on his face.

Suddenly, I'm sweating because that look—it's the exact same one he wore the night two years ago when he kicked me out of his house. "Lucas . . . is everything all right?" I ask tentatively. Then a thought hits me, and I swallow hard. "Is Sinjin okay?"

He hasn't mentioned his bandmate since last night when Cal and Wyatt stopped by the house in Nashville, and I'm wondering if he's just heard bad news.

Jamming his phone into his pocket with tight, jerky motions, Lucas bobs his head. "He's going to be fine." He pushes away from the desk and eases down on the coffee table in front of me. My lips part just a little when he draws my hands into his, stroking the rough pads of his thumbs in long circular motions along the insides of my wrists. "I've got to take care of something here in town, but I won't be gone long. You'll be okay here?"

"Yes," I whisper. Impulsively, I bend forward and run my lips along his jawline, feeling my heart bang fiercely inside of my chest at the sound of his breathing, which is suddenly unsteady. I can't resist wondering what he would've said if I told him no, if I asked him to stay here with me instead.

He changes clothes quickly and then leaves, promising as he closes the door behind him that he'll be back before I realize he's gone. I don't mind his absence, at least not for a little while, because it gives me an opportunity to admire the view of Atlanta from our room's balcony and check out the master bedroom. I'd be lying if I didn't admit to myself how anxious I am to test the four-poster king-sized bed with Lucas.

After I take a long bath where I shave my legs and wash my hair, I wrap up in an oversized bathrobe, courtesy of the hotel, and curl up on the sofa. For the next hour, I spend my time making phone calls and answering e-mails, both his and mine.

When I call Gram, she sounds relieved to speak to me. "Are you doing all right?" she asks.

"Yeah, I'm fine, I . . ." I start, pausing when I hear her sniffling. "Gram, what's going on?"

"It's Rebecca," she says. I listen, stone-faced, pacing back and forth because it's impossible for me to sit still now, as she tells me about how my mom has gotten into a fight in prison with several other inmates after stealing a pair of shoes. I feel that bitter feeling in the pit of my stomach, the shame, as she talks about Mom having to be sent to the county hospital for surgery.

"Will she be all right?" I ask, but it's mostly out of love for my grandmother.

"They'll keep her there for a few more days and she'll be on medical lockdown once she goes back. But I don't understand why she'd take someone's shoes, Sienna. I put money in her account there. I give her as much as . . ."

I freeze, clenching my free hand in the front of my bathrobe. It looks like I won't have to confront Gram about my mother. She's revealed that she's been going to visit Mom herself, but I wish with everything inside of me that I could be the one suffering instead of her.

My grandmother has stopped talking now. I hear her sobbing quietly on the other end and a creaking noise. She must be in bed. I ball my hands into fists, banging them into the couch.

"Gram, I can't yell at you about going to see her. I'm not going to argue with you or any of that because I've got *no* room to talk, but please, please, please stop letting her take advantage of you."

A few years ago, when Mom's whereabouts were discovered after she skipped town, the bounty hunters had caught up to her approximately two days after the three hundred grand cash bond Gram paid was forfeited to the court. If my mother's worthless ass had been caught just forty-eight hours earlier, Gram would never be in this situation.

But even after Mom screwed her over, tried to talk Seth, who was just a teenager, into taking the rap for her—even then Gram stood by her side.

My grandmother, with all of her kindness and humility, deserves so much better than my mom. Seth and I deserve so much better than our mother, and though I hate to admit it, more than our dad, too.

Because a phone call every other week and the occasional awkward visit on holidays was about the equivalent of a hello from the homeless man who trolls the coffee shop I go to for Tomas in Los Angeles each morning.

Taking a deep breath, I make the decision to tell my grand-mother exactly what I'm thinking. "You deserve more than her."

"I know," Gram says, her voice catching on a sob. "It's hard—what with the house and Rebecca. I don't know whether I'm coming or going anymore."

"Don't worry, I'll be home soon and we'll take care of every-thing. I swear it."

"It's hard," she says once more. "I-I've got to get to bed, sweet-heart. I'm going to go back to the hospital for your mom tomor-row morning and I've got a doctor's appointment of my own. But baby, I love you so much."

"Love you, too."

When I hang up, I sink down onto the floor beside the couch, barely able to think because of the headache blurring my vision. Lucas finds me like this with my face buried in my hands, grind-ing my teeth furiously.

"Don't gri—" he starts, but then he sucks in a mouthful of air, striding across the marble foyer and into the living room in a matter of seconds. He cups my face between his strong, rough hands. "What the hell is going on?"

"I'm fine."

"Sienna," he says in a cautioning voice, and I glance up at him, revealing my tear-streaked face. He rolls his body down

the side of the couch until he's right beside me. It's almost comi-
cal, how absolutely helpless he looks when confronted with my
tears, but he pulls me into his arms. Lucas Wolfe, the most
commanding man I've ever met, lets me sob onto the front of his
flawless white T-shirt, allows me to drip mascara all over it and
his tattooed skin.

I sniffle. "My mom got beat up in prison."

Holding me by my shoulders, he pulls away from me slightly,
placing just enough space between the two of us so that he can
look into my blue eyes and feel me out. He frowns, rubbing his
lips together. "I'm taking it you're not exactly sad about your
mom getting an ass-whipping."

I laugh, in spite of the tears, and drag the backs of my hands
across my face. "God, no. She's had it coming for years. It's
just—" I let out a small, strangled sound and he buries his head
in my hair again, stroking the back of my neck, making me feel
safe.

"You can say anything to me, Sienna."

"It's my grandma, you know. My mom's been so awful to her,
and yet Gram keeps taking the kicks over and over again. It just
hurts. It hurts so fucking bad."

Lucas murmurs that he understands, but I can't miss how
his voice hitches. How it feels as if there is something left unsaid
between the two of us.

But he listens to me sob, listens to every complaint I have
about Mom. It's like a dam bursts and I tell him everything,
breaking every dating rule in the book. When he firmly tells me

to go to sleep, tucking me into the four-poster bed in the master bedroom and climbing up beside me, the unsaid words are clear to me simply by the way he looks down into my eyes.

What I had said to him earlier about Gram—about her taking the kicks repetitively—that person used to be me.

16

I wake up the next morning with Lucas still in bed with me, his arm draped protectively around my waist. Reluctantly, I shrug away from him and push myself up into a sitting position, cringing at the throbbing sensation that's focused right between my eyes. His eyes open, alert, and he frowns when he takes in my expression.

"You going to be all right?" he asks, stifling a yawn as he rolls out of bed. I nod, and he flicks his gaze over to the digital clock on the nightstand. When he sees the time, 9:29 a.m., he groans loudly, scratching his fingers through his tousled dark hair. "Fuck me, we overslept. Guess that's the cost of . . ."

Smoothing down wild strands of my own hair, I run my tongue across dry lips. Forgetting my headache for a moment, I slide onto my knees, facing him. "The cost of what?"

"You really want to know?"

"Yes," I whisper, squinting at him as I massage my temples. "Honestly."

He bends down, walks his hands forward on the mattress until our faces are a couple of inches apart. "Last night with you was a first," he murmurs.

My brow knits together into a frown. "We didn't make lo—"

His clears his throat, cutting me off, and shakes his head. Sliding the tip of his finger along my face, he says, "I don't do overnights."

My breath hitches. "Ever?"

Lucas slides my bottom lip between his thumb and forefinger, nodding slowly. "Not in a long-ass time. Not until you," he confirms. "Now, get dressed before I break my promise right here and now and spend my morning inside of you."

God, I wish he wouldn't say things like that and then expect me to go about my day as if everything were normal. How can anything be normal when he tells me that I'm a first for him?

Still, I manage a tight smile as I get out of the bed and head to the bathroom. Fortunately for my sake, my headache is dulled by the shower, but the piping-hot water does nothing for the way he's gotten me worked up, both emotionally and physically.

Lucas is already dressed when I finally come out of the shower, sitting on the sofa and tossing back yet another Red Bull. "We're going to meet my parents today," he tells me, grinning as he skims his hazel eyes up the length of my body.

I pull my robe snugly around myself and give him a hesitant look. "First sleeping with me all night and now a meet-and-greet with the parents."

Shaking his head, he laughs. "I know. What other shit can I possibly surprise you with, huh?"

"You took the words right out of my mouth," I reply in a dry voice, and his gaze automatically zeroes in on my lips.

I choose my clothes with extra care, going for a long-sleeved lacy black top, a skinny black pencil skirt, and my mile-high pumps.

"You look good enough to taste," he whispers, standing and meeting me halfway when I come out of the bedroom. He pulls the hairpins from my hair, messing his fingers through the apple-scented locks. "Mmm, so much better."

He hasn't mentioned anything about last night other than sleeping together, and I'm not about to bring up our heart-to-heart talk about my fucked-up family. Instead I mold my body to his, sighing at the way his heart feels against the side of my face.

"I might as well throw away every hairpin in my overnight bag," I complain through a smile.

He grins, cocking his head to the side so that his hair falls over his forehead. I reach up to push it back, but he grabs my hands, kissing my inner wrists as he gives me a dangerous look. "You should've realized that days ago."

When we leave the suite a few minutes later and get onto the elevator, he entwines our fingers together. I don't look up at him, but I don't have to.

The gesture and everything he's told me already says so much.

He releases my hand the moment the doors open and we step into the lobby. We're immediately rushed by the nosy documentary maker I met in the studio two days ago, and he begins briefing Lucas on how today needs to go down. He grants me a curious once-over and a courteous greeting, but other than that he doesn't say much to me. As I walk behind them, typing notes on my Samsung tablet and trying not to roll my eyes, it takes a lot of effort not to point out that nothing about this documentary seems very realistic. He's even prepping Lucas about how to act around his own parents.

And speaking of Lucas's parents . . .

Biting my lip, I send Kylie a message asking what I should expect. I know this is probably something I should have asked her before, but a few days ago my feelings were nowhere near this strong for Lucas. Something has happened between us, just as he promised. I don't want to make a fool of myself in front of their folks or leave a horrible impression that might last forever.

Because this evening I plan on accepting the rest of his offer. Aside from rescuing my grandmother's house—which I can safely say I've done at this point—there's nothing I've wanted more in a very long time than to be Lucas's.

My cell phone goes off and I check the message from Kylie. *Dude, my parents love everyone. They liked my ex-husband, so you can run naked through their yard if you want and still be okay.*

A moment later, she sends another message. *But really, don't run through their yard naked.*

Feeling a sudden sense of relief, I take Lucas's hand as he helps me into the limousine that will take us around Atlanta for the day. He touches my skin a little too long, skimming the tip of his thumb over my knuckles. I flush. Stare out the window. Wish that he hadn't pulled away.

The documentary maker leans forward, a slow smile forming

on his pale face, but Lucas shoots him a look. The cameraman is the last person to climb inside the limo. Lucas and the creator of the documentary—which I find out is called *Rock on the Road*— sit on one side of the car, and I sit with the camera guy on the other so I won't be seen on film. The whole time Lucas talks about his life growing up in Atlanta, he's staring at me and not the camera.

"I played baseball—first baseman—at that high school over there my freshman year." He points out the window at a school on the right side of the street. It's a private religious academy, much to my surprise. "Took a hit in the balls with a baseball and that shit ended pretty quickly," he adds, rolling his eyes dramatically for the sake of the camera.

"What about the music? What would you say had the biggest impact on your sound growing up?" the documentary guy presses.

Lucas looks deep in thought, though I have a feeling he's just pretending. These questions have more than likely been asked by hundreds of reporters in more scenarios than he can count.

"My dad. He was a huge Metallica fan. I—uh—may have been in a Metallica cover band with Sinjin and Wyatt once upon a time ago," he says.

Metallica. I cock my eyebrow at him and he gives me a shrug and a grin. "Google is your friend," he mouths.

The limousine slows down to the crawl necessary for residential communities. When we stop, pulling up to the curb of a brown and white bungalow, a woman who looks like a pint-sized version of Kylie, minus the multicolored hair, comes out onto the front porch, smiling brightly.

"I hope you cooked," Lucas drawls as soon as he gets out of the car, and his mom races down the front steps toward us.

"You know I did," she says in a voice brimming with emotion.

By the way she hugs Lucas, pulling him fiercely to her and burying her face into his chest, she's either been prepped by the documentary maker as well or Lucas goes home just about as often as I do. I'm leaning toward the second and wondering what kind of past he has here. By the obvious affection he has for his mother and the adoration he showed when talking about his dad in the limo, I don't think he feels anything other than love toward his parents.

As soon as everyone is inside of the Wolfes' cramped living room, Lucas's mother turns to him and asks, "Where's Kylie?" She glances at me as I sit down on the piano bench, and lifts a dark eyebrow. "Is she at the hotel?"

"She had an emergency to take care of in California," Lucas explains easily. He winks at me. "Don't worry, Ma, she'll be here for Easter."

I bite the inside of my cheek to keep from grinning. His Georgian accent seems to magically appear when he's with his mom, and I make a note to tease him about it later since he'd given me such shit when we first met about my own accent. Plus, I think it's sexy as hell that he's almost twenty-nine but respects his mother enough not to tell her his sister is partying in New Orleans and spending extra time with . . . *housekeeping*.

Mrs. Wolfe turns out to be just as kind and charming as Kylie, speaking to the camera with a natural ease as she boasts about her kids. Lucas's dad shows up halfway into the filming.

He's got on a sweaty golf shirt, but he hugs me when I introduce myself as Kylie's temporary replacement.

"She didn't send any of that champagne, did she?" he whispers into my ear, and I grin.

The mood in the Wolfes' home is happy, easygoing, but as each minute rolls by, I find myself withdrawing. I have to remind myself more than once that I have Gram, that my grandparents were just as wonderful as anyone else's parents as I witness Lucas interacting with his mom and dad.

Somehow, I manage to keep the feelings of jealousy at bay.

"Lucas not giving you too much trouble?" Mrs. Wolfe asks, and it takes me a second to realize the question is meant for me. I meet her brown eyes and nearly die because though they're smiling, it's so obvious she knows there's something between her son and me.

So I clear my throat and give her the best answer I can come up with in such an awkward situation: "He tells me that Google is my friend at least ten times a day."

Everyone in the small living room laughs, and after that, the documentary maker shifts the discussion to some of Lucas's most outrageous quotes and his parents' opinion of them.

When it's time for us to leave, a couple of hours after our arrival, both Mr. and Mrs. Wolfe give me a hug good-bye and embrace Lucas. "Before I forget," his mom says, stopping him before he gets into the limousine, "Sam's been trying to get in touch with you. Said it was—"

"Already taken care of," Lucas tells her, his voice tight, almost rude. She doesn't notice it, but I can clearly see that his face is drawn into a harsh frown as he hugs his mom one last time. Whoever Sam is, I'd bet money he's one of those things keeping Lucas from coming to Atlanta regularly.

When we ditch the camera crew and I have Lucas all to myself in the limo, he tells me to come over onto his lap. I climb across the seats a little too eagerly, sliding my bottom down on top of him. He splays his hands out on either side of it, grinning at how I squirm beneath his touch.

"I want you naked, doing that all over me later," he whispers in a suggestive voice, as he squeezes my bottom.

"How much later?" I gasp, as his lips find my neck. He slides the tip of his tongue along my collarbone, whispering in between kisses how delicious I taste. "How much later?" I demand again, and he growls, pushing me back gently so that we're eye to eye, nose to nose.

"Lunch with Cilla won't take long and then we'll—"

I freeze as soon as he says her name, the rest of his words suddenly drowned out and becoming a warbled mess. Pulling completely away from him, I hug my arms around my stomach. "I didn't know Cilla Craig was in Atlanta." Despite all my best efforts to control myself, there's a hint of wariness in my voice.

Fucking jealousy.

He opens my arms, spinning me around so that my back is to him. Drawing me into his lap again, he caresses my breasts, flutters his fingers softly against my nipples and then twists them just enough to send vibrations through me.

"That's what we're here for," he says between strokes, between kisses on the back of my neck. "Besides the documentary, the only other reason I came to Atlanta is for Cilla's birthday party tomorrow."

"Oh," I say curtly.

He doesn't seem to notice how angry I am by the time we arrive at the restaurant, or how my hand goes slack in his as he guides me inside. I almost want to retract my invitation to let him touch me even though I know doing so would be silly and a waste of time—at this point, he'll simply refuse to stop.

Though I'm hoping that Cilla's beauty is a product of Photoshop and MAC, she turns out to be just as stunning as she is on all the magazine covers and in the music videos. Lucas introduces me as Kylie's temp, and she nods at me, giving me a hint of a smile. Cilla's got this husky, sexy voice that turns heads when she laughs and she orders Bud Light and a messy cheeseburger even though neither is on the menu.

"How's Shannon and Daniel?" Cilla asks, taking a swig of beer.

It's not until Lucas laughs and answers her with "Just came from over there, actually. You better stop by and see them while you're in town" that I realize Shannon and Daniel are his parents' first names.

She winks at him. "Screw you if you thought I'd miss out on your mom's cake."

I purse my lips together because Lucas had suggested we leave before I got to try any of the dessert his mother had offered us.

EMILY SNOW

Cilla doesn't say much to me—she's mostly focused on Lucas—but at one point, she tosses her mane of inky black hair over one shoulder and stares me down. "So, Pepper, how'd you get caught up with Luke?" she demands. "Because I didn't even know Kylie knew what a vacation was. That kid works way too much."

Holy fuck, she just called me Pepper. I feel my skin flush with anger. I want to reach across the table and slap the lazy grin off her face. I start to give her a sharp retort, but Lucas answers for me. "Sienna worked on the set of one of my music videos a few years ago. She does wardrobe back in Los Angeles."

"Fun," Cilla says, though she doesn't look like she means it and I'm glad I never had to work on a Wicked Lambs music video.

The rest of lunch seems to drag by at an uncomfortably slow pace. Each second I spend watching Cilla and Lucas catch up is difficult. They laugh and seem so in sync with one another that my stomach pitches viciously. I stare at a scuff in the floor, at a stain on one of the waitresses' starched white aprons—anything to keep from listening to them.

Finally, I excuse myself. I linger in the restroom longer than appropriate before going out to face them again. When I reach the table, Lucas is paying the check.

Cilla grins up at me. "I was just inviting Luke—and you, of course—to come over and—"

"I'm good, thanks," I say, not even willing to hear what she's got to say. Lucas's hazel eyes narrow into tight slits, but I glance away from his face.

I don't give a shit what he thinks right now.

We're quiet during the limo ride back to the hotel, sitting on opposite sides of the backseat with our bodies stiff with tension. But the moment we walk through the door of the suite, he drags me to him, pinning my hands above my head and forcing my lips apart until my knees go slack. He kisses me, urgently, deeply— so hard that it leaves my lips feeling tender and bruised.

Then, carefully, he pushes me away from him. Keeping his voice level, he points to the chair by the desk. "Sit down, Sienna."

"No, I'm not going to—"

"Sit. Down," he repeats. I'm fuming and my body is trembling, but I sink down, my bottom hanging off the edge of the chair. I clench my hands on the armrests the moment Cilla's name comes out of his mouth. He wants to know why I was so rude to her, and I shrug. "Be honest with me, okay? What the fuck were you thinking?"

I turn my face away from him when I speak because I don't trust my emotions.

"She looked me over like I wasn't fit to lick her motorcycle boots." Silently, I add, *And she looked at you like I look at you. I'm afraid of your past together. I'm afraid of Cilla period because I don't want you with her.*

I won't tell him all my fears, but I don't want to hold back either. Squeezing my eyes closed, I whisper in a ragged voice, "I was thinking how bad *I* want you."

He takes my face between his hands and kisses my lips again, sending my body into a frenzy. "Don't tell me you're threatened

EMILY SNOW

by Cilla," he hisses against my mouth. I nod my head and he tangles his hands in my hair, releasing a low growl from the back of his throat. "You drive me fucking crazy, Sienna. She's one of my best friends—we grew up together—but she's not you. Never in a million years."

It feels so good to hear him say those words, and I circle my arms around his neck. "I want you," I tell him again, pulling away. "I want to be that person you need."

"I won't believe that until you've calmed down, until you're absolutely sure," he warns, but I grind my body against his. "Stop or I will punish you this time."

I take his hand, pressing it between my legs. He cups my chin, turns my face until our eyes connect, hazel to blue. Releasing a groan, he sets me away from him and removes his own T-shirt. I watch, holding my breath and drinking in the sight of his toned, tattooed chest and arms, as he rips the fabric into several long strips.

"What are you—?"

"Be quiet and get naked."

I strip down so fast he cocks an eyebrow as he comes toward me. He tosses one of the hotel towels on the chair. "Sit down," he says, and I slide into the seat. He kneels down in front of me. When I reach out to stroke his hair, he catches my wrist, tethering it to the arm of the chair. I gasp. Giving me a dangerous look, he ties my other wrist to the opposite side of the chair. Then, spreading my legs wide apart so that I'm completely exposed to him, he binds my ankles to the legs of the chair.

"Lucas, I—"

He covers my mouth with the tips of his fingers, bending his head to touch me. I squirm, grasping at air with my own fingers. For what seems like eternity, he tastes and bites and sucks. When I'm close to coming, when I'm rocking back and forth in the chair almost violently and bucking my hips to his mouth, he stops.

"I'm going to make a phone call. Run an errand," he whispers, untying me, making sure to skim his rough fingertips against the most sensitive areas of my body. Inside of my wrists . . . between my thighs . . . under my breasts.

"You are not to touch yourself until I return, do you under-stand?" he demands.

I nod as he helps me to my feet. Opening my legs with his hand, he nudges his finger inside of me. "Do you understand?" he repeats in a harsh voice.

"Yes . . . Lucas."

The moment he leaves our suite, I skulk into the bathroom.

17

"You were in there a very long time, Si," Lucas muses, startling me, as I pad out of the bathroom a little while later. Clutching my hand over my heart, I press my bottom up against the desk and stare across the room at him. He's sitting in the seat he'd bound me to less than an hour ago, quietly strumming his guitar. Heat floods my body because I can't help thinking about how his mouth had teased my body. How he'd warned me not to come. How he'd left me wanting more, wanting him to finish.

"I was dirty from—"

"You were touching yourself."

He's not asking me, he's telling me what I've been doing. Before I can think of something witty to say, I blurt out, "You refused to finish."

Lucas drops his hazel eyes down to his guitar and strums out the opening notes of a song that's so familiar—so full of meaning for both of us—it causes my throat to go dry. "All Over You."

The exact same song that started all this for us two years ago. "Is that what you want now, Sienna? For me to finish? To take you all the way?" he asks, his voice strained.

"Yes," I whisper.

"You're mine?"

I nod my head, unable to speak as I splay my hands out flat on the desk behind me. "I'm yours."

He rises to his feet, placing the guitar at the side of the bed. Now, I've got his full attention. Static runs through my body, making every inch of me feel as if I've been electrocuted, as he takes slow steps toward me.

His hands travel down the sides of my body slowly, as if he can't get enough of touching me. Finally, he stops at my hips, gripping the soft fabric of my robe between his long fingers. He jerks me to him, so close I can almost taste the spearmint gum he's recently chewed. "Do you trust me?" he murmurs against my lips. When I don't answer, because I'm unsure of what to say, he releases a sexy noise from the back of his throat. "Turn around."

"Why? So you can spank me like a little kid?" I demand, re- calling some of his earlier threats. There's a sarcastic edge to my voice—one that lures a slow spreading grin from Lucas. God, why does he have to look so beautiful, so *perfect,* and yet so sin- fully dangerous?

"Not at all like a child," he promises.

Shivering, I face the desk and bend over, placing my fore- arms and hands down on the wood. Lucas moves behind me, brushing my hair away from my neck, and I exhale deeply as his lips burn a trail from the right to left side of my shoulder blades. I would be stupid if I said I wasn't the tiniest bit frightened, but the other feelings that course through me—blurry and wonderful and intoxicatingly confusing—trump the fear.

"I'm crazy for wanting this," I say breathlessly. Crazy and sadistic and careless.

And so fucking alive it burns.

"I want you crazy for me," he growls. "I want—"

"Every part of me," I finish for him, glancing over my shoulder just in time to see a grin spread across his face.

"Abso-fucking-lutely."

Lucas removes the white robe from my body, leaving me bare. His fingers are feather soft as he guides my hips further away from the desk and bows my back so that my bottom is jutted up at him.

"I'm obsessed with your body. With you," he whispers, gliding his fingertips down my skin—which is still slightly damp from my shower—down my hips, past my thighs. He kneels down behind me, and I glance back at him, startled. "Trust me," he says before kissing the small of my back. Then, carefully, he spreads my legs apart and repositions my feet so that there's a wide space between them.

When he stands up, his hard body slightly skimming mine along the way, I moan. "Lucas . . ."

He swats my left ass cheek with the palm of his hand, the same palm that was playing such beautiful music only minutes ago. It's not hard enough to bruise, but the sting is enough to make me shiver.

In pain.

Anticipation.

Need.

Punishment lasts for approximately two more swats, one for each side of my bottom and then Lucas kisses the base of my neck. My shoulder blades arch together. For a moment, I feel him go completely still. "You sure you still want this, Sienna?"

"More than anything."

The dark cotton blindfold drapes over my eyes.

Suddenly, I feel bare, deliciously blinded to the world around me. On the outside, I'm patient as I wait for his next move, but my heart is throbbing. My breath is coming out in short, choppy wisps.

Please . . .

Running one of his hands down my arm, he intertwines my fingers with his and tugs me around to face him. "I need to be inside of you. I want . . ." His voice trails off, but I bob my head up and down, press my body as close to his as possible.

He doesn't have to say another word because I know exactly what it is Lucas Wolfe wants from me. And I'm strong enough to give it to him. When I say the words, a ripple of pleasure flows through me. It settles into the pit of my belly. "Please . . . Lucas." I sound timid and confident, all at once.

I gasp as he lifts my body effortlessly and slides my bottom onto the wide desk behind us. There's part of me that's dying to see the expression on his face—whether or not his hazel eyes have darkened or if he's staring at me with animalistic lust—but I love the way my senses seem heightened. The way my skin tingles in some places before he even touches me, almost as if it's sensing his next move.

He slides his hands between my thighs, splaying his rough fingertips on my smooth skin. Slowly his fingers move up, and I feel one—no, two—slide inside of me, delving into the wetness. My knees buckle together. He opens them back apart and positions his body between them.

I grind my teeth together to keep from moaning, and I feel a tiny sting across my right breast, as he flicks me with . . . *something*. Momentarily surprised, I gasp. Then I wiggle my hips against his hand.

His fingers push and pull, filling me, taking me under until I arch my back and cry out. "Please," I say, barely recognizing my own voice and he gives a raw chuckle.

A second later, I get the sweet release he refused to give me a couple of hours ago.

"You're so fucking delicious . . . all mine," he murmurs into my skin.

I pray he's nowhere close to being done.

At last, Lucas tugs the blindfold down. I blink rapidly as my eyes adjust to the light. When they finally focus in on him, he brings his fingers to his mouth. Teasingly, he flicks his tongue over the tips, tasting me. I groan and reach out to him, but he captures my fingers in his hand, kissing them, tasting them, too.

When he guides my hand to his cock, I'm hesitant at first. What if he only wants to tease me again and has no intention of having sex with me? What if—

He nods his head and closes my grip around his shaft. "I'm

yours, Sienna," he says. When my breath catches, and I squeeze him harder, he nods again. "Yours."

I run my hand up and down the length of his hardness, slow at first, and then faster, tighter until he's moaning. He shoves away from me for a moment, staring down at me with a look that's enough to make me come without even being touched. Then, lifting me up and off the desk, he cups my bottom in his hands. His cock slides inside of me in one breathtaking thrust.

The room seems to tilt on its side.

He shudders when I tighten myself around him—my arms circling his neck, legs locked together around his waist and the length of him clenched deep inside of me.

And suddenly, my back is to the wall and his hands have left my ass to tangle into my long red hair. He drives his cock into me, slides my body up so that I lose him, lose *this*. Then he grinds his hips up.

He's inside of me again.

Out.

In.

Gritting my teeth, I say, "Oooh, Lucas"—another sting, this time my left breast—"I want to fucking come again."

"Not yet, not until I say so," he says, shaking his head so that his hair falls against my face. Then he crushes his lips to mine. I taste Red Bull and spearmint gum and myself. His tongue and cock seem to be working in unison, exploring and demanding until I'm incoherent.

Until I'm begging him.

Then he lets go of my hair. It spills between our faces, clinging to our slick skin. His hand squeezes between our bodies, and he rubs my clit between his thumb and forefinger. "Now," he growls. A few moments later, I'm crying out, squeezing my legs around him.

I'm falling.

Hard.

Fast.

And in more ways than one.

A moment later, he shivers, and presses his hands into the perspiration at the small of my back. Keeping himself inside of me, he carries me into the bathroom. When he unravels our bodies, he kisses the tips of my fingers.

His eyes never leave mine.

Not when he starts the shower and we wash each other's bodies, using our hands and the soap to draw on each other's skin.

Not even when we towel each other off.

"You're mine," I say, and he nods.

"Why didn't you ever reach out to me before?" Lucas whispers to me much later as we lie in bed face-to-face, our arms wrapped tightly around each other as if the world will end if we so much as let go for a moment.

It's the first time he's spoken directly about what happened between us two years ago during the video shoot for "All Over You" without a mocking edge to his voice. Suddenly uncomfortable, I shift, rubbing the bottom of my foot along his muscular calf. "Honestly?" I ask, remembering how he'd shown up at my front door the day after telling me to get the fuck out of his house. Tori had dealt with him; she'd been all too happy to tell him off for me.

"Yeah, the truth."

Swallowing hard, I nod. "I didn't want to get hurt," I say. "I mean, you'd already told me you didn't want me. I was just scared to hear what you had to say because—"

"I'm sorry." He takes my hand into his, linking our fingers. "I'm so fucking sorry I hurt you." There's so much emotion in his voice right now that my throat constricts painfully.

Why did he have to bring this up? Why now?

I squeeze my eyes together, in an effort to hold back tears, and he kisses the corner of one where the dampness is already hot against my skin. "It's okay," I finally say, taking a deep breath before I look at him again. He shakes his head slowly, a tight look crossing his face.

"No, it's not. I could've had you like two years ago if I hadn't been so . . ."

My breath catches in my throat, nearly choking me, but I manage to ask, "If you weren't so what?"

Lucas gives me a sad smile. "So fucking stupid."

Then he reaches around me, touching the base of my neck gently, and draws my face nearer to his. His lips seek mine out, warm and demanding, and I moan as his tongue parts mine, slipping into my mouth.

"God, what have you done to me?" he growls when he finally breaks away. He rolls over, finally releasing his hold on my body, and stretches his long arms behind his head. "You have no fuck-ing idea, do you?"

When I shake my head, he continues, "I've never wanted to protect someone like I do you. I've never"—he shudders and closes his eyes for a moment—"wanted to make something work this much despite how many things can go to shit."

"Me, too," I say, but he gives me a look as if I don't under-stand.

Then, for what seems like an eternity, Lucas gazes up into the darkness.

After a while, I decide I've had enough silence. It scares me when Lucas is like this and I want him speaking to me, touching me. "I said yes. I have to say that I may be the biggest groupie tease who's ever lived," I say, attempting to lighten the mood. It must work, because he lets out a throaty laugh and turns his head to stare at me.

"Yeah, you did, but you're not a groupie. Never like that."

"I want you again," I whisper, and a look of desire sweeps over his features.

"Say the word," he growls.

"Please, Lucas?"

And then we're all over each other again, exploring, squeez-ing. Tasting.

It's only later—after he's asleep, snoring lightly and I'm left alone in the silence of our luxury hotel room—that I find the object he flicked my breasts with earlier tonight in the palm of his hand.

It's a black and red guitar pick.

18

Lucas's 7:00 a.m. wake-up rule flies out the window once again the next morning because we both oversleep. The sound of the hotel room's telephone ringing in our ears is what drags us out of bed a little after nine. Groggily, I scramble over him, shivering when he gives my hip a squeeze. Grinning down at his handsome face, I push my hair away from where it's fallen over my eyes and answer the phone. I'm immediately greeted by a chilly female voice.

"Kylie?"

Because I'm filling in for Lucas's sister and I figure this is probably one of his business contacts, I say, "Uh-huh?"

"Put Lucas on the phone, it's Sam."

Sam. I mouth the name a few times, trying to remember where I've heard it. When Lucas grips my shoulder and gives me a questioning stare, it suddenly hits me. This is the person his mother had mentioned yesterday just before we left his parents' house, the person whose name had made every muscle in his body tense up in anger. And she's a woman. I bite my bottom lip, clutching the phone until I feel like I'm seconds away from shattering it.

"I'm sorry, you—"

"Don't you dare try that I'm-sorry-you've-reached-the-wrong-room shit with me. I talked to your mom, she said you're there, so put him on the goddamn phone," Sam says in a tight voice. When I don't jump to do her bidding right away, she gasps. "Wait—*Kylie?* Who the fuck is this?" She screeches the last few words, and I cringe, pulling the phone away from my ear before she starts up again.

Lucas is sitting up in bed now, staring down at the receiver and wearing a blank expression. "It's Sam," I say, hoping to elicit some kind of reaction from him. When nothing happens and he continues to glare at the phone like it's a ticking bomb, a chill races through me, turning my blood to ice.

Now I want to know who Sam is just as badly as she wants to know my identity.

He takes the phone from my hands, grasping it as forcefully as I had only moments before. The only difference is he's flushed and trembling. "Leave," he orders me. There's no cruelty behind his words or any emotion at all, for that matter, but I feel numb as I slide off the bed and shrug into the bathrobe I'd tossed on the floor last night.

"Call if you need me," I say in a helpless voice, turning around to glance at him as I leave the room. I pull the door closed behind me, wondering if I should leave the hotel suite while he takes his call.

Instead, I sit down on the oversized couch in the living room, hugging my knees to my chest. I grab the TV remote from the coffee table and turn it on, trying my best to focus on the first thing I come to—some trashy talk show about a woman and the six men who were possibly her baby's daddy.

"Kent, you are not little Madison's fa—" the host begins, but all I can hear is Lucas's conversation with Sam in the other room.

"I told you not to contact me while I'm here," he growls. There's a long pause and then he adds, "Really? Are you fucking kidding me?"

I jab the volume button on the remote to tune him out, but it doesn't do me any good. And every snippet of what Lucas is saying to Sam only intensifies the cramps clawing at my chest.

". . . you can't keep doing this to me," he yells.

What? What the hell is she doing to him?

Then there's silence for a little while. I pretend like I'm interested in the woman on the giant flat-screen TV who's weeping at yet another negative DNA test result. I pretend like I'm not at all spying on Lucas.

". . . it's *nobody,* just . . ." He pauses, and I can hear a guttural noise rip from his throat. "I'm sending you money. I'll send you whatever you want, but you can't expect me to do this with you for the rest of my life."

I flinch. Is Lucas in some sort of trouble with Sam? And then, a more frightening thought comes to me: Is Lucas involved with drugs, just like Sinjin? I grind my teeth, hard and fast.

Then I hear him say something that causes me to shudder.

EMILY SNOW

"You psycho bitch, sometimes I wish you would just go to them and get it over with."

Go to whom? Get what over with?

I hear the sound of something slamming repeatedly followed by the pipes in the bathroom turning on. I tighten my grip around my legs, hearing a loud buzz in my ears, wishing I could sink into this couch and disappear for a while. When Lucas comes out of the shower nearly an hour later, there's a bloodstained towel wrapped around his knuckles.

"Lucas . . . what's going on?" I whisper.

He sits down on the opposite end of the couch. "Just somebody I used to"—he cringes and his face pinches—"make music with."

I dip my blue eyes to his bloody hand, my forehead pulling together into a painful frown. "Sounds like it was some really shitty music."

"The worst." Then he gives me a strained smile and motions me over to him. "Come here," he says.

When I hesitate, he groans and rakes both hands through his wet hair. The towel falls away from his hand and onto the carpet, revealing a vicious slash across his knuckles. He gives me a pleading look that's so unlike Lucas, it makes my chest feel as if something is twisting inside of it. "You're angry. And you've hurt yourself. Maybe I should go out for a little while and let you—"

His fingers wrap around mine, tugging me gently to him and into his lap. We're both breathing heavily, staring at each other with wide eyes, as he brushes strands of hair back from my face. "I don't give a fuck about my hand, Si. And I don't want you to go anywhere."

242

Then he covers my lips with his mouth, drowning out all the questions I have left to ask him. Lucas kisses me like I'm his last meal, like he's never tasted me before, even though he had me many, many times last night. One of the fingers on his uninjured hand slides into my mouth, between our lips, and I nibble on the tip of it.

When I pull away, it takes me a moment to gather my bearings. "Are you sure everything is all right?" I finally question, nervously rubbing my palms up and down the front of the white terry-cloth robe.

"Now it is."

A moment later Lucas stands, with me straddling him, and carries me back to the bedroom. I cringe when my eyes lock on the broken hotel phone. It's lying facedown on the floor by the nightstand, and when a little sound escapes from the back of my throat, he stares down at me with apologetic eyes.

"They'll charge me for it," he explains. He must not realize that I could care less about the hotel getting pissed over a ruined telephone—Lucas could buy millions of the same model if he wanted to. I'm worried about why he smashed it to pieces in the first place.

I'm worried about what Sam—a woman who was bad for music—said to him to make him fly off the handle.

He places me on the bed, and I scoot up to the headboard, shivering as he tugs my robe away from my body in one swift motion. "You look like sin," he tells me, climbing on top of me slowly, his every move sensual and deliberate.

"Lucas?" I ask, and he kisses me.

He traces his tongue around my lips twice before saying, "Mmm-hmm?"

"Will you talk about it?"

He pushes himself off of me just enough to study my expression. "Sienna . . ." he groans, and a surge of panic races through me.

"When you're ready?"

"Yeah . . . when I'm ready. But for now, let's just have this, okay?" When I nod my agreement, a half smile—one that doesn't reach his hazel eyes—drags the corners of his lips up.

Then, he keeps his promise of eating strawberries, courtesy of the minifridge, and me. It's in this bed that Lucas finally gets the chance to cuff me, turning me over on my stomach and sliding himself in and out of my body until I'm left sobbing with pleasure.

After we've made love twice, he tugs me to him, pressing his lips in between my shoulder blades. "I can't get enough of you. I'll *never* be able to get enough of you," he murmurs in a voice that sounds slightly dazed. I arch my back and sigh.

"Me neither."

And it's here, in this bed, that I come to terms with the fact that I've fallen in love with Lucas Wolfe.

We spend the majority of the day in bed, snorting over daytime television and talking about everything from my fascination with pianos and his guitar collection to me confronting my mother about everything screwed up she's done to my family over the last several years.

"You'll have to fucking talk to her eventually, Si," Lucas says after I tell him I've not had contact with Mom in more than a year.

"I will," I say, but he doesn't look convinced.

"You're going to wait until she gets out and shows up on your doorstep, aren't you?"

I roll my eyes, digging my hands into the corner of the sheet covering us. "I will eventually." If Lucas isn't willing to talk about his issues with Sam—whoever she is—he shouldn't expect me to lay all my feelings out on the table. Forcing a smile onto my face, I change the subject before we end up ruining the rest of the evening. "Enough about my family, now it's my turn."

"Shoot."

"Why did you move to Nashville?"

Lucas blows a stray strand of hair from my face, twisting his lips to the side before responding. "I was burnt out. Couldn't write for shit—couldn't do anything, for that matter—so I sprung for a change of scenery."

"Did you know it was my gram's house you were bidding on?" I ask, splaying my hand out on the dagger-filled heart on his chest, and he releases a hoarse laugh.

"No, Kylie found it for me. The only thing I said was I wanted to live in Nashville . . . she handled the rest."

Tracing the tip of my finger around the outline of a silver dagger, I lift an eyebrow and sit up a little to examine his expression. "A million other places and you picked Nashville?" He nods and it's my turn to laugh. "Nice," I say. I rest my head on his chest, loving the way his hand skims up my back and over my shoulder to tangle into my hair.

We're quiet for a little bit, letting the sound of Stone Sour on the nightstand radio fill the silence, until I finally whisper, "So now that you're not going to live in Nashville, what'll you do?"

He lifts a strand of my long red hair from where it's fallen on his shoulder, sliding it back and forth between his fingers. "I'll go back to L.A. with you."

"My ten days are about to end, Mr. Wolfe," I tease.

"We both knew this would be more than ten days, Si."

No, I hadn't. I had no idea what I was walking into when I signed Lucas's contract, but I nod, unable to speak because of the giant lump that's formed inside my throat.

"I hate to do this, but . . ." He glances over my shoulder at the clock, and I follow his eyes to see that it's 7:45 p.m.

"Cilla's birthday party," I murmur, and he confirms this by shrugging his tattooed shoulders.

"I'd much rather be in bed with you." But he's already getting up and heading in the direction of the bathroom.

My dress for the party is the sexiest piece of clothing I've ever owned. It's short and black, made of scalloped lace with a cutout back. When Lucas sees me in it, his hazel eyes darken until they seem more brown than green, and he promises me that tonight, my dress will become binds for each of the four posters of the bed.

Every nerve in my body responds just thinking about it, and when I tell him what he's done to me, he slides my dress around my hips and kneels down in front of me.

"I want to fuck you right now," he murmurs, cupping my bottom. He bends his head until his forehead rests against the lace of my panties. My legs tremble, and when his eyes come up to meet mine, when he trails slow, hot kisses across my calf, I know I'm lost.

We're a half hour late getting downstairs to the car that's waiting for us.

19

Cilla's twenty-eighth birthday party is being held at a swanky Atlanta nightclub, and I immediately recognize several of her guests from TV and magazine covers. Lucas stays close by my side as we mingle among his friends and other rockers who look at him like he's a god.

"This is Gavin Cooley," Lucas says, introducing me to the front man of Dark Fiction, a heavy metal band I sometimes listen to when I work out and want to feel like I'm kicking my own ass. Gavin gives me a long once-over, staring at my legs a little too long, so I stare back, from the top of his spiked blond hair to the tips of his boots. Lucas clears his throat, giving Gavin a dark look as he tightens his grip on my waist. Gavin tosses back a shot glass full of clear liquor and responds with a gradual, lazy grin.

"So you're Lucas's new girl? The chick from YouTube?" he asks me in a thick Southern accent.

"Kylie's temp while she's away," I correct him, and both of his eyebrows lift like he's trying to keep from laughing.

"*Yeah? Well, tell Ky I said hey, will you?*"

Lucas cocks his head to one side and gives him a brisk nod. "Will do," he drawls. When Gavin wanders off in search of his date for the evening, I glance up at Lucas, wrinkling the tip of my nose.

"Please don't tell me him and Kylie—" I start but he snorts, shaking his head.

"Nah, he tried his shit on her a couple of years ago and she kneed him in the balls." Then someone else yells Lucas's name, along with several expletives, and we turn together to see the guitarist for Wicked Lambs waving him over to the brightly lit bar. "Come on, Mickey and I go way back."

Any other person would be starstruck around so many musicians, but I'm not. I only have eyes for Lucas. I play my part well, standing by his side as his personal assistant, but wanting him more than anything.

Once we get a moment alone and he makes sure nobody's looking, Lucas coaxes me into a darkened corner with him, kissing me deeply and sucking on my left earlobe. I gasp, and he glides his fingers inside of me, causing me to almost lose control on the spot.

"Soon," he promises, cupping my face with his bandage-wrapped hand, and I moan softly against the heel of his palm.

As soon as we rejoin the crowd, Cilla's latest boyfriend, the bass guitarist for an up-and-coming band from Ohio, seeks Lucas out. I start to pull away from Lucas's grip, smiling up at him when he frowns.

"You okay?" he asks, his voice fierce, protective.

"Bathroom," I murmur, and even though he nods, his fingertips linger on mine a moment longer. I hug my arms around myself as I navigate through the noise and chaos in search of the restrooms, which are located at the back of the club. As I'm passing an empty lounge, a long-nailed hand closes around my wrist, pulling me inside and slamming me up against the wall. I expect to see Cilla—she's been prancing around drunk off her ass most of the night and singing bad nineties music—so I'm surprised when a different face hovers in front of me.

She's beautiful—with henna-red hair in a pixie cut and a heart-shaped face—but so are most of the women here tonight. What really strikes me about this particular woman are her large gray eyes. They're unfocused and wild. Scary. My heartbeat picks up.

"So you're Luke's little bitch?" she demands between clenched teeth, pressing all her body weight—which isn't very much considering she's short and rail thin—against me.

"I'm his personal assistant," I say, repeating the spiel I've been feeding to everyone I've come in contact with tonight. Even then, the word doesn't sound quite right or believable.

The gray-eyed woman opens her mouth to say something, but then her face changes from furious to a look of understanding and back to livid again. "So you're the bitch from the phone this morning, huh?"

I suck in a deep breath through my nose. "Sam?" I blurt out.

Her lips curl up into a sneer, and she bobs her head. "Yeah,

I'm Sam and if you go near him again, I swear to God I'll ruin you," she says. "I swear to God I'll—"

I've never automatically disliked someone before getting to know them, but Sam is quickly becoming the first. Flushing, I shove her away from me. She stumbles backward, wobbling on her high-heeled boots and glaring at me. "You'll what?" I demand. "And just who the hell are you anyway?"

This woman makes me feel like I'm on one of those trashy talk shows I'd watched this morning while she and Lucas argued on the phone. It makes my stomach churn.

"I'll ruin him," Sam promises, drawing herself up to her full height. She chooses not to answer my second question, baring straight white teeth at me instead. "And I'll fuck you over, too."

That feeling of dread that I felt when Lucas was talking to Sam comes back to me, hitting me hard, and it's impossible to get it to go away this time. Who the hell is she? And what does she have on Lucas that lets her provoke such a nasty response from him? That gives her enough courage to threaten me?

"Stay away from me," I warn, brushing her aside so I can leave. She grabs my arm again, this time raking her nails into my skin. And this time, something inside of me snaps. I slam *her* up against the wall. So hard that the back of her head makes a loud thumping noise.

It doesn't even faze her.

She laughs like a crazy person, shaking her head from side to side, and saying, "You have no idea who you're talking to, slut."

"Hey!" a voice shouts out. Both of our heads snap to see Cilla standing in the doorway, her eyes squinted and a shot glass in each hand. "What the fuck are you doing in here?" She touches the earpiece she's wearing, hissing, "Security!"

I almost expect Cilla to have me escorted away by the two bouncers who start over just moments after they're called, but instead, it's Sam she tells to literally fuck off and burn in hell.

"Still giving blow jobs to sell records, Priscilla?" Sam hisses and Cilla cocks her head to one side, giving the other woman a frosty smile.

"Shoot up anything good lately?" Dropping her gaze to Sam's inner elbow, Cilla lifts her shoulders. "Stupid question, huh?"

Growling, Sam takes a step toward Cilla. "You seriously want to try that shit with me?"

"You don't scare me at all, cunt, so do your worst," Cilla snarls. A moment later, two bouncers arrive and she steps out of the way, sweeping her arm out at Sam. I stare at her helplessly as she finishes off one of her drinks, ranting about how incompetent the security she hired turned out to be.

Sam shoots me one final look, shrugs off the bouncers, and stalks off.

Staring after her, I rub my hand across the spot on my arm where she'd clawed me with her long fingernails. I startle when a gentle hand touches my shoulder, and I turn to see Cilla standing behind me, holding both shot glasses in one hand, with her lips pursed into a thin pink line.

"You all right?" she asks me, and I shake my head.

"You know, I'm not your biggest fan because you're with Luke, but nobody deserves to have to deal with people like Samantha," she says through gritted teeth. "God knows she's put Lucas through enough."

The way Cilla says his name speaks volumes, and my body goes rigid. "You're in love with him," I say, and she nods.

"For God's sake, don't give me that crybaby look, Pepper. He doesn't even know I exist when you're around and besides, I'm his best friend. I'm just . . . *Cilla*," she says, her voice taking on a bitter bite when she whispers her own name.

"I love him, too."

Her shoulders tremble as she laughs at me. She downs her shot, and shakes her head from side to side as if she feels sorry for me. "Then you'd better watch your ass because Sam is . . . ugh."

"Who *is* she to him?"

Cilla's beautiful face is suddenly surprised, but she recovers quickly. "Sam's his ex-wife, babe."

Cilla leaves me alone so that I can finally go to the restroom, but I'm so flustered I don't even use it. Instead, I splash water on my face, smearing my makeup. Staring at myself in the streaked mirror, I grip the edges of the counter and attempt to gather my thoughts.

Sam is Lucas's ex-wife.

Lucas had been married at some point—a fact he'd failed to mention to me on more than one occasion, including this morning after Sam called our hotel room.

All my research on him and his constant bullshit about Google being my friend had never prepared me for this.

When I finally control my breathing enough to face the crowd of his friends again, I exit the bathroom. As soon as I turn the corner, I run into a tall, hard body, and I clench my teeth as I bring my gaze up to meet his face.

"I'm ready to go," I growl.

He doesn't tell me to stop grinding my teeth or argue with me. A brief flicker of something—defeat, maybe, or guilt—passes over his features and he gives me a curt nod. "Car's already waiting."

The ride back to the Four Seasons turns out to be yet another one of those painfully quiet moments between us, one that squeezes my heart a little harder every quarter mile. Lucas's face is an impeccably controlled mask, but whenever a streetlight touches the inside of the car, I see a muscle twitching dangerously in his cheek. I should be the one who's angry. Not once has Lucas ever mentioned having an ex-wife, especially one as fucked up and psycho as Sam. But then again, Lucas doesn't mention anything about his life aside from music.

As we ride the elevator up to our suite, standing on opposite sides of the metal car, a horrible feeling slinks its way through my chest. As soon as we enter the room, I toss my bag onto the couch. All the contents spill out, but right now I really don't give a shit.

"Sit down," he orders, but I shake my head, wringing my hands together.

I remain standing, on the opposite end of the coffee table, glaring at him. "Why didn't you tell me about her?" I demand. "About Sam?"

"Sit down," he says again.

"Why? So you can feed me more bull?"

"Just . . . please?"

And I obey. Partly because my legs are quivering too violently to keep up my current stance and the other part because I know this conversation will never happen unless I comply with him. I lean forward, waiting for him to say something—anything—to me.

"I fucked up," he says, and I let out a broken sound that's somewhere between a sob and a snort.

"That's all you can say? Don't you realize you could've just told me? That I'd have much rather heard it from you instead of getting mauled by some psycho at your best friend's birthday party?" Automatically, my fingers close around my upper arm where the skin is still raw from Sam's nails.

Rubbing his hands over his face, Lucas slides down in front of me to sit on the edge of the coffee table. "She'll destroy you if I'm with you," he says in a detached voice, causing me to scoff.

"By what? Clawing me to death?" When his hazel eyes lift to mine, I inhale a deep gasp of air because he looks so tortured, so furious. "I can take of myself, Lucas. You're the one who's been telling me to stand up for myself and—"

He cuts my words off. "Sienna . . . I can't—" Heaving a sigh that's so full of agony it nearly rips my heart out of my chest, Lucas glances away from my face at the thick carpeted floor. "You've got to go."

I feel everything inside of me shut down, as he refuses to

look into my eyes. "What the fuck are you talking about?" I demand at last.

"I'm dismissing you. You've fulfilled the terms of our contract," he says.

I bolt up off the couch, but his strong hands cup my shoulders, steadying me. I clench my fingers into his shirt and pull him close to me. "No. *No*. I've got two days left. Lucas, tell me what's going on," I plead. Then a thought occurs to me as I remember something his mother said to him yesterday afternoon. "When we got to Atlanta yesterday and you left, you went to see Sam, didn't you?"

The expression on his face says it all. I draw in a breath that makes my lungs feel like they're surrounded by ice.

"It's not what you're thinking," he says at last.

"Then tell me what it is."

"I've got to keep her away from you. You can't possibly—the thought of her . . ." Then he shrugs away from me, standing up. My eyes follow his every movement as he walks back and forth across the narrow space in front of the television. "Sienna, please just leave," he finally says.

I shake my head, and he drags his hands through his thick dark hair, making a low, violent noise. "God, Sienna, just fucking go, okay? The house is yours. You're done. Just go before I call security on you."

He doesn't sound like the Lucas I know. He doesn't sound like anyone I've ever known. My heart is beating wildly as I draw myself to my feet and take a tentative step toward him. He backs up in the direction of the foyer, shaking his head.

"So, that's it, huh?" I demand, tears rolling down my cheeks, singeing my skin. "What happened to all that shit about keeping me, Lucas? All your lies about me being a first for you?"

"I've given you a house. I don't fucking owe you anything else," he says, his voice a sharp, cold knife shoved into the pit of my stomach. Even then, I refuse to let it end like this. I open my mouth to argue with him more but he turns his back to me. He clenches his hands—the exact same hands that touched me so intimately hours before—into tight fists by his sides. "Concierge is taking care of your flight to Nashville. Be out before I return tomorrow."

I'm shaking so hard that it's impossible for me to speak. I hold myself close, wheezing. When the words do come to me, it's too late.

He's already left, slamming the door behind him.

Slamming the door on what could've been.

20

"I'm flying to Atlanta," Tori announces angrily for the third time in the last fifteen minutes.

I stare down at the plane ticket on the coffee table a few inches away from my face. It's pulled halfway out of an envelope so that I'm able to see the flight details, and I suppress a shudder. "Why? I'm flying to Nashville in a couple of hours," I say, my voice deflated.

"So you won't have to be alone, Si."

Sitting up, I slide back into the corner of the couch and wipe the bottom of my sleeve across my eyes. I clear my throat, flinching at how badly it burns to do so. "I'll be fine."

Tori releases a long hiss. I hear her squeezing something frantically on the other line—a brand-new stress ball, more than likely. "You wouldn't have called me if you were fine."

True. So true it brings me dangerously close to crumbling all over again. After spending hours sitting on the couch with my arms wrapped around my body to hold myself together last night, I'd finally fallen asleep shortly after 3:00 a.m. Up until then, there'd been some part of me that believed that Lucas would come back to the hotel room. Up until then, even though I could barely see through swollen eyes—could hardly swallow because of a raw throat—I'd believed there was still time left for him to make things right.

Instead, I'd been awoken at seven by the concierge at the door—an older woman who wore a kind smile and spoke in a gentle voice as she handed me the envelope. I'd found not only a ticket inside but a check from Lucas, written in the same precise handwriting that had been on the sheet of paper he gave me in the fondue restaurant in Nashville.

That's when I'd called Tori.

Because I felt used and cheap.

Because I felt alone.

"I'll be fine," I croak out at last, evoking a sigh from Tori.

My best friend is quiet for a moment, and I'm certain she's seconds away from raising hell, but when she finally speaks, her voice is quiet. "Do you want me to come to Nashville, then?" she asks, and I make a sound of protest. "It's nothing for me to take time off for work for you—you know that, right?"

Slowly, I bob my head. "Yeah, I know. And trust me, I love you for that. This is just something that I have to do . . ." When my voice breaks, Tori finishes the sentence for me.

"Alone."

We end the call less than a minute later, after I give her my word that I'll call her as soon as my flight touches down in Nashville a few hours later. Then, giving the hotel room door one final look, I slide off the sofa, grabbing the envelope with my ticket and the check. Somebody else would take Lucas's money—and he's written the check for an astronomical amount, at least as far as I'm concerned—and run with it, but I refuse to.

I rip the check into tiny pieces, each tear causing the barbs in my chest to dig a little deeper. Then I flush them away and set about getting ready to go home.

Alone.

When I arrive in Nashville a little after two thirty, I call my bank to discover that there's just seven hundred and fifty dollars left in my account. Because I'm not quite ready to face my grandmother, I use half of that money to secure a small rental car.

"You'll get a hundred and fifty dollars back after you return the car," the kid behind the Hertz counter explains in a bored voice. He jabs his finger at a section of small print located on the back of my rental contract, and I drop my eyes to it. "If you need to extend your rental, call this number."

All I'm able to do is nod as I take the packet of paperwork from him with shaky fingers.

Hoisting my bag higher onto my shoulder, I go off in search of my car, which turns out to be a tiny Mazda 3 that reeks of stale fast food, sweat, and latex condoms.

As I leave the airport, I blast the radio, playing the most bubblegum pop station I can find so there's no chance I'll have to hear Lucas Wolfe's voice sliding over me as I drive.

I've not cried since leaving the Four Seasons this morning,

and to be honest, I'm not sure there are any tears left, but I know that right now the sound of his voice would destroy me.

Because then I'd remember everything he'd said to me. How he'd deceived me, and how stupid I was to believe we'd be more. Hearing Lucas's voice would just force me to come to terms with the fact that at the moment I realized I was in love with him, things between us had just ended.

I drive around for two hours, unsure of where I should go or what I should do. I know what it's like to be used. My mom had made sure I was well equipped with that knowledge over the years. Yet somehow, this betrayal feels so much worse even though I'd spent only a few days with Lucas.

The sad part is, I find myself hoping it is all a horrible dream, wanting to wake up, to open my eyes and kiss him. Wanting him to devour me just a little more.

When my phone rings, I don't even look to see who's calling me. I just answer. Exist. Kylie's crying when I lift the receiver to my ear.

"Please tell me he didn't," she sobs.

A tiny portion of the numbness fades, and I feel a headache splintering the center of my skull. I nearly swerve off the road, causing the driver in the car behind me to lay down on his horn. "Why does it matter?" I ask her in a stressed voice.

"He's letting her control him. I checked his— He sent her a wire this morning for two hundred and fifty grand and then I called him, and . . ."

More of my detachment from reality floats away, constricting my throat. "Sam?" I ask hoarsely. I vividly remember her words to me last night at Cilla's party, and Lucas's argument with her yesterday morning. I'd been trying to put all of it out of my head, but Kylie is slowly bringing everything back.

I hate this.

"She's got something on him, Sienna. I've got no fucking clue what it is, but she threatened him. She doesn't want him happy. She's—"

But now, I know exactly what Sam is. She is the queen of hearts inside the stopwatch. Sam is calling the shots on Lucas, so he feels he has to call them on everyone else, on me.

The rest of the numbness is gone now, leaving a nauseating pain in the middle of my chest. I pull over at a gas station and rest my head on the steering wheel. "Kylie, I'll call you back," I whisper. She's still talking, begging me not to go, when I draw the phone from my ear. I hang up on her, powering it down completely.

And then, the tears return, burning my face and leaving my shoulders shaking.

When everything is said and done, and after I spend the night feeling sorry for myself in a seedy pay-by-the hour motel, I go back to Gram's house. I'd called her before I left my hotel, feeding her another line of bull about just getting back in town from Los Angeles, so she's expecting me. Her eyes are damp when she meets me outside on the porch and it takes everything not to cry, too.

Stop blubbering, I tell myself. *You've cried enough, so suck it the hell up.*

"You're back," Gram says, embracing me the moment I reach her.

I drop my bags to the wood boards and breathe in her scent of vanilla and Chanel, nodding. "Only for a few days."

She presses her hands to either side of my face, her wedding ring cold against my skin, and smiles sadly. "I wish it were longer."

"Me, too," I whisper. This trip has made me realize just how much I wish I could come home to Nashville and stay for good.

As Gram leads me into the familiar cinnamon-scented house where the best of my childhood memories were made, I grip my bags tighter. I'd failed. Not at getting Gram this house back, but I'd failed to keep my heart intact. Gram's still smiling—a gentle, bittersweet look—when we go into the family room and sit side by side on the old leather sofa.

"I should probably go ahead and tell you that the new owner, Mr. Wolfe, won't be moving to Nashville after all. He's very generously offered to give me the house back," she says. I feign surprise, gasping, and her grip tightens around me. "Sienna, I know where you've been."

My blood runs cold as I lean back slowly, ashamedly, to meet her gaze. "What?"

"When we went to see your mom yesterday, Seth told me. Now, don't get angry with him. He was only trying to give me some peace of mind, but to be honest . . ."

"God, Gram," I say, but she squeezes my hand, lifting my chin up with the other.

"It's all right, Sienna."

No, it wasn't. Not by a long shot.

And then I hear myself spilling everything. I leave out the specifics, of course, but she listens, hanging on to every word I have to say. I put enthusiasm into my voice; make my actions lively and happy.

After I've finished, Gram holds me close, just like she used to do every time Mom screwed up when I was a kid. She doesn't ask any more questions of me, even though I know they're on her mind and she's fully aware there's so much more to what's happened between me and Lucas.

"You and Seth are two of the greatest things that have ever happened to me."

"I know, Gram. I don't know where I'd be without you," I murmur, digging my fingers into her sweater, holding on for support.

Late that evening, as I'm erasing my Facebook account, a short message from Lucas arrives in my personal e-mail inbox. As I read it, I'm forced to bite the inside of my cheek to keep from crying again. Or from grinding my teeth.

Sienna,

It's sad that I can't even come up with a decent explanation for myself. Then again, maybe that's because I've never had to or wanted to explain my actions before you. I know that by trying to protect you, I've hurt you. I know you must want me to fucking die right now, and I'm so sorry.

Lucas

I start to erase it—because really, what good does replying do—but then I find myself hitting reply. I find myself typing a message that's just as short but so much more succinct than what he's given me.

> *Dear Lucas,*
>
> *One of these days, you're going to have to stand up for yourself. No matter what someone's holding over your head. When you do, you'll be able to accept that there are people who love you. When you do, maybe you'll be able to tell me why you'd rather protect me by keeping me in the dark and pushing me away instead of keeping me close.*
>
> *Sienna*

I don't dwell on what I've said or read over it fifty times like I would have done a few short weeks ago.

I just hit send.

21

For the first week after I return to Los Angeles, to the life I thought I'd made for myself, I still expect Lucas to show up at my door just like he'd done when he kicked me out of his house two years ago.

He never shows, so I try to move on, heartbroken.

But while my heart feels weaker than it was before, I know that I am so much stronger. So much more my own person.

Of course, even that realization does very little for the fact that at first it's impossible to avoid everything dealing with or reminding me of Lucas. He still finds me—on a giant ad for Your Toxic Sequel's new album on the side of a bus and staring across from me in a magazine carousel in the grocery store checkout. Photos from the shoot he did in Nashville. A month or two ago, I'd have plucked another magazine from the shelf and covered his face, but why bother?

By the time Micah, a mutual friend of mine and Tori's who's

been stopping by our apartment more and more often just to see her, puts on an entire Your Toxic Sequel playlist at a get-together we have to celebrate Tori's twenty-fourth birthday, I'm numb enough to Lucas that I don't even flinch.

"This song rocks," Micah says, coming over to me with a shit-eating grin stretched across his face as "All Over You" blasts through our tiny living room. I shrug and pick at a string hanging from the hem of the strapless dress I'd borrowed from Tori. It's like a shirt on me, but she swore to every higher power I looked amazing.

"It does," I say in a disinterested voice.

Tori's not so nonchalant about Micah's choice of songs. She pulls him aside, her dark eyes wild, as she hisses, "You don't play Lucas Wolfe's crappy-ass music here, Micah Daniel, or I will—"

But I save him, worming my body between the two of them. Even when she's wearing five-inch stilettos, I'm still taller than Tori, and I glance down into her eyes, giving her a tight smile.

"It's one of their best songs," I say.

Micah agrees a little too fast. I give him a sympathetic look as he slinks away. I mean, he doesn't actually know what's going on or why Tori is bitching at him.

It's not Micah's fault Lucas dismissed me.

Jabbing a purple-painted fingernail at Tori, I narrow my eyes. "Don't be a bitch, okay? I can fight my own battles, but that"—I nod my head toward the iPod dock on our entertainment center—"is definitely not one of them."

Tori's mouth drops open and she stares at me. I can hear the sound of her hands intertwining nervously with each other.

I guarantee she's wishing for a stress ball and as soon as we're done here, she'll probably go and rummage around in her night-stand drawer searching for a new one.

"You're kind of a ball-buster now," she says at last, a hesitant smile replacing her frown. "I don't know whether to kiss you or head-butt you in the tit."

"You're so eloquent," I tease, and she stretches her neck up and touches her lips to my cheek. "And you're drunk. Come on."

Then I grab her hand, pull her back to the middle of the floor as fast as her needle heels will carry her. And as we mingle with our friends, and I hear Lucas's voice making naughty, sexy promises, I decide I'm all right.

After Tori's birthday party, I go on with my life effortlessly. I'm more attentive than I've ever been. More alert to details in my job. This makes Tomas giddy enough to overlook the fact that I shut him down—kindly, of course—every time he tries to run all over me.

Tori stops worrying.

And Lucas still doesn't show up at my door, not that I expect him to anymore.

Two months after returning home to California, I come home from work to find a letter from Kylie. I almost slide it to the bottom of the stack of mail I plan to tackle this weekend, but then I sigh. She's sent it in a pretty linen envelope and I take care when opening it, so as not to tear through the bold cursive red ink. When I pull the neatly folded square sheet of paper out, something else comes along with it, floating down to the floor and landing right-side up.

It's a check for $4,800, and it's made out to me.

Kylie's written a memo at the bottom left-hand corner: *24 hours/day x 8 days @ $25 an hour. Thanks.*

"What's that?" Tori demands, slinking out of her bedroom and around the corner. She's dressed up, and it doesn't take much for me to guess she's got another date with Micah.

Staring down at the check, I rub my fingers back and forth over the thin paper. "Kylie Martin's sent me money for working for Lucas." Then I read portions of the actual note aloud. "'For your trouble.'"

I skip over the part that says *God . . . Sienna, please contact me. Send me a message on Facebook or call me or something. And don't be prideful and not cash this check. You earned it and if it doesn't clear my account in ten days, I will take the cash personally to your grandma.*

Tori walks over to the counter and shimmies herself up on top of it. Hugging her knees, she says, "And she thinks that's supposed to be enough for her brother screwing you over? Dude, you should send that shit back and tell her no thanks."

"I'm cashing it," I reply firmly.

Not because I'm money hungry or anything like that but because this money is enough to get me somewhere I *need* to go.

Tori rolls her dark eyes but says nothing. A few hours later, after I've eaten dinner and completed an ass-kicking exercise video by myself—I'm starting to see crazy definition in my abs—I sneak away to my room. It takes me all of thirty seconds to reactivate all my social media accounts, and while I'm doing this, I dial Kylie's number.

"Kylie?" I whisper, the moment she picks up. She lets out a long sigh of relief.

"And here I was thinking you forgot about me," she says, the grin in her voice too impossible to hide.

"We're running away together, remember? And you're knocking me up with your blue-haired love child."

The next morning, to Tomas's shock and irritation, I turn in my notice for *Echo Falls*. He actually places his iPad down on his desk in order to give the matter at hand his full attention. He glares down at the formal letter I typed up last night after getting off the phone with Kylie. Listening to her enthusiasm about music and the scene in New Orleans where she's currently living had pretty much solidified my decision to say good-bye to doing wardrobe for the TV show and to California itself.

I could do what I loved anywhere. And the anywhere I wanted to be was Tennessee—more specifically, Nashville.

"You're only giving me two weeks," Tomas says hotly, his voice bringing me back to the present, and I nod my head slowly.

"That's usually how it works," I reply.

"We're getting into the most complex goddamn part of the whole storyline, the most costume changes, and you're only giving me two weeks."

"There are costume and wardrobe people willing to give their babies up to work on this show. Trust me, you'll find someone else."

I hear him tell me to not return tomorrow, hear him claim

that as soon as someone contacts him regarding a reference for me, he'll tell them what a selfish cunt I am. How I was incompetent when doing my job. I leave him talking without so much as a backward glance, but I *hear* everything.

That evening, when I take Tori out to dinner and tell her my plans to move, she cries dramatically. "I'm not mad," she sniffles. "I just— Who's going to watch me drink peppermint schnapps on Fridays and warn me about sleeping with randoms."

I laugh so hard I choke on the Coke that I'm drinking. "Stacy's looking for a place to stay," I point out, referring to one of our friends she often goes clubbing with. As if she has a cutoff valve, Tori stops crying and her beautiful face creases into a frown.

"Ugh, not a good idea. Stacy has new randoms every other night. Maybe I'll just get a puppy. Or, you know, a boyfriend like Micah because he's got an enormous dick. But probably a puppy," she says, smiling.

I would've still moved whether Tori liked it or not, but knowing I have her blessing makes things so much easier.

I try several times to give Tori some of the money Kylie sent me, but she refuses it. "No, that money covers a lot of blood, sweat, and tears." When I waggle an eyebrow at her, she rolls her eyes and begrudgingly says, "Okay, a lot of sweat and tears, but you earned it."

On the day I say good-bye to our apartment and California, my little brother shows up first thing in the morning at my door wearing his usual faded polo and baseball cap. He'd arrived to help me move late last night but had insisted he stay at a nearby hotel.

"You sure you want to leave this place? Because"—a big grin slinks across his face—"I could really get used to visiting."

I groan, letting him in. "Ugh, I don't even want to know what you did last night," I mutter.

He winks at Tori, who's sniffling on the couch. "What's the matter with you?"

She flashes dark, warning eyes at him and wipes her nose with a Kleenex. "Don't be a douche, Seth." Then she turns to me. "Why is he here again?"

I laugh. "Be nice." But she glares at Seth once more, as he digs into a container of cookies sitting on the countertop, helping himself.

After everything is loaded into my old Mercury a couple of hours later and Seth is waiting impatiently behind the steering wheel, I'm certain I'll have full body bruises the next day because Tori can't get enough of hugging me good-bye.

"I'm going to miss you so much," she mumbles into my chest during the seventh or eighth embrace. I take this opportunity to slip three grand—my share of the bills for two months—into her back pocket.

She pulls away from me and drags the money out of her pocket. Pursing her lips, she puts a hand on her hip and tries to shove it back in my direction with the other. I shake my head. "You agreed to it two nights ago," I inform her. When she cocks her eyebrow, looking at me like I'm telling her the biggest lie ever thought of, I nod. "When we went out to dinner with Micah and you were giving him the eyes. I said—and I quote—I'm paying two months of bills when I leave and you said yes."

"You sneaky fucking *bitch*," she says, laughing and drying tears.

I realize I'm doing the same thing.

"Listening's a virtue, dear friend. Google it."

EPILOGUE

My life in Nashville is better than anything I could've ever imagined. I live with Gram. I connect with friends I've not spoken to since my mother's arrest, as well as Ashley, who drags me along to all of her boyfriend's cover band gigs. I don't see Mom, but I know it's inevitable that I will.

I meet new guys and have the occasional one-night stand. None of them is anything like *him,* but I'm glad.

There are no physical or emotional binds with the guys I have sex with once or twice.

And then I start getting clients. Personal shopper. Wardrobe consultant for music videos—country music, but I'll take it because I absolutely adore my work. And every time someone hires me, I'm told Kylie Martin referred them.

I've got to give it to her, she's good for business.

I speak to Tori every day, and I make it a point to contact Kylie every few days as well, either by phone or instant message. She asks me a million questions about work, Gram, and even Seth. I ask her about the guy she's been seeing—someone she met at an awards show after-party—and why she picked her new hair color. It's fire-engine red and white blond now and I absolutely loathe it.

She laughs when I tell her outright that she looks like a Spice Girl.

Not once does she mention Lucas or Sam and I don't ask.

But then, in the middle of July on a sticky night when Gram has gone to play bingo, Kylie texts me at five minutes 'til nine, telling me to turn on my TV. Gives me the exact channel.

It's a music video station.

There's a banner running across the bottom, advertising Lucas Wolfe's solo video premiere. My phone vibrates in my hand. I look down at it to find another text from Kylie.

Just . . . watch the goddamn video. Pretty please for me.

This is one of those moments where I seriously consider changing my phone number, but I roll my eyes and slide down in my grandmother's recliner. I place my cell phone on the coffee table. The video begins at exactly 9:00 p.m., and it's different from any Your Toxic Sequel video—almost poetic. Lucas is sitting on a stool, blindfolded. Instead of lip-synching along to the music, he's holding up giant flash cards.

It takes me a few moments to realize the song, a moody, sexy ballad called "Ten Days," uses the background music Lucas and

I wrote together, on the night he bent me over the piano. It takes me an additional couple of seconds—because the sudden wetness in my thin cotton panties is a distraction—to comprehend that the words on the cards aren't words at all, but numbers that count down from ten to one.

And then I finally understand that the cards he's holding up every two or three lines indicate a message within the song meant exclusively for me.

It's an outrageous, Lucas-eque way of getting in touch with me. Keeping absolutely silent, I listen to the rest of the song, mentally repeating each line that contains a piece of the puzzle. And as the music pulses in my ears, I feel a thousand silk ribbons wrap around my heart and squeeze.

8. *But you're probably saying*
7. *fuck me right now because I*
6. *screwed you when you wanted to*
5. *trust me. You've still got two*
4. *days left, so I'm giving you*
3. *the honest truth, saying sorry, making it right.*
2. *Just . . .*

The pit of my stomach aches with the familiar pang of longing and fear as I wait for him to hold up the final card, the missing piece of the message. That old, weak part of me tells me that I should turn off this video now; that I should forget Lucas because all he'll cause me is more hurt.

I tell that part of me to shut the hell up.

I'm breathless when the music ends, and then Lucas pulls down the blindfold and holds up the last flash card to nothing but silence. He looks tired, like he hasn't slept in weeks. My chest constricts painfully. Has he been taking care of himself?

My front door shakes. Someone drums hard on the wood, the tempo fast, rhythmic. Suddenly, I've got this vivid image of that day in court months ago—how Lucas had drummed his long fingers on the table in front of him.

I cross the room, biting the inside of my cheek hard enough to draw blood. The moment that I fling the door open—that I raise my gaze to his hazel eyes—Lucas finishes the song. "Say that what happened isn't *it* for us," he sings. He lifts his rough hand to stroke the side of my face, and I shiver. That instinctive need to grind my teeth together returns.

He doesn't admonish me.

He doesn't even seem to notice it.

"What are you doing here, Lucas?" I demand. My voice is so soft, naked.

"You've got two days left," he says, roughly.

"And you dismissed me."

"You signed a contract. Besides, I'm a fucking idiot."

His words take my breath away. I grip the corner of the door, squeezing it with all my might. What makes him think that he can waltz back into my life after months apart? What makes him think that—?

"I'm not going to give this up," Lucas growls.

He drags me into his arms before I can react to what he's

said, closing them around me. At first, I don't know what to do or say because being in his arms still feels so good. I just stand there, in the doorway, with my arms hanging limply by my side and my body betraying me. But then he says it again. And again. Lucas, the man who once kicked me out of his house for not putting out, who's pushed me away at every turn, is telling me he doesn't want to let me go.

No, that he *won't* let me go.

At last, I look up at him again. His dark hair falls into his eyes, but he blows the strands away, his breath fanning my face.

"What you did hurt, Lucas. You wanted me to give myself to you just so you could tell me to screw off," I whisper harshly. "And now you want me again."

He pulls my body a little closer, so that I can feel all of him. His heart is slamming just as violently as mine, and I dig my hands into the hem of his shirt.

"I've always wanted you. It just took me a while to tell the shit holding me back to fuck off."

"Sam?"

He nods. "If you're with me, she will try to ruin me. She'll try to ruin you because she knows I love you. You've got to know that. You've got to know what she has on me—"

Shaking my head, I press my hand over his mouth, partially in disbelief at what he's just said, and in part because I want to savor this moment. He loves me. Lucas-fucking-Wolfe loves me. I untangle my other hand from the fabric of his shirt.

"Damn you, Lucas." I sigh.

"I know you're angry and I know that it'll take work, but I just want you to try. To give getting through my fuck-ups together a chance. I need to know that you can give a shit about me again."

And I don't care about Sam or the skeletons in his closet because it's all stuff that can be overcome. I only know that he's here. Holding me. Touching me. Devouring me.

The red ribbons constricting my heart slowly unravel, fall to the ground. Free me.

"A lot can happen in the two days I owe you," I say, burying my face into his shoulder. I squeeze my eyes together. And I breathe him in. "But you're right—you are an idiot if you thought I ever stopped loving you."

"I love you, too, Sienna."

ACKNOWLEDGMENTS

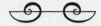

To my girls in "The Naughty Mafia," Ava Black, Kelli Maine, Kristen Proby, and Michelle Valentine—thank you so much for your incredible support. <3 you all!

To Tanya Keetch—thanks so much for your awesome editing and the wonderful instant messages. You rock, babe.

To Cris Soriaga Hadarly for all the support and FANTAS-TIC trailers and to Kim Person, who has been so supportive of this book since it first went up on Goodreads—you two are great!

To the bloggers who've pimped my books, THANK YOU! I appreciate all the time and effort you've put into reading and reviewing my work.

To my agent, Rebecca Friedman, and her assistant, Abby—you ladies are amazing. Thanks for answering all my questions and being so kick-ass.

ACKNOWLEDGMENTS

Thank you so much to my family and my best friend, Angela, for supporting my writing and believing in me.

And to my readers . . . a giant THANK-YOU for reading my books and showing so much love and support. I love you guys!

ABOUT THE AUTHOR

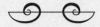

Emily Snow is the *New York Times* and *USA Today* bestselling author of the Devoured erotic romance series and new adult novel *Tidal*. She loves books, sexy bad boys, and really loud rock music, so naturally, she writes stories about all three. She lives in Virginia.

Visit her online at www.emilysnowbooks.com, or follow her on Twitter @EmilySnowBks.

Find out how
Sienna and Lucas's
story began.

Read

ALL OVER YOU

Out now, from Touchstone Books

1

Lucas

"You're leaving?" a hoarse, feminine voice demands, breaking the silence in the dark hotel room. Every muscle in my back goes stiff, and I pause where I'm standing a few feet away from the bed and the naked woman lying in it. A moment passes before I give her a curt nod. Yanking my black T-shirt over my head, I sit down on the edge of the hotel mattress and shove my feet into the motorcycle boots she'd taken off me earlier on my order.

"Got a shoot in the morning," I tell her, my voice bored. But even if my band wasn't doing a music video this week, I wouldn't stay with her. After we were done and she'd closed her eyes, falling asleep, I'd come up with a plan. Unravel those hands from the hotel bedposts and sneak out unnoticed. Now that she was alert again and staring right at me, that strategy was blown to shit.

The woman sighs as she nudges her knee back and forth across my lower back in an attempt to get me to look at her. I don't. "That's too bad, Mr. Wolfe. I thought we could go for round three," she says suggestively.

The mattress squeaks, and I know she's grinding her hips into it. I let her do this for another ninety seconds before I turn around, slowly. She's kicked the rumpled sheets away from her petite body, and her legs are spread apart, inviting me in. Arching her back upward, she strains against the satin binds, biting her bottom lip and moaning softly.

Cocking my head to the side, I quirk the corner of my mouth. "Not tonight."

"Why not?" she asks, her voice taking on a pout. The sensuality doesn't extend to her dark eyes. They're giant and desperate and only make me more intent to leave this hotel room and take my ass back home where nobody would question me.

"Look, Megan—"

She gasps, just like I expect her to. "Mara," she corrects me. "My name is Mara."

I know that—I don't forget the names of the women I tie up—but I give her a sardonic look. Narrow my hazel eyes into thin slits. "*Mara,* I don't do overnights."

Or relationships, because my ex-wife would rip anyone I tried to be with to pieces.

Mara turns her head, and her inky black hair falls around her flushed face and on the piles of pillows bunched up beneath her head. She focuses her gaze on something across the room, and I follow it to a trio of oil paintings hanging several inches over the flatscreen TV. I hear her breathing heavily, deep drags in and out of her pierced nose. There's this part of me that wants to feel a pull toward her. That wants to turn around and crawl back in bed and completely own this woman, even if there's that risk of Sam going apeshit.

Instead, when I turn my eyes back to Mara, I reach for her wrists, skimming her palms with the pads of my fingers as I loosen the fabric and pull it over her hands. Her skin is still slick, and when she rolls to her side to turn completely away from me, the strap prints on her ass—just below her back dimples—are vivid, despite the dim lighting.

I watch her sides expand as she breathes, the way the flowery tattoo that completely covers it moves up and down. "You won't call me again, huh?" Mara asks.

Normally, I don't explain. There's no reason to when we both know the answer—Mara's a groupie, and I'd been clear about what she was to *me* at the beginning of the evening as I blindfolded her. But for some reason, I say, "No." I trace my fingertips across her hips. She shivers, a tiny gasp coming from her throat, and I add, "I've got no plans to ever call you again."

She nods. "Didn't think so. Thank you . . . Lucas."

I leave the room—a room that I've been to more times than I can count—wearing a bored look. In the elevator, a tall blonde looks up from the man she's groping to give me a long, hard once-over. Her green eyes go wide as she mouths my name, and my lips twitch, but I say nothing. When I exit out the back, to where my car is waiting in its usual spot, the night guard inclines his head, giving me a polite and goddamn knowing smile.

"Have a wonderful evening, Mr. Wolfe."

Yeah, real wonderful.

I've always been a fan of early mornings—the workout and long shower and writing—so I'm wide awake, playing my guitar, when my assistant shuffles into my music room a few minutes after eight the next day. She slams a few plastic bags down on the carpeted floor, cursing and barely missing a signed guitar that cost more than her yearly salary. My eyebrow shoots up, but I don't stop strumming.

"I've got a punching bag downstairs," I suggest. "I'd rather you beat the shit out of it before you wreck my house."

She gives me a dark look before she begins to dig through the bags, looking for something. "Go screw yourself, Lucas."

"Not very sisterly." Setting the Les Paul to the side, I lean back in my leather chair—so far that the front legs come off the floor—and glance across the room at my younger sister. Red-faced, with black and blue hair, Kylie looks like shit. When I tell her this, she snorts.

"Thanks for the compliment." She finally finds what she's been searching for and comes over, plunks a rectangular pink cardboard box on the music bench a few feet away from me, and gestures to it grandly, blowing strands of hair out of her eyes. "I brought you breakfast. Enjoy."

"Doughnuts," I reply sarcastically. "Yum."

She sits on the bench, throwing open the box and digging in. "You don't have to be a dick all the time. Or such a picky eater."

Now I snort. "Says the picky girl who won't even touch cheese."

Kylie ignores me, focusing instead on the schedule for today. "You've got the shoot at"—she rolls her dark eyes, drags out her iPhone, and punches the screen a few times—"ten thirty. Three or four days . . . as long as everyone cooperates."

Meaning Sinjin's not messed up out of his mind and Wyatt's not fucking everything on set with a pussy. I nod, suddenly aware that this shoot will probably take a good week or two just because my band can't get their shit together long enough to make a decent video.

I clench my fist for a moment before shutting the notebook I'd been working in before my sister showed up. Sensing my irritation, Kylie gives me a forced smile and pats my hand. Hers are sticky with doughnut icing, and my mouth drags into a frown.

"I'm sure it won't be too bad." But even as she tries to cheer me up, it's easy to see that she's still agitated. I wipe the back of my hand on the inside of my shirt and cast her the most pleasant look I can muster.

"You remember the last shoot, right?"

Kylie cringes but recovers fast. "I've heard they got a pretty actress for you to pretend to sleep with." Her voice takes on that high-pitched tone people use to lure their kids to the dentist.

"I'm jumping for fucking joy."

"God, you suck. Too bad they can't get a body double for you," she says, reaching out to wipe her own hands down the front of my shirt. A low growl releases from the back of my throat and she looks up into my eyes, laughing—a genuine one.

Then Kylie stands, digging in her giant bag as she walks to the door. "Going to drop your laundry off at the cleaner and pick up your lame-ass groceries."

"Could you possibly sound any more miserable about that?" I ask.

She spins around and grins widely, a cigarette dangling from the corner of her lips. Oh, yeah, she's pissed—she hasn't touched one in months. "Give me a raise and I'll sound as cheerful as you want."

I don't remind her that she makes twenty-five bucks an hour because all she'll do is give me shit and a million reasons why she deserves more.

When she comes back with bags of groceries and a dry-cleaning receipt an hour later, I'm dressed. She looks less irritated than she did this morning, so I don't bring it up as she drives me to the set where day one of shooting will take place. As we walk into the studio together, it's obvious this is the last place she wants to be right now. She lags a few steps behind me, dragging her feet and making an annoying scraping noise across the concrete.

"Do you have somewhere to be?" I demand impatiently, tossing a glare over my shoulder at her.

Her face scrunches into a painful expression. "No, I just—"

"You're running late," a deep voice says, and before I turn to face Wyatt, I don't miss the way Kylie's face flushes. Not this shit again.

"Right on time," I say, turning sideways so that I can look between the two of them. Kylie glares down at the floor and mumbles something and Wyatt's shit-eating grin suddenly doesn't seem so relaxed when he walks closer to us, cell phone in hand.

And as I stand here, caught between a decade of push and pull between my best friend and little sister, I feel sick to my stomach. I feel like the biggest hypocrite who's ever lived.

"Where's this actress I'm supposed to pretend screw?" It's the first thing that rolls past my lips, but apparently it does the trick. Kylie looks up, grinning, and Wyatt rolls his eyes and goes back to sending messages. Probably to a woman because that's the way he and Kylie operate. They're together, they break up, and then they date—or in Kylie's case—marry other people. Over and over again.

As I stride in the direction of my personal dressing room, I cast one final glance over my shoulder at my sister and Wyatt, whose faces are inches away from each other and flushed with anger. They're bitching at each other in hushed tones and when I turn the corner, I realize that there's this twisted part of me that's thankful for Sam—thankful that my ex is screwed up to the point of keeping me out of relationships.

Don't miss any of the *DEVOURED* series!

All Over You
9781476744124

Consumed
9781476744131

Available now!

Hollywood starlet Willow Avery is out of rehab, with only one chance left to redeem herself before she's officially on every director's crap list. When she accepts the lead in a new beach drama, Willow finds herself in Hawaii training with Cooper, a gorgeous Australian surfer with the bluest eyes she's ever seen and the sexiest accent she's ever heard. Cooper's different from the men she's used to. He doesn't want to use her. And he refuses to let her fail.

This fall, look for *LUCKY ME*

Nineteen-year-old Delilah returns to college with one explicit warning from her parents: No more gambling or they'll cut off her tuition payment and bring her home to attend community college in Honolulu. Delilah's obsession for poker may spell doom for her education—unless she can help her cute RA make the money he needs.

Available wherever books are sold or at www.simonandschuster.com

TOUCHSTONE
A Division of Simon & Schuster
A CBS COMPANY